YOU WILL NEVER LEAVE

A PSYCHOLOGICAL SUSPENSE THRILLER

N. L. HINKENS

Text copyright @ 2020 Norma Hinkens

Published by Dunecadia Publishing, California

ISBN: 978-1-947890-21-3

Cover by: **www.derangeddoctordesign.com**

Editing by: **www.jeanette-morris.com/first-impressions-writing**

❀ Created with Vellum

"What's the nearest campground on the map?" Matt asked, squinting through the windshield of his 2016 Ford F-250. "We can't keep driving in this rain. It's getting worse by the minute."

Blair pulled the camper travel guide from the side pocket on the passenger door and flipped it open to the page she'd previously marked with a yellow Post-it note. She'd relied on the downloaded maps on her iPad for most of the trip so far, but without Wi-Fi she had no way to search for an alternative campground to the one they'd planned on. They hadn't intended on making camp for at least another couple of hours, but the weather conditions had been deteriorating over the course of the afternoon, and she could sense Matt's temper percolating into the red zone.

With a resigned sigh, she traced a fingernail along their route on the map, trying to pinpoint where they were at present. Her husband hadn't been the same since his last deployment and subsequent medical discharge. The injury to his leg nagged at him, but it was the change on the inside that worried Blair the most. Little things set him off—even a sound or a smell could trigger an unwelcome flashback and all the emotions that went along with it. Apparently, war made men's tempers as volatile as the hand grenades they lobbed at each other. But the rage that had served Matt in battle had no place in their home. Although Blair had only admitted as much to her therapist, she'd actually been afraid of Matt when he'd first returned from Afghanistan—all the unprovoked outbursts, the night terrors. Even when his anger subsided, he'd seemed numb, and unfeeling, a distant relative to the warm and gregarious man she'd married.

Months of intensive therapy had helped stabilize his emotions, especially the guilt and depression over bringing home several buddies from his battalion in caskets. Now, he and Blair were spending the next three months traveling around the States in his father's travel trailer to allow him some time and peace to heal, away from the jostling crowds that unnerved him, while enjoying some of North America's finest camping spots and national parks along the way. Matt loved the mountains, and the idea of staying in a new spot every night appealed to him. He got restless easily—another side effect of too many back-to-back adrenaline-filled days with the smell of death all around him.

"There's a campground up ahead called Bird Creek," Blair said. "About six miles off the main highway. It's a twisty, mountainous drive in, no hookups or showers—just an outhouse—and it only has eight spots. But it's near a lake, picturesque, no doubt." She turned the planner sideways to gauge the distance better. "Black Rock, where we were headed, is another sixty miles or so."

Matt flattened his lips as he flicked the windshield wipers up to maximum velocity. "Bird Creek it is. I've had enough of this non-stop rain."

The official diagnosis of PTSD had been hard for Matt to accept at first. But Blair had insisted he face it head on and deal with it before they considered starting a family. She wasn't about to subject any future children to the kind of hair-trigger eruptions she'd witnessed since Matt's return. In those frightening feral moments, it felt as if anything could happen. In fact, that was the main reason she'd insisted Matt leave his Glock behind on this trip. It was the one thing they'd argued back-and-forth about before they'd set out.

"What are we supposed to do if we encounter a bear, or a cougar, or even a rattler?" Matt complained. "It's foolhardy to head out for a three-month camping trip around the most remote parts of the States without a weapon."

"We'll take the proper precautions," Blair countered. "I'm bringing bear spray, hiking bells, and a whistle."

Matt cracked his knuckles, looking increasingly exasperated. "Come on, Blair. You really think a grizzly's gonna turn and run 'cause you're whistling at it? And it's not just the wildlife we need to be concerned about. What if we bump into some crazy mountain man with a rifle in the middle of a remote forest?"

"Now you're being ridiculous. It would give me more peace of mind not to have to sleep with a loaded gun beneath our pillow for the next ninety days." Blair raised a palm to stop Matt interrupting her. "And before you say anything, I know you'd keep it loaded because you tell me often enough that an empty chamber won't help in a moment of crisis." She hesitated before adding quietly, "You're not at war anymore, Matt."

In the end, Blair had enlisted the help of Matt's therapist to convince him to leave the Glock in the safe at home. The therapist had agreed it would be better to undertake the camping trip without dragging along "a weapon of war," as she'd dubbed it, that might inadvertently trigger traumatic memories. Truth be told, if circumstances had been different, Blair might have opted to bring the gun. Bear spray hadn't proven very effective for the young couple in the movie, *Backcountry*, which, against her better judgement, she'd watched on Netflix before leaving on this trip. They weren't planning to head up to Alaska until the end of June, but she was already nervous about the prospect of hiking in some of North America's most remote terrain—home to some of its fiercest wildlife.

"I think that's the road we need to take up ahead," she said, squinting through the rain-mottled windshield. The incessant whirring and slapping of the wipers was grating on her nerves, but doing little to combat the poor visibility.

"Where? Don't let me drive past it." Matt stepped on the brakes, leaning forward in his seat to peer through the lashing rain.

When they reached the turnoff for the campground, Matt swung wide onto a gravel road and began winding his way along the mountainous route to Bird Creek. After climbing for a mile or two, the road narrowed making the drive even more treacherous.

"Not very scenic," Blair commented. "It looks as if this area was burned recently."

"More important, there's nowhere to pass if we meet a vehicle," Matt muttered. "There better be a turnout or two along the way or we're screwed. I can't back up here."

Blair inhaled and exhaled slowly. She wondered if she'd done the right thing in giving her husband the option to abandon their plans to reach Black Rock tonight. She could almost feel the tension radiating off him. Not that she blamed him, given the circumstances. Towing his father's trailer up a mountainous gravel road in a blinding deluge was not exactly the relaxing getaway he'd signed up for. More akin to the kind of high-octane military operations they were hoping to relegate to his past.

A short time later, they passed a turnout half-filled with a rockslide and several blackened tree trunks that had slid down the mountain. Blair threw Matt a disquieted look. "Sketchy. I wouldn't want to be parked there when that debris comes tumbling down."

"No kidding!" Matt gritted his teeth. "Hopefully, we won't need to pull over to let anyone pass. I doubt too many campers will venture down this road hauling a trailer. If they've any sense, they'll wait out this storm. That's if there's anyone up there to begin with."

"We're probably not the only ones who decided to bail on driving any farther in this rain. Better plan on company."

Matt shrugged. "We don't have to hang out with them. In this weather, we've got a good excuse to stay hunkered down in the trailer."

Blair turned and looked out the side window. She didn't relish the idea of isolating themselves again. She would have enjoyed getting to know some of the other campers around a fire in the evening—playing cards, or cornhole, and swapping stories. They'd met some interesting people even though they'd only been on the road for three weeks. But Matt rarely wanted to socialize with anyone beyond a perfunctory greeting.

Still, she was determined to make this about her husband's healing first and foremost. Any socializing they did would be on his schedule and only to the extent that he felt comfortable—his therapist's advice. Matt had a heightened tendency to sense danger everywhere—a survival tactic from his stint at war—which kept him keyed-up and on edge around strangers. Blair's main goal for this trip was to return home at the end with a healthy husband, well-adjusted and ready to begin civilian life, set up a business, and start the family they both wanted.

Glancing across at him, she noticed he was gripping the wheel tightly with both hands. It almost unnerved her more than seeing him drive one-handed, with the other elbow casually resting on an armrest or hanging out the window, as he usually did. Her stomach tightened when she caught a glimpse of the view through Matt's side window. The drop-off on his side of the road into the ravine below was getting steeper all the time. She couldn't help wondering if this was bringing back unwanted memories of driving an army truck along the precipitous, mountain roads in Afghanistan, fearful that, at any minute, a roadside bomb would take out their convoy. Matt was one of the lucky ones who'd survived such an attack.

Blair let out a sigh of relief when they passed mile marker four—not too much farther to go now. The road itself was in reasonable condition, but it was unnerving to think about meeting another vehicle, or the even more disturbing possibility that a volley of rocks might come tumbling down the side of the mountain.

After a couple more bone-shaking miles, they spotted Bird Creek Campground ahead on the right. Blair rubbed her temples with the tips of her fingers, grateful to have made it here without incident. She sensed Matt had had about all he could take for one day. A flat tire or something equally crippling in this weather would have fried his circuit board entirely. Now they could kick back and relax, cook up a stir fry, maybe play some cards, and get a good night's sleep. There wouldn't be any of the usual setting up camp outside in this kind of weather. Ordinarily, it was a ritual they both enjoyed—gathering wood, getting a fire going, arranging their folding chairs beneath the awning, and watching the flickering flames. Enjoying the healing power of nature along with the relative luxury of not having to sleep on the ground in a tent. For that, Blair was particularly thankful to her father-in-law. Matt had first suggested a backpacking trip until his father had pointed out that it was too early in the year to be assured of decent weather.

"We're not the first ones here," Matt said, a note of disappointment in his voice, as they rumbled down the root-ridden road to the campsites.

"At least the campground was spared the fires," Blair said, keeping her tone upbeat. "It's pretty here, backing up to the forest."

She counted four other camping parties in total as they trundled along sizing up the open spots. A young couple who'd evidently pulled in just a few minutes before them were still in the process of unhitching their truck from their trailer. Blair waved at them in passing and the woman waved back in a friendly manner. A little farther along, a Tahoe was parked next to a small, stylish, teardrop-shaped travel trailer that Blair instantly fell in love with. A few sites past the outhouse, a nondescript camper van was tucked into a secluded, shady spot. The last remaining occupied site sported a beat-up Toyota Tacoma pickup and a small trailer that looked like it had circumnavigated the globe one time too many.

"Pretty tight spots. You wouldn't be able to fit a forty-footer in here," Matt said, circling around the loop one more time to assess the remaining open sites. He slowed down and pointed to the site adjoining the beat-up truck and trailer. "This one looks reasonably flat, and it's not too close to the outhouse. I'll back in so the slide has more room to open away from those trees. Do you want to jump out and guide me?"

Blair slipped on her raincoat and threw her hood up over her head. After stepping out into the downpour, she took up a position where Matt could spot her in his side mirror. Waving through the rain like an air traffic controller, she

N. L. HINKENS

directed him left a few inches to line the trailer up and then
made a fist when he'd backed it in as far as he could go.

"Nicely done," she said, when he opened the door and
joined her. "Got it the first time."

"Helps to have a top-notch assistant," he joked, winking at
her as he unhitched the trailer from the truck. "Thank good-
ness for automatic levelers. I'd hate to be trying to block
these tires in this rain."

He flicked the switch to bring down the tongue jack and
then activated the levelers. A familiar whirring began, and
the trailer trembled as the stabilizers made contact with the
ground beneath.

"That'll do it. Let's get back inside," Blair said, just as a tall,
lean man in bright yellow rain gear came into view. A large
German shepherd loped along at his side. Blair eyed it
cautiously. She wasn't crazy about dogs to begin with, but big
ones in particular scared her. Their deep-throated growling
unnerved her. It all went back to being bitten as a child when
a stranger's dog had gotten off the leash at the playground
and made a beeline for her. Blair unconsciously traced her
forefinger over the scar on the back of her left wrist which
had required ten stitches and an ice cream sundae to make
right.

Determined to quash her fear in an effort to be neigh-
borly, and encourage Matt to do the same, she nailed a
cheery greeting as the man approached. "Hi, I'm Blair
Dawson. This is my husband, Matt."

The man nodded to them. "Sam." He gestured to his dog.
"And this is Duke."

"We just pulled in and got set up," Blair said, taking in the
young man's chiseled jaw and blue eyes that conveyed a
dispirited air at odds with his rugged good looks. "We were
hoping to make it to Black Rock but decided to get out of the
weather. Where are you from?"

"All over." Sam ran an eye over their trailer. "Nice rig."

"It's my father-in-law's," Blair explained.

Sam gestured through the trees to the dilapidated trailer and truck parked in the site next to them. "Me and Duke are next door. Holler if you need anything."

"Thanks," Matt cut in abruptly. "Right now, we need to hunker down and dry off."

Sam threw him a guarded look, before unleashing Duke and striding across to his trailer.

Matt and Blair hurried inside and kicked off their boots. After hanging up their coats in the shower, Blair turned on the gas to boil some water. "This rain calls for a cup of afternoon cocoa."

Matt switched on the generator and flicked the switch to open up the slide that expanded the living area to a comfortable size. "What did you think of that fellah, Sam?" he asked, sinking down on the couch.

Blair spooned hot cocoa mix into two mugs and then reached for the kettle, weighing her answer. She'd become used to Matt's initial suspicions of everyone and had learned not to react too strongly to his loaded comments. "He seemed okay. I'm not fond of dogs, so that was one strike against him, but Duke was well-trained."

A rut formed on Matt's brow. "He was evasive—he's hiding something."

Blair tensed, stirring the hot chocolate slowly. They hadn't been inside five minutes and he was already exhibiting paranoid behavior, suspecting the first person they met of harboring some deep, dark secret. She allowed a thoughtful pause to pass before answering, "I don't know how you got that impression. We only exchanged a few words with him. He came across as friendly enough to me; told us to holler if we needed anything."

Matt's voice grew testy. "You asked him a direct question

and he deflected. What does *all over* mean? Nothing, that's what."

"What does it matter?" Blair said. "Why should we care where he's from?"

"It might matter. He could be dangerous. Did you notice he never smiled once?"

Blair handed Matt a mug of hot chocolate, resisting the temptation to point out that he hadn't as much as split his lips in a grin either. "So he wasn't chatty. He was probably half-frozen, and all he wanted to do was get inside his trailer and dry off."

Matt placed his mug in a cupholder and walked over to the trailer door. He locked it and then jiggled it several times to make sure it was secure. "You haven't been in the kind of situations I've been in, Blair. I know when things don't add up, and my gut's telling me there's something off about that guy."

2

*T*he hot chocolate soon warmed their bellies but did little to dissolve Matt's tension. He continued to speculate about Sam, his slovenly trailer—which Matt suspected he was living out of—and his menacing German shepherd.

"He looks like a homeless drug addict. He could be dangerous. They'll do anything to feed their habit," Matt grumbled. "I'm not sure we should stay here tonight after all."

"It's too late to blaze a trail to Black Rock now. We can make an early start in the morning." Blair grimaced inwardly as she drained the dregs in her mug. She might as well resign herself to a long, unsettled night with Matt reliving buried terrors, jerking awake, pacing their trailer, and checking and rechecking the lock on the door. Once he'd worked himself up into this agitated frame of mind, there was no talking him out of it. Driving in the torrential rain had slowly been raising his stress level, especially the last few treacherous miles into the campground, and now he'd earmarked Sam as a potential enemy target instead of a fellow traveler they could enjoy a game of cards and a beer with—well, maybe not a beer. Alcohol was not a good companion to Matt's PTSD.

By late afternoon, the rain finally let up. "Let's get out and stretch our legs for a bit, check out the campground before it gets dark," Blair proposed. "We've been sitting around all day."

Matt got to his feet and peered out the window at Sam's trailer, partially visible through the trees. "Okay, it's probably a good idea to scout out the other campers before nightfall anyway."

After pulling on their coats and boots, they made their way outside. Blair stopped to inhale the pine-scented, rain-drenched earth. The ground always smelled lush after a good soaking, releasing the best of itself in return for the refreshment it had enjoyed. A faint hint of charred timber from the scorched mountainside hung in the air. She peered up at the sky searching for a hint of blue, but the iron cast hue overhead sent a clear message that the rain would be back with a vengeance. They needed to make the most of this brief respite to explore their surroundings.

She reached for Matt's hand and together they walked down from their campsite to the muddy road. Hopefully a little touch therapy would take his anxiety down a notch or two.

"That hiking trail over there leads up to a lake." Blair pointed to a wooden trail marker. "Might be good fishing, but it's probably too muddy to check it out today."

"It's going to start dumping again anyway," Matt grumbled.

They glanced at Sam's trailer in passing, but there was no sign of him or Duke. Walking on, Blair cast a curious glance at the deserted-looking camper van in the site next to Sam's rig.

"Looks like they've been here a while," she observed.

"No lights on or any other signs of life," Matt said. "That's odd. I can't imagine where someone would go in this weather. I don't like it."

"Maybe it's a friend of Sam's," Blair suggested in an overly patient tone. "They could be hanging out in his trailer."

Matt grunted in response, as if to convey his skepticism that Sam had any friends.

Continuing on, they passed an empty campsite, the weathered outhouse and water pump, and then the stylish trailer Blair had admired on the way in.

"Someone's home," she commented. "The generator's running."

They proceeded around the corner to the campsite where the young couple had been setting up earlier. The lights were on in the trailer and they could hear music playing.

"We could stop by and introduce ourselves," Blair suggested, yearning for a bit of company to pass the long evening that lay ahead of them. "The woman gave us a friendly wave on the way in."

Matt picked up his pace. "Too intrusive. We'll bump into them out and about at some point anyway. Let's turn around before it starts pelting down again."

On their return trip, a tiny, fit-looking, gray-haired woman in Ugg boots, black yoga pants and a blush-colored sweatshirt exited the teardrop-shaped trailer and walked over to get something out of the Tahoe. She slammed the car door shut and straightened up, spotting Matt and Blair trudging along on the other side of the road.

"Hi!" she yelled breezily, fluttering her fingers at them. "You must be the couple who pulled in a little bit ago."

Blair tugged on Matt's hand, and they crossed the road and walked up to the campsite to introduce themselves.

"I'm Hazel," the woman chirped, gracing them with a

warm smile. "Are you planning on staying here for a few nights?"

"We were actually on our way to Black Rock," Blair explained, "but we had to abandon that plan when it started dumping. Matt didn't want to be driving another sixty miles in lashing rain."

"I don't blame you one bit." Hazel cocked a motherly brow at Matt. "You're welcome to come in for a cup of tea or a glass of wine. I can't imagine anyone's going to start a fire this evening." She tilted her head back and assessed the sky. "Looks like we've got some more weather to look forward to."

Blair pinned a searching look on Matt. "Up to you, if you're not too tired after driving." She was giving him an out if he needed it—secretly hoping he'd opt to be sociable and relax for a change. Hazel didn't come across as the type to set off any alarm bells.

After a beat of silence, Matt answered with a shrug. "Sure, we'll stop in for a few minutes."

Blair rewarded him with a broad smile. Evidently, his earlier paranoia concerning their camping companions had subsided, or at least he was making an effort to put it behind him.

"I've been craving some company," Hazel admitted, winking at them as she led the way up the steps to her trailer.

"This is absolutely gorgeous!" Blair exclaimed as she removed her boots at the door.

"Well-constructed too," Matt said admiringly, running his fingers over the riveted door seam.

"Thanks, feel free to take a look around," Hazel offered.

"Is this a custom interior?" Blair asked, as she and Matt checked out the stylish appointments and layout.

"Semi-custom. I bought it new," Hazel replied, gesturing for her to take a seat at the small dining table. "I fell in love with the design the minute I saw it. I didn't want something ugly if I was going to be spending any length of time in it."

"I take it you do a lot of camping?" Matt said, sitting down next to Blair.

Hazel laughed. "I do now. I'm a retired nurse. I rented out my home and I've been traveling for the past year-and-a-half." She reached for the sunflower yellow kettle on the stove top. "Would you prefer tea, or perhaps a glass of home-made blueberry wine?"

"Tea would be great," Blair responded.

"Tea for me too, please," Matt added.

Alcohol was something they'd both avoided ever since Matt's diagnosis. It was sort of an unwritten rule between them that they would remain teetotalers, at least as long as he was working on his recovery, which Blair was beginning to fear might take a lifetime.

"Have you visited all lower forty-eight states yet?" Blair asked.

Hazel gave a wry grin as she filled the kettle. "The truth is, I haven't made it very far at all. I'm writing a book—trying to at least."

Matt raised his brows. "What's it about?"

"Holistic self-care and homeopathic ways to treat disease —ways the government doesn't want you to know about."

Blair could feel Matt tensing at her side, his stranger radar suddenly on full alert.

A shadow passed over Hazel's face as she sat back down at the table. "My younger sister passed away of pancreatic cancer several years ago. She was only forty-eight. An excruciating death. Not one I'd wish on anyone. I've always been interested in homeopathic medicine, but after she died, I went all in. I forage for plants and herbs and make my own tinctures now. As a former nurse, I'm sick of watching people die."

"I'm sorry," Blair said quietly. "That must have been very hard to lose your sister so young."

"It was," Hazel acknowledged, tucking a stray gray curl behind her ear. "But I'm determined to finish this book and dedicate it to her. That way something good will have come out of her suffering."

The kettle boiled and Hazel got up to make the tea. She set three steaming mugs down on the table, and then reached for a Tupperware container of cookies and peeled off the lid. "Don't worry, these are healthy. Almond flour, coconut oil, and no sugar."

Matt eyed them dubiously. "No sugar, how does that work?"

"Try one," Hazel urged. "You won't even notice it's missing. I use stevia to replace it—it's a plant-based sugar substitute."

Matt reached for a cookie and took a bite. He raised his brows approvingly. "They're not half bad."

Hazel and Blair exchanged an amused look. Blair had already decided she liked this quirky older woman. That was the thing about camping. You always ran into interesting people and they all had a story.

"So what are you two doing out here mid-week in April?" Hazel asked.

Matt stopped chewing and reached for his mug, leaving Blair to answer the question.

"Matt just finished his military active duty, and we're starting up a landscaping business together. I'm a landscape architect," Blair said. "We decided to take a few months off to travel round the States first. Everyone keeps telling us we won't have time later when we're trying to grow a business and raise a family, so we thought why not, it's now or never."

Hazel nodded, casting a perceptive glance across at Matt. "Military, huh?"

Blair had a feeling she suspected there was more to the story. Hopefully, she wouldn't pry.

"Have you met any of the other campers yet?" Matt asked, eliminating any opportunity for Hazel to probe further.

"Of course!" She chuckled. "As you've seen, I make a habit of introducing myself to everyone. The young couple next to me pulled in right before you got here—Whitney and Logan. I actually bumped into them this morning at a gas station and told them about this place. They were looking for somewhere quiet and off the beaten track. I tried to lure them over here earlier with my homemade cookies, but he wasn't having any part of it. They're on their honeymoon, so I suspect we won't be seeing much of them."

"What about Sam, the guy with the German shepherd? Have you talked to him?" Matt went on.

Hazel gave a pensive nod. "Now that's a sad story. He arrived here shortly after me. He's a free climber—you know, one of those extreme athletes. He lost his climbing buddy, Andy, a couple of months back in a terrible accident. He fell to his death. Sam was the one who found the body."

Blair threw a horrified glance at Matt. No wonder Sam had struck her as melancholic—the poor guy was grieving the tragic loss of his climbing partner. "That's so sad. He must be really broken up about it."

"The worst thing about it is that he has survivor's guilt," Hazel rambled on. "They were tied together when they fell. The rope snapped, but somehow Sam landed on a ledge and didn't go down all the way."

Matt lifted his mug and took a hearty swig of tea, trying to mask his emotions. Blair could see a flicker of guilt in his expression. He'd totally misjudged Sam. Matt knew better than anyone what it felt like to lose a buddy you had risked life and limb with.

17

"What about the camper van?" Blair prodded. "It doesn't look like there are any lights on, or any signs of life."

Hazel threaded her fingers through her shoulder-length gray curls. "Haven't seen anyone go in or out. Sam says there's a group of hunters tent camping up by the lake about a mile or so from here. Maybe the owner's with them."

"We should get back before the rain starts up again," Matt said, setting down his mug. "Thanks for the tea, Hazel."

"You're welcome. It was a pleasure to meet you both, and I'm sure I'll see you out and about tomorrow."

"SHE'S FRIENDLY," Blair said as they walked back down to the road.

"Nosy, you mean. Asks way too many questions," Matt muttered. "In everyone's business already. And a conspiracy theorist to boot. You heard what she said about the government. She's a kook."

Blair decided not to grace his comments with a response. Granted, Hazel had a bit of a hippy flair in her approach to life, but she'd been nothing but fun and friendly as far as Blair was concerned.

They were almost back at their trailer when they heard the sound of a vehicle approaching from behind. They stepped to one side to let an older model RV go by. Blair raised a hand and waved at the couple inside. The woman kept her eyes forward, a pinched look on her face, but the man raised a meaty paw and waved back.

"This place is getting more popular by the minute," Blair remarked.

"Only because there's nowhere else to stop between here and Black Rock," Matt said, watching the RV lumber on down the root-ridden dirt road. "She didn't look too happy about it. At this rate, they'll just about get that rig parked before it's too dark to see what they're doing."

They continued retracing their steps to their trailer, slowing their pace when they reached the campsite next to the outhouse where the new arrivals were attempting to back in their RV. Blair and Matt watched in silence as the man drove backward and forward trying to position the thirty-foot RV between the fire pit and the trees.

"Poor guy's struggling." Matt shook his head. "And his wife's no help. I'd better go guide him in."

"Good idea," Blair replied.

Matt made his way over and spoke a few words to the man through the slider window on the driver side. Afterward he took up a position at the back of the campsite and directed the stranger as he began backing in once again. After a couple of attempts, he was finally in position.

Blair walked over and stood next to her husband, waiting to greet the couple. To her surprise, the woman threw them a scant glance and then disappeared into the back of the RV. A moment later, the man came down the steps and stuck out a burly hand. Tall, bearded, and broad-shouldered, he looked to be in his sixties. "Appreciate the help. I'm Harvey Ross." He gestured over his shoulder. "My wife, Sandy, went to lie down." He hesitated. "She's not feeling well."

"That's too bad. I hope she feels better soon," Blair said. "If we can help with anything, we're just around the corner in the gray and silver trailer."

Harvey gave a tight smile. "Thanks."

"Need any help getting your rig leveled?" Matt asked. "Doesn't look like you have automatic stabilizers. Got any wedges or leveling blocks?"

Harvey frowned and scratched his head. "Blocks ... let me see, I'll have to ask Sandy where she put them." He climbed back inside and made his way to the bedroom at the rear.

Matt shook his head in a bewildered fashion. "Weird. He can't park his rig and he can't remember where his gear is. Maybe he's starting to lose it."

Harvey reappeared several minutes later and made his way back down the steps. "Sandy thinks they're in the storage compartment on this side." He unlocked the hatch and rummaged around inside before producing the plastic leveling blocks.

"I'm going to leave you two guys to finish up here while I head back to start dinner," Blair said. "Nice to meet you, Harvey."

She smiled to herself as she strolled back to her trailer. Nothing like a little male bonding over a project. Maybe this detour would prove beneficial for Matt after all.

BLAIR HAD JUST FINISHED ADDING the vegetables she'd chopped into the wok with some chicken, when Matt arrived back. "Are they all settled in?"

Matt kicked off his boots and threw himself down on the couch. "They are now. That guy doesn't know what he's doing. I finally had to take the wheel and drive the RV up on the blocks for him."

"What about his wife?" Blair asked. "Did you get to meet her?"

Matt's expression darkened. "We might have another crazy neighbor on our hands. She never came out to introduce herself, but she can't have been that sick. I caught her peeking through the curtain at me when I was leaving."

3

$\mathcal{B}$lair frowned to herself as she stirred the chicken and vegetables around in the pan. Sandy's abrupt disappearance had seemed a bit rude but, in all fairness, Harvey had explained that she wasn't feeling well. "Just because Sandy was looking out the window at you doesn't mean she's crazy, Matt. Curious would be a better word."

"She was spying on me. Don't you find it odd that she didn't even come out to say hello? I don't think she's sick at all."

"Maybe she's agoraphobic," Blair said with a shrug.

Matt grunted. "Just a fancier term for crazy."

Biting back her frustration, Blair set down the ladle with a clatter and joined Matt on the couch. She reached for his hand and released a tired breath. "Surely you, above all people, should have some empathy for her. Whether she's agoraphobic, or recovering from some illness or another, she's obviously not up to meeting people. You understand that feeling better than most. Why are you being so hard on her?"

Matt groaned and slid down on the couch. "I don't wanna

be around any more crazy people. I've seen enough screwed up soldiers to last me a lifetime. People are unpredictable when they're messed up. I just need the rest of the population to be normal." He scratched at his shoulder, not meeting her gaze. "That's what this camping trip was supposed to be about—normalizing things. Seems like everyone we've met here so far is damaged goods."

"They're not so different from us, then. We have our issues too. You need to start trusting a little more—give people the benefit of the doubt before you judge them. Like Sam—poor guy."

Blair leaned over and kissed Matt on the lips, before getting up to check on their dinner. She did a quick taste test and then turned off the gas. "Stir fry's ready. Why don't you grab the soy sauce and some sparkling water?"

Matt dragged himself to his feet and set the table while Blair busied herself ladling out a plateful of stir fry for each of them. "We can still leave first thing in the morning, if you want," she said, as they sat down to eat.

Matt swallowed a mouthful of food and nodded. "Let's do that. This place is getting crowded."

BLAIR BOLTED UPRIGHT IN BED, rubbing her eyes in confusion as she looked around. At first, she thought she was dreaming, but the loud thumping on the trailer door wasn't a figment of her imagination. Scrabbling for her phone, she peered at the screen, bleary-eyed. Six-fifteen in the morning. She stumbled out of her sleeping bag, inadvertently elbowing Matt in the process. He stirred and shifted onto one elbow, blinking uncomprehendingly at her. As soon as the pounding on the door registered in his brain, he yanked at the zipper on his bag and leapt to his feet. "Who's there?" he demanded.

"Easy!" Blair said. "I'll get it. Maybe Sandy's sick or something." She pulled a sweatshirt over her head, shivering in the brisk, morning air. Matt flew past her in his boxers, peering through the blinds before cautiously cracking the door. "Sam! What's up?"

"Are you ... are you guys okay?" he asked in a wavering voice.

Blair joined Matt at the door, her pulse quickening at the sight of Sam hunched over on the doorstep, white as a sheet, his arresting blue eyes swimming in fear. She flung the door open, reached for his arm and tugged him inside. "Come in! What's wrong? Is it Duke?"

Sam shook his head, a haunted look gripping him. "He's fine. I left him in the trailer."

"Sit down, I'll make some coffee," Blair said.

"What's going on?" Matt asked.

Sam slumped down at the dining table and plunged his hands through his hair. "I can't believe it."

Matt slid onto the bench opposite him. "Talk to me. What's wrong, man?"

Sam gulped a mouthful of air, seemingly at a loss as to how to proceed. "I came here to forget ..."

Blair winced at the anguish in his voice as she spooned coffee grounds into the French press. He must be referring to his climbing partner who'd fallen to his death.

"And now this," Sam went on, almost as though he was talking to himself.

"Now *what*?" Matt demanded, an impatient edge creeping into his voice. "Has something happened?"

Sam loosed a ragged breath before composing himself. "I took Duke for a walk this morning on the hiking trail that leads up to the lake. Halfway up, I let him off the leash for a bit. All of a sudden, he began barking like crazy and took off. I thought he might have spotted a bear or something. I freaked out and started whistling for him, but he didn't come

23

back. When I caught up to him, he was sniffing at something beneath the brush."

Sam fastened a panic-stricken gaze on Matt. "It was a body—a man. I was afraid it was you at first, but he was older, bald." Sam shook his head, scrunching up his eyes as though to block the memory from resurfacing.

Blair swallowed down the bile rising up her throat. Her hands trembled and the spoon she was holding fell into the sink with a loud rattle.

Matt flashed her a concerned look before turning his attention back to Sam. "Any idea what happened to him?"

Sam wrung his hands on the table in front of him. "I didn't look too closely. He was half-buried in the undergrowth. But I think there was a ... a knife sticking out of his belly."

Blair let out a horrified bleat, reaching for the edge of the counter for support.

Matt's expression darkened. His chest heaved silently up and down as he clenched and unclenched his fists, as though weighing up everything Sam had told them. He got to his feet and began to pace. "He can't have been dead for long if the body hasn't been disturbed by animals."

"What are you thinking?" Blair asked, recognizing by his agitated demeanor that he was chewing on something.

He came to a sudden halt, his posture rigid. "There's a good chance the killer's still out there."

Blair stole a frightened look in Sam's direction. "Are you sure he was stabbed? Maybe he had a heart attack or something."

Sam rubbed a hand across the stubble on his jaw. "I can take you to the body if you want to see for yourselves."

They fell silent for a long moment, and then Blair said, "We're going to have to bury him."

"Not if he's been stabbed," Matt responded, his face set in

a stiff frown. "We can't move him. We have to notify the authorities."

"Then we should take some pictures at least," Blair proposed. "Maybe bring Hazel with us. She's a retired nurse, so she might be able to confirm how he died."

Sam frowned. "What about the other campers? Shouldn't we tell them what's happened—warn them? Like you said, the killer could still be out there."

Matt drew his brows together. "Let's hold off until we verify it was murder. No sense in freaking everyone out prematurely."

Sam got to his feet. "If we're going back up to the body, I'm bringing Duke."

Matt escorted him to the door. "We'll fetch Hazel and meet you back here in a few minutes."

"I'll bring my phone," Blair said, unplugging it from the charger. "It's got a good camera."

Matt disappeared into the bedroom and emerged a moment later, dressed in jeans and a thick sweatshirt.

After donning their outerwear, they locked the door behind them and strode off in the direction of Hazel's trailer. Blair rubbed her arms briskly in the cold air as they walked. The wind was kicking up and the threat of another stormy day hung in the air. Matt's eyes roved constantly over the road ahead and behind them, ensuring no one was lurking in the shadows. An ominous air as heavy as the pregnant clouds above them had settled over the campground, dispelling any hope of the beneficial detour Blair had naively hoped might unfold.

When they reached Hazel's trailer, Blair rapped her knuckles on the door. "Hazel! It's Blair and Matt. We need your help." She listened for a moment, and then hammered on the door again. "Anyone home?"

"Try knocking on her bedroom window," Matt suggested. "She might still be asleep."

"I don't want to give her a heart attack," Blair said. "I'll try the door one more time first." She knocked again and held her breath, listening for footsteps. After a moment, she heard a muffled call from inside the trailer, and then the sound of the door being unlocked. Seconds later, Hazel cracked the door a few inches and peered out at them in a semi-comatose trance, her wiry, gray hair standing on end. Her eyes flicked a calculating look from Blair to Matt. "Everything all right?"

"Sam found a body," Blair blurted out. "On the hiking trail up to the lake."

Hazel's eyes widened, her expression alert. "Is it one of the other campers?"

Matt shook his head. "Sam doesn't recognize him."

"Him?" Hazel echoed.

"It's an older man," Matt responded.

Hazel opened the door all the way and motioned for them to come inside. She sank down on the couch maintaining a calm demeanor as she attempted to smooth her tousled hair. "And Sam's sure this man is ... dead?"

Blair nodded. "He thinks he was stabbed in the stomach. Can you come with us and take a look? We need to confirm what's happened and then one of us will have to head out and notify the authorities."

Hazel rubbed her fingers back-and-forth across her forehead as if digesting everything she'd been told. "Let me put on some clothes." She disappeared into the bathroom and stepped out a few minutes later fully dressed in the same outfit she'd worn the day before. "So, assuming this guy was killed," she said, pulling her hair into a ponytail. "The killer could still be out there—hiding along the trail somewhere. Maybe we should arm ourselves."

"There's safety in numbers," Matt answered. "Sam's

coming too. No one's going to attack a group of four with a German shepherd in tow. Let's confirm that this guy was killed first before we start worrying about how to defend ourselves." He pulled out a folding survival knife and flashed the blade briefly in front of Hazel. "If it makes you feel any better, I have this."

Hazel slipped her arms into a black puffer jacket and pulled a wool cap down over her ears. She grabbed a pair of rubber gloves from beneath the sink and stuffed them into her pockets. "All right, let's do this."

Matt watched as she locked her trailer door behind her. "Check it again, make sure it's locked," he insisted.

Hazel raised her brows a fraction but did as he asked.

They hurried back to find Sam leaning against Matt's truck waiting for them, Duke at his feet. Hazel walked right up to Sam and embraced him. "I'm so sorry you were the one to find him."

Sam twisted his lips. "It was like it was happening all over again—finding Andy."

Matt threw a harried glance over his shoulder. "Let's walk and talk. I want to get there and back before the other campers are up and about. No sense in freaking the honeymooners out before we know what we're dealing with. Or Harvey and his sick wife, either."

"He's talking about the older couple who pulled in late yesterday afternoon," Blair explained to Hazel and Sam. "Harvey's wife, Sandy, is sick. I'm not sure what's wrong with her. We didn't get to talk to her."

They made their way down the road and onto the hiking trail. Duke trotted obediently at Sam's side, sniffing at interesting scents in passing.

"That's one smart dog," Hazel commented.

Sam gave an appreciative nod. "He's a good companion."

Blair cast a wary glance over at Duke. He seemed to have

gathered that she wasn't a dog person and was keeping his distance. By the same token, she was thankful to have him along. She felt the same way about dogs as she did about guns. She didn't care for them, but she could appreciate that they had their place and purpose in the right hands.

"How much farther?" Hazel asked.

"About a quarter mile or so," Sam replied. "The body's not too far off the trail. Whoever killed him didn't make much effort to bury him. Just stacked a bunch of brush on top."

Blair's stomach churned. As horrific as it sounded, everything Sam had told them so far seemed to indicate that the man had been murdered. Why else had the body been covered up? She couldn't help wondering if someone from the hunting party camping up by the lake had killed the man. After all, Sam seemed to think he'd died of a stab wound. And a hunting party would have no shortage of knives. She felt sick thinking about how this was going to affect Matt. His insomnia would be in overdrive tonight. Of all the things that could have happened to them—she'd take a flat tire over this any day. They'd set out on this trip to get away from Matt's bloody memories of war. But it seemed death was destined to follow him wherever he went.

They fell silent when Sam informed them that they were almost at the spot. Apart from the early morning twittering of birds in the trees overhead, and the occasional squelching sound of the group's footsteps along the muddy trail, an eerie stillness permeated the atmosphere. Almost as if the whole forest was holding its breath, waiting for a verdict. Blair couldn't help but notice that Matt had taken up the rear, his military instincts kicking in. If the killer was roaming the wooded mountainside, he had no intention of being caught by surprise.

Duke broke the silence with a series of resonant barks as he suddenly darted across to the left side of the trail, straining against his leash. Sam led the way through the undergrowth, coming to a halt next to a pile of brush stacked in front of a fallen log. "This is the place."

They gathered around and stared down in horror at the dirt-covered face of an elderly man peeking out from beneath the brush. He looked to be in his early seventies. A beetle scurried down his veined cheek and disappeared under the collar of his checked shirt. A shiver went down Blair's spine. An ominous reminder that it wouldn't be long before an army of insects descended on the body, intent on claiming their share of the spoils. They had to get an ambulance out here as quickly as possible.

Hazel knelt next to the man and pulled on her yellow rubber gloves. She brushed a leafy twig from the torso and leaned down to examine the wound on his belly.

"Any other stab wounds?" Matt asked, his eyes still roaming their perimeter.

"I don't think so," Hazel said, continuing her careful inspection of the body. She checked the man's arms and legs for any sign of injury and then pulled down his collar and studied his neck.

Matt darted another furtive glance around them and took a knee next to the body. He stared at it for a long moment before locking eyes with Hazel. "Are you seeing what I'm seeing?"

"Blood in the eyes, heavy bruising around the neck—possible ligature marks." She got to her feet slowly and pulled off her gloves. "The stab wound was inflicted after he died. Someone strangled him."

4

*B*lair flinched when an ice-cold raindrop landed on the back of her neck. She cast a harried glance up at the darkening sky as she threw up her hood. "We need to make a plan. It's about to start pouring again."

Matt clenched his jaw and began pacing. "Whatever we do, we can't move the body. We should cover it up as best we can without disturbing it and then head back to the campground. We need to get everyone together, let the others know what's going on, and decide who's going to head down the mountain to notify the police." He came to a sudden halt as if something had occurred to him, and then hunkered down next to the body and dug through the man's pockets. After a moment, he let out a frustrated breath and stood back up. "No ID. Blair, get out your phone and take some pictures."

She fished around in her coat and pulled out her phone with shaking fingers. Reluctantly, she moved closer to the body. "Should I ... I mean ... do we need close-ups?"

"Yes, close-ups of his face and side profile," Hazel said. "Also, the wound on his stomach, and the knife—there's a brand name on the handle. Then we'll need a few full-length photos that show his approximate height and the position of the body."

Out of the corner of her eye, Blair caught Sam turning away, his shoulders sagging as though the weight of it all was too much for him to bear. He patted Duke's head distractedly, staring into the distance at the hunters' tents up at the lake.

"Better get a move on," Matt urged. "The rain's really starting to come down now."

Blair took a series of shots from various angles and then slipped her phone into her coat pocket. "That'll have to do. I don't want to ruin my phone in this rain."

Matt reached for some brush and began to scatter it loosely over the body.

"There's no guarantee the body will still be here by the time the police arrive," Hazel said sounding dubious. "Maybe we should wrap him in a tarp and bring him back to the campground with us."

"For now, we should treat it as a crime scene," Matt said. "We can reconsider if the police don't make it here before dark."

The rain pummeled them relentlessly on their return trip to the campground, and, within minutes, the first crackle of thunder pealed out overhead. The trail quickly morphed into a mud bath and, more than once, Blair almost lost her footing. They could scarcely see five feet in front of them, which made the hike back down a terrifying proposition. The only consolation was that the killer's visibility would be equally hampered if he was anywhere in the vicinity.

As they staggered into the campground, Matt yelled to Blair above the ruckus, "Take Hazel and Sam inside. I'm going to knock on the other trailers and round up everyone so we can figure out what to do."

Blair unlocked the trailer with icy fingers, and Hazel

stumbled inside after her. Shivering, they pulled off their coats and muddy boots and dumped everything by the door.

"Where did Sam go?" Blair asked.

"He's taking Duke back to his trailer," Hazel replied. "He'll be right over."

On autopilot, Blair lit the stove and filled the kettle, then cranked up the heat before exhaling a long whoosh. "I'm in shock. Any theories on what happened out there, or who he is?"

"No idea," Hazel replied, rubbing her hands together and blowing into them.

"He could be one of the hunters camping up by the lake," Blair suggested.

"It's possible." A flicker of a frown crossed Hazel's face. "Or perhaps that's his camper van—next to Sam's trailer. For all we know, one of the hunters could have killed him."

"I have to admit, the thought struck me too," Blair said as she lined up some mugs on the countertop and lifted down a small Tupperware container of sugar. "I feel bad in a way. I mean, I haven't even met them, yet here I am speculating that one of them is a murderer. And I'm always telling my husband not to judge people."

Hazel fixed a penetrating gaze on Blair. "None of us knows each other at all. That makes us vulnerable."

Blair shifted her stance uncomfortably. "Now you sound just like Matt. He tends to be a bit paranoid about strangers."

"You'll live longer that way than being too naive," Hazel retorted.

They broke off their conversation as the door flew open and Matt came in out of the howling wind, followed by Harvey and the young honeymooners.

"This is Logan and Whitney," Matt said, unbuttoning his jacket.

Blair nodded to them. "Hi, I'm Blair, Matt's wife, nice to—"

"I'm not sure what this is all about," Logan cut in, shaking the water out of his shaggy, blond hair and looking around the room with narrowed eyes. "Was it absolutely necessary to drag us out in the middle of a storm?"

"It's freezing out there," Whitney complained in a breathless, high-pitched twang. She hugged her arms dramatically around her body. "And we saw lightning on the way over."

"We'll get to the point of the meeting in a minute," Matt said. "Why don't you all take a seat and make yourselves comfortable while we wait for Sam."

Whitney and Logan sat down on the couch while Harvey sank his large frame into one of the captain's chairs opposite them.

"Is your wife not coming?" Blair inquired, handing around steaming mugs of coffee and tea.

Harvey wrinkled his brow. "Sandy's not well enough to come out in this downpour."

"I'm sorry to hear your wife's not doing so good," Hazel responded. "Is she recovering from the flu or something? It's going around."

Harvey scratched the back of his neck, revealing an ace of spades tattoo on his inner wrist. Blair had never been a fan of tattoos, but when Matt had come back from his last deployment with an inked helmet resting on a rifle emblazoned on his left shoulder to commemorate his fallen comrades, she'd decided the tribute outweighed her preconceived notions about body art.

"Sandy has cancer." Harvey let out a weighty sigh. "She finished her final round of chemo last month. We were hoping to get the all clear from her doctor, but the latest scans were ... not good." He frowned, as if recollecting the moment they'd been given the dire news. "She's frail and on a bunch of medication—it makes her all groggy and confused. They wanted to talk to us about hospice, but we decided we'd rather take off in our RV. Sometimes you've just got to take what you can get, when you can get it."

Blair flashed him a sympathetic smile as she positioned herself on the end of the dining bench. As a military wife, she knew only too well what it was like to live in a state of limbo, never sure of how much time you might have left together, making every moment count.

She cast a quick glance around the room full of strangers. You never really knew who was closest to the end of their life. Logan and Whitney were the youngest among them. But sometimes the young died first. That thought had plagued her every day of Matt's deployment. She took a hasty sip of her coffee, shaking her head free of her morbid thoughts. "Do you think Sam's okay?" she ventured. "Maybe I should go over there and check on him."

Matt leaned back against the countertop, arms folded in front of him. "If he doesn't show up in the next minute or two, I'll go over there. He's probably sorting his dog out."

He'd barely uttered the words before the door rattled and a half-drowned Sam stumbled through. "Sorry," he gasped. "The thunder freaked Duke out. I couldn't get him settled." He sank down on the other side of the dining table opposite Blair.

"Coffee?" she asked.

He shook his head. "I'm good, thanks."

Blair reached for her mug and cradled it in her hands. Sam's face and hair were drenched from the rain, but his eyes looked red-rimmed from crying. She had a hunch it wasn't Duke who had held him up. Coming across the body earlier had likely reignited the trauma of finding his friend's battered body at the bottom of the mountain. Matt was right —they had inadvertently ended up at a campground full of damaged people.

Matt cleared his throat and raised his voice to drown out the incessant drumming of rain on the roof. "All right, I'll get right to it. The reason we called this meeting is because Sam discovered a man's body on the hiking trail going up to the lake when he was out walking his dog earlier this morning."

Whitney's eyes grew large as pools. She snuggled closer to Logan on the couch, tucking her manicured fingers around his arm.

Harvey drew his shaggy brows together. "Any ID on him?"

Matt shook his head. "Negative. He looks to be in his seventies."

Harvey blinked and interlaced his fingers in his lap, digesting the information.

"Did he fall or something?" Logan asked, darting a confused look around the room.

Matt and Hazel exchanged the briefest of glances.

"Stab wound to the stomach," Matt answered. "Blair took some pictures as evidence, in case animals get to the body before forensics."

Whitney let out a tiny yelp like a puppy in distress.

Logan jerked his knee up and down in an irritated fashion. "So what does this have to do with us?"

"We need to notify law enforcement, for starters," Hazel said.

"It's storming like crazy out there," Logan scoffed. "The whole sky lit up while we were walking over here. And the campground's swimming in water. How are we supposed to get out to notify the police?"

Matt raised a hand to placate him. "Nobody's going anywhere until the storm abates. Once it does, I'll take my truck and blaze a trail to the nearest town while the rest of you wait here."

Logan narrowed his eyes to calculating slits. "Whitney and I can't hang around. As soon as the weather clears, we're out of here. We need to get back for work. We were supposed to leave this afternoon."

"I thought you were on your honeymoon," Blair said.

Whitney shot Logan a loaded look.

"We're on the tail end of it," Logan responded with a smug smile. "We don't have unlimited time off to cruise around at our leisure. Some of us have jobs to get back to."

Matt tapped a finger to his jaw, studying him. "Like it or not, we're all caught up in this now. You can't leave until the police clear you. None of us can."

For a moment no one spoke. The torrential rain on the roof above them grew ever more insistent.

"What do you mean *clear* us?" Logan demanded, an ugly snarl forming on his face. "Are you suggesting one of us had something to do with this?"

"I'm not suggesting anything," Matt replied. "I'm telling you we're all suspects in the eyes of the law simply by way of being here."

"That may be, but some of us have obligations," Harvey piped up. "It's not like the police can't interview us back home." He lifted his chin in Logan's direction. "He's got work and I've got a sick wife. Sandy's been going downhill in the last forty-eight hours. I need to get her to a hospital."

"The road back to the highway's too treacherous to drive your RV on in these conditions. As soon as the storm clears, I'll head out," Matt said. "Worst case scenario, I'll leave first thing in the morning. As soon as I get a signal, I'll call 911 for police and an ambulance. Until then, everyone needs to stay put."

"If none of us killed him," Whitney said, looking around the room questioningly, "then who did?"

"My guess is one of the hunters up by the lake," Logan replied. "They probably got into a fight or something."

"I could hike up there and find out if they know anything," Sam offered.

"Are you crazy?" Whitney arched a plucked brow at him. "We should be talking about how we're going to stay safe here overnight."

"She's right," Hazel said. "If there's a killer prowling around out there, I don't want to be taken by surprise in the middle—"

Her voice trailed off at the sound of someone rattling the handle on the trailer door. A collective gasp reverberated around the room. Matt darted to the window and peered cautiously around the blind. "It's a woman. She's holding a coat over her head."

"How do we know the killer's not a woman?" Whitney wailed.

Matt shot Harvey a questioning look. "Is that your wife?"

"What? Don't tell me she ventured out in this weather," Harvey exclaimed, jumping to his feet. He peered over Matt's shoulder. "Yeah, it's her all right."

Matt immediately wrenched open the door and helped the soaked woman inside.

Blair pulled out a blanket and draped it around Sandy's shoulders. Matt escorted the frail, shivering woman over to the captain's chair Harvey had vacated and pushed her gently down in it. A soft sigh escaped her lips and her head lolled forward.

"What were you thinking coming out in this rain?" Harvey scolded, as he adjusted the blanket around her. "We need to get you back to bed."

Sandy's feverish eyes darted around the group assembled

37

in the trailer, and then lit on Blair, a hint of desperation emanating from them. "What's … going on here?"

Blair silently acknowledged the subtle shake of Harvey's head. Understandably, he didn't want her upsetting his wife with the news of the body. She was distressed enough already and seemed disoriented from her medication.

"Your husband's right," Blair said softly. "It's best if you go back to bed, Sandy. We were just discussing the storm. Matt was discouraging anyone from trying to leave until it's over."

She peered down at her coffee and pretended to take a sip. She hated lying to the woman, but it was up to Harvey whether to tell his wife about the body they'd discovered—he knew best whether she could handle the news or not.

"I'm going to take Sandy back to our RV," Harvey announced, hoisting his wife to her feet. "She needs to rest."

Sandy started to say something, but quickly dissolved into a harsh coughing fit.

Harvey threw a helpless look around the room. "She really shouldn't be out of bed." He helped her hobble toward the door, but she struggled to keep her balance.

"I'll come with you." Hazel jumped up and grabbed Sandy's other arm. "I might have something in my trailer for that cough."

"That won't be necessary," Harvey said, sounding miffed. "I can handle her medication."

"At least let me help you walk her back," Hazel insisted.

When the door shut behind them, Logan let out a long, low whistle. "Good riddance. Spewing her germs all around."

Blair threw him a reproving look. "It's not contagious. She's got cancer. By the sound of it, she might be dying of it."

Logan stood and stretched. "Yeah, well, we could all be dead by tomorrow the way things are going. If we're done here, Whitney and I are going to head back."

He helped his young wife into her coat, and they disappeared, arm-in-arm, into the rain, letting the door slam unceremoniously behind them.

"He's a piece of work," Sam said as he got to his feet. "I should get back to Duke."

Matt nodded. "I don't foresee being able to drive out of here any time soon. We can talk later about each of us taking a shift tonight to keep an eye on things—just in case we have a prowler at Bird Creek."

AFTER SAM EXITED THE TRAILER, Matt locked the door and checked it fastidiously.

"Why didn't you tell the others the man was strangled?" Blair asked when Matt sank down on the couch next to her. "I saw you and Hazel exchange a look."

He furrowed his brow. "You keep acting like we can trust everybody. It's always good to keep some details on the QT that only the killer would know. Obviously Hazel and Sam know the truth, but there's nothing we can do about that, unfortunately."

"What do you mean *unfortunately*? It was a good thing Hazel came with us. She spotted the injuries on the man's neck."

Matt twisted his lips. "Which is why I'm not buying the whole holistic-book-writing retired nurse story. Did you hear her? She sounded like a crime scene investigator if you ask me. There's more to her than meets the eye."

"You're making wild assumptions. This whole incident has everyone on edge."

"You'd better believe it," Matt retorted. "We're talking about murder here. Don't mention anything to the others about the man being strangled until the police get here."

Blair shot him a skeptical look. "You don't seriously think a pair of honeymooners, or an elderly couple wrestling with a cancer diagnosis had anything to do with killing him, do you?"

Matt rubbed his thumb over the stubble on his jaw. "There's only a small pool of possibilities. It's too soon to rule out anybody."

5

By late afternoon, the storm had worked itself into a violent tempest buffeting the trailer so hard that Blair feared it would rip the roof off. The road circling through the campground was a churned-up mess of mud and downed branches, and visibility was close to zero. There was no chance of driving a vehicle out of Bird Creek any time soon.

"I'm going to take one of our radios over to Sam and see about setting up some kind of shift to keep watch tonight," Matt said, shoving his feet into his damp boots. "We need to make sure there's someone awake at all times in the event the killer makes an appearance."

"Highly unlikely in this weather, don't you think?" Blair said.

Matt shrugged as he exited the trailer. "I'm not taking any chances. We need to be prepared. No one else is coming to our rescue."

Twenty minutes later, he returned, soaked through and shivering, barely able to make it up the steps to the trailer without being blown sideways.

"It's evil out there. I've never seen anything like it," he said, pulling off his boots.

"Did you get some kind of rotation worked out with Sam?" Blair asked.

"Yeah, I'm taking the first shift from ten until two, and then Sam will trade off with me."

"I hope Hazel will be all right on her own."

"She'll be fine as long as she stays put. She has a solid rig, and it's new, so it won't have any leaks." Matt peeled off his damp socks and hung them up in the bathroom. "I'm starving. What do we have to eat for dinner?"

After surveying the contents of the refrigerator, Blair settled on making some turkey and cheese sandwiches and heating up some soup. Afterward, they whiled away the remainder of the evening playing Monopoly, Scrabble, and various card games, but it was impossible to focus on anything other than the growling monster outside. Every time a crack of lightning split the sky, Matt flinched as if it were a gunshot. At nine-thirty, they abandoned any attempt to make the evening more bearable and packed up the games. Blair decided to turn in while Matt checked his radio and settled in for the first shift of the night.

After tossing and turning for what seemed like forever, Blair finally drifted off against a backdrop of banshee gusts and yammering rain.

She woke with a start in the early hours to a low rumbling, the grinding of boulders shifting like gears, the cracking and snapping of trees—matchsticks in the hands of giants. Vicious and violent sounds that ripped away the fog of sleep. A sense of impending doom filled her, triggering a sudden surge of adrenaline. Foggy with sleep, her first delirious thought was that a train was rumbling through the campground. She unzipped her sleeping bag and shook Matt, awake.

"Get up!" she screamed in his ear as he rubbed his eyes in sluggish confusion. "Something's wrong!"

Matt groaned. "I only got to bed a couple of hours ago."

Blair prodded him urgently in the chest. "Do you hear that? That rumbling—what is it?"

He yawned and swung his legs resignedly over the edge of the bed.

All of a sudden, a thunderous noise unlike anything Blair had ever heard before shook the trailer—the sound of the earth's innards being ripped apart. The hairs on the back of her neck stood up.

"What's happening?" she shrieked as she threw back the covers. "Is it an earthquake?"

Matt leaped into action, grabbing his sweatpants and hoodie. "I don't know. Stay here." He dashed across to the door, pulled on his boots, and reached for the high beam flashlight clipped to the wall.

"Where are you going?" Blair yelled. "You can't go out there. It's too dangerous."

"I'm only going to take a quick look. Get the emergency pack ready, just in case."

"In case what?" Blair called after him. The door slammed shut on her unanswered question. She hurriedly pulled on the clothes she'd abandoned in a pile next to the bed, her brain firing in several different directions at once. What if their campground was swallowed up in the quake? Should they check on the others? Hazel was on her own and Sandy was sick. Should they gather together in one trailer so they could help each other, or was it safer for them all to stay put? She wished with all her heart that they'd kept going to Black Rock and never made the fateful decision to turn off the highway and overnight in this nightmarish place.

Fully clothed, she opened the closet and began rummaging around beneath their clothes for the emergency pack. She was sure Matt had tossed it in here to make space for his iPad and walkie talkies in the cabinet near the driver's seat. Her panic mounted when she remembered moving it into a plastic storage tub of miscellaneous items that Matt had loaded into one of the compartments beneath the trailer, never thinking they might actually need it. She had no choice but to brave the elements to retrieve it. Digging around in the kitchen drawer, she found the small flashlight she'd stashed there for emergencies. To her frustration, the batteries were dead. She slammed the drawer shut and reached for her phone instead—the built-in flashlight would have to suffice.

After gearing up in her boots and jacket, she darted to the door of their camping trailer and wrenched it open, gasping at the force of the wind that blew her backward. "Matt! Are you out here?" She waited, heart thumping, but couldn't hear anything above the howling of the storm and pneumatic pounding of the rain on their truck and trailer. Doggedly, she staggered down the steps and then froze, staring in horror at the hillside beyond their campsite. Her heart hammered out a frenzied rhythm. The mountain backing up to the camp-ground was seething and rippling beneath the steely eye of a watchful moon, as though birthing some monster from the deep. One by one, towering pine trees toppled forward, pros-trate in the wake of a ponderous torrent of mud, truck-sized granite boulders and debris snaking down the slopes in an ever-widening swathe. Blistering fear prickled her skin. Had the earthquake shifted the whole mountain? "Matt!" she shouted helplessly into the wind. Her throat felt like it had closed over with fear. Where was he?

Cautiously, she felt her way along the body of the trailer to the storage compartment. She turned the knob on the hatch and reached inside for the plastic tub, trying to make sure the wind didn't rip the hatch off in the process. Tugging the tub toward her, she flipped open the lid, and then froze at the spine-tingling realization that someone was standing directly behind her.

The violence of the storm seemed to fade into the background as the thundering of her heart took over her senses. Before she could react, a hand gripped her shoulder and she instinctively let out a blood-curdling scream. Letting go of the tub, she spun around to see Sam staring at her, hair plastered across his forehead, water streaming down his face. Nerves taut with fear, her thoughts tumbled over themselves in quick succession. What was he doing out here? How long had he been standing there?

"Are you all right, Blair?" he asked, his eyes crinkling with concern.

At that moment, Matt came running up to them, saving her from having to formulate a response. "Everything all right?" His eyes darted uncertainly from her to Sam and back. "I heard you cry out."

"Yes … I … was looking for the emergency pack," Blair stammered. "Sam spooked me."

"I saw the light outside the trailer," he explained. "I wanted to make sure you guys were okay."

"Let's go inside," Matt said. "We need to talk."

Blair swiftly retrieved the emergency pack before shoving the tub back into the compartment and closing up the hatch.

Back inside the trailer they convened at the dining table, shaking the water out of their hair like dogs attempting to dry off.

Blair pinned an anxious gaze on Matt. "Did you see anything? It looked like the mountain was moving."

"It sounded like an earthquake," Sam added.

Matt swiped at the water dripping from the end of his nose. "It's too dark to say for sure, but I think it was a mudslide. I'm guessing the deluge of rain was too much for the burned sections of the mountains. The force of the water must have washed everything down."

"We're not in any danger, are we?" Blair asked.

"We're not directly in the path of the slide," Matt said. "But that doesn't mean there won't be another one. We might not be so lucky a second time."

"What about the hunters camping up by the lake?" Sam asked.

Matt scratched the back of his neck, looking decidedly uncomfortable. "I don't know. We'll have to wait until it's light out to see."

They fell silent for a moment or two, digesting the implications. If the hunters' tents lay in the mudslide's path, they wouldn't have had a chance—they wouldn't even have known what hit them.

Sam got to his feet. "I need to get back to Duke. There's nothing we can do until it's light out."

Matt nodded. "I don't know about you, but we're getting out of here today, rain or no rain. It's too dangerous to stay. We'll clear the road if we have to. If the others know what's good for them, they'll leave with us. We can caravan out to the main highway to make sure everyone makes it safely. As soon as we get a signal, I'll call 911 and arrange to meet the police at a rest stop or somewhere safe. They'll probably want to interview us."

Sam nodded. "Makes sense. I'm with you. See you later."

Once he'd exited the trailer, Blair got up to brew some coffee. Matt reached for her by the wrist and pulled her back down. "What was Sam doing over here?"

She frowned, yanking her hand out of his grip. "You heard him—making sure everything was all right."

"I told you to stay put inside the trailer."

"You also told me to get the emergency pack."

Matt gave her a chagrined look. "I forgot it was in the

outside storage compartment. Pretty stupid place to put it in retrospect. Why did you scream?"

"Sam startled me, that's all," Blair assured him. "I wasn't in any danger."

"You don't know that. We don't know anything about him —other than what he's told us. It could all be a pack of lies."

"What are you saying? You're acting like Sam's the killer. That doesn't make any sense—"

"I don't know who he is, Blair. And neither do you. You can't ever be alone with him, or anyone else from the campground, for that matter."

"Fair enough. But I didn't know he was there."

A nerve twitched in Matt's cheek. "That's the part that scares me."

"I don't think he deliberately snuck up on me," Blair said. "The storm was so loud; I couldn't possibly have heard him approach."

Matt's gaze bored into her. "Exactly! That's my point! Why didn't he yell out to you to make sure he didn't freak you out?"

Blair turned away without responding. Matt had a valid argument. It had unnerved her when Sam had reached for her shoulder without saying a word. She couldn't help wondering what might have happened if Matt hadn't shown up when he did.

6

By nine o'clock that morning, the wind and rain had subsided enough to venture outside and take a closer look at what had transpired overnight. After digging out their binoculars, Matt and Blair donned their outerwear and locked the trailer behind them.

"Let's head up the hiking trail a bit and see if we can get a better view of the mudslide," Matt proposed.

Blair slipped the binoculars' strap around her neck and tucked her hands into her pockets to keep warm. "Should we ask Sam to come with us?"

"No!" Matt said, a forced calmness in his voice. "Let's just go ourselves. We can update him when we get back."

Blair frowned to herself as they set off. Apparently, Matt's suspicions about Sam were back in full force.

They'd only gone a quarter mile or so when they saw the first tell-tale signs of mud oozing across the hiking trail.

"I'd no idea it came this close to the campground," Matt remarked, in a somber tone. "Looks like we dodged a bullet last night. We should get out of Bird Creek as soon as possible. I don't want to take any chances of getting caught in a second slide."

"I'm good with that," Blair said. "This place hasn't exactly turned out to be the idyllic retreat I pictured. More like one unending nightmare since we got here."

They walked on for another couple of hundred feet or so before coming to an abrupt stop at the shocking sight that lay directly ahead. A forty-foot wide swathe of black mud, massive boulders, uprooted trees, and miscellaneous brush had obliterated the trail to the lake. For a moment they stood frozen to the spot, digesting the horrifying implications of the scene of devastation before them.

"The police are never going to find that man's body now. Good thing we took photographs." Matt shook his head in disbelief, eying the horizon. "Any sign of the hunters?"

Blair lifted the binoculars and surveyed the area. She panned slowly to the left, tracing the path of the slide back to its origin on the scarred mountainside that had succumbed to the storm. Her stomach churned as the sickening reality took hold. The mudslide had torn straight through the hunters' campsite and obliterated every trace of them. Shaking, she slipped the binoculars over her head and handed them to Matt. "You need to see this."

He stared silently through the lens. For a long moment, he said nothing. Then, he abruptly hunkered down and scrubbed his hands over his face. "It's like it wiped them from the face of the earth. Unbelievable. I've never seen anything like this before."

"Do you think there are survivors?" Blair asked.

Matt straightened up and inhaled a deep breath. "I doubt it, but we need to find out before we get out of here. Let's head back to the trailer and round up some supplies first."

They wasted no time retracing their steps along the churned-up trail, each lost in their own grim thoughts. When they arrived back at the campground, Sam came out of his trailer to meet them, Duke at his heels.

Blair could sense Matt's hackles rising, but Sam seemed oblivious to any tension between them. He gestured to the binoculars in Matt's hands. "See anything?"

"It was a mudslide." Matt moved his jaw side-to-side, as if contemplating whether to continue the conversation or leave it at that. "The burned section of the mountain gave way. The debris blasted straight through the campsite up by the lake and crossed the hiking trail. Not sure if any of the hunters made it out alive or not. We're going up there now to have a look around."

An anguished look flickered in Sam's eyes. "I'll grab some rope and come with you. Duke can help locate any survivors."

Matt pressed his lips together and gave a tight nod, acknowledging that Duke would be an asset. Then he turned to Blair. "Why don't you ask Hazel to join us too? We might need her medical expertise. And knock on Whitney's and Logan's door and let them know what's going on. We could use their help to search the area. I'll fill in Harvey and Sandy."

Blair hurried off, casting a curious eye over the uninhabited camper van in passing. She couldn't help wondering if the killer had been caught up in the mudslide and his body washed away with his victim's? Either way, it would be up to the police to put the pieces together now and figure out who the van belonged to. As soon as she and Matt had searched for any survivors, they were going to blaze a trail out of this wretched campground before anything else happened.

When she reached Logan's and Whitney's trailer, she hammered on the door repeatedly, stepping back when Logan stuck a tousled head out. "Yeah?"

Blair quickly brought him up to speed. "It's absolute destruction out there. The mudslide went straight through the hunters' campsite. We could use your help looking for survivors."

Yawning, Logan tugged a hand through his hair. "I thought it was an earthquake—Whitney was freaking out. Some honeymoon this is turning out to be."

Blair shot him a look of pained exasperation. "It sucks for all of us, but right now, there could be people out there who need our help."

Logan scratched his chest, a look of irritation on his face. "Don't wait for us. I only got to sleep a little while ago. We'll catch up with you. I need some coffee first."

Before Blair had a chance to respond, he closed the door in her face. She let out a snort of disgust as she turned on her heel and set out for Hazel's trailer. She wasn't going to hold her breath waiting on Whitney and Logan to show up and join the search party. She had a hunch they would hitch up their trailer and blast out of here the first chance they got.

Hazel spotted her through the window and waved a hand in acknowledgement. "I was just getting ready to head over your way," she said, yanking the door open. "Was that an earthquake last night?"

"Mudslide," Blair responded.

Hazel's eyes widened. "Did it come close to us?"

"It went straight through the hunters' campsite by the lake and crossed the hiking trail. We're heading up there now to look for survivors. We could use your help in case anyone's injured."

"Of course," Hazel agreed, springing into action. "Come on in. I'll grab some supplies." She went into the bedroom and resurfaced a moment later clutching a medical bag. "If there are any serious injuries, we might need a stretcher to bring them back," she said, as she pulled on her Parka and boots.

"We'll cross that bridge when we come to it," Blair replied.

"We have a tarp in the back of our truck we can use, but there's no sense in hauling a bunch of supplies with us until we know what we're dealing with." She didn't add that she held out little hope of finding any survivors in the mudslide's path. Hazel hadn't seen the devastation she'd witnessed.

Matt and Sam were busy sorting through a tub of climbing gear at Sam's trailer when Blair showed up with Hazel in tow. Matt had donned his waterproof tactical gear and Sam was kitted out in waders and a heavy-duty raincoat and pants. Evidently, they were planning on trudging deep into the mud if need be.

Matt nodded to Hazel. "Thanks for coming. We might need your expertise if we find anyone alive."

"I never imagined for one minute it was a mudslide," Hazel said.

"I'm guessing the burned side of the mountain couldn't absorb any more rain. With all the vegetation gone, there was nothing to stop the dirt giving way." Matt reached for a shovel leaning up against Sam's trailer. "Are Logan and Whitney joining us?"

Blair twisted her lips. "I wouldn't hold your breath. I have a sneaking suspicion they're going to bail out of here now that the storm's passed."

"Figures," Matt said gruffly. "That Logan's a waste of space. And Whitney's not much better—she's an airhead."

"Give them a break," Blair soothed. "They're on their honeymoon. Did you talk to Harvey?"

Matt nodded. "I told him to stay put and keep the door locked."

Sam grabbed a hiking pole and a coil of rope.

"All right, let's get moving." Matt strode off, leading the charge, his shovel resting on his shoulder.

They set out along the trail at a brisk pace, Duke eagerly sniffing out the route ahead of them. When they reached the mudslide, they took turns surveying the gouged-out mountainside in the distance through the binoculars.

"The campsite by the lake's decimated," Hazel said in a hushed tone. "It will be a miracle if anyone survived. Looks like a battlefield out there."

Matt flinched, his expression hardening as he stared off into the distance.

Blair clenched her hands into fists in her pockets. She could tell his thoughts were traveling far beyond the horizon to the road in Afghanistan where his comrades had fallen.

Realizing her gaffe, Hazel grimaced and threw Blair a helpless look.

She gave a subtle shake of her head, hoping Hazel would take the hint and drop it. Apologizing now would only underscore the analogy.

"Let's make our way up to the original campsite and look around the area," Matt suggested. "We can spread out from there."

With Duke firmly leashed, Sam took the lead, prodding tentatively at the ground in front of him with his hiking pole to test the depth of the mud. A distinct smell of ash hung in the air from the scorched earth that had been stripped from the fire-scarred mountainside. Blair and Hazel followed behind Sam with Matt taking up the rear. Blair's mind was abuzz imagining what the hunters' final moments must have been like before the catastrophic debris flow of mud, trees, and boulders thundered over their tents like a cavalcade of tanks. It was hard to imagine anyone could have lived through such an onslaught, but it would be on their consciences forever if they didn't make some attempt to look for survivors before they left.

Progress was painfully slow as Sam meticulously tested the mud in front of him each step of the way. Every so often, one of them yelled out, *Is anyone there?* or *Can anyone hear me?*

but there was never a response. As they moved steadily forward toward the lake, Hazel suddenly let out a yelp and pointed to her left. "Over there! I see something. Looks like a backpack."

"Wait here!" Sam said. He turned and began picking his way gingerly over to the pack. Reaching down, he grabbed hold of one of the straps and hoisted it aloft. The others watched with bated breath as he prodded the surrounding area with the pole, while Duke sniffed around. Satisfied that no one was buried in the vicinity, Sam carefully unzipped the pack and rooted through it. After a few minutes, he slung it over his shoulder and made his way back to the group. "There's no ID inside, not even a hunting license. Just some camping food and supplies."

"We'll have to bring back any personal possessions we come across," Matt said. "The families will need to identify them." For a brief moment, his gaze met Blair's, and she glimpsed the emotions he was wrestling with.

"I think I see part of a tent or something wrapped around a tree," Sam said, pointing off into the distance.

Blair panned the area with the binoculars and then let out a gasp. "You're right! It's fabric of some kind. Let's check it out."

Single file, with Sam leading the way once more, they continued traversing the swathe of mud, rocks, and debris until they neared the tree where a shredded tent was flapping feebly like a wounded butterfly. Sam held up a hand to halt them. "The mud's getting deeper," he yelled back. "It's above my knees. You girls might want to wait here."

Blair handed Matt the binoculars. "Take them, in case you spot something else."

He and Sam proceeded with caution. It wasn't long before the mud was squelching up to their thighs. Blair and Hazel watched with apprehension as the men ploughed on toward the tree. After wrangling with the tent remnant for several minutes, Sam finally succeeded in freeing it. He rolled it up and stuffed it into the hunting backpack on his shoulder. For the next twenty minutes or so, he and Matt methodically poked and prodded at the mud in the surrounding area with their pole and shovel, before abandoning their efforts.

Matt straightened up and cupped his hands to his mouth. "Anyone out there?" He turned his head expectantly in every direction like a bird observing its surroundings, waiting for a moment or two before yelling again, "Can anyone hear me?"

Blair scrunched up her eyes in concentration as she scoured the area for any signs of life, a head poking up from the mud, a hand waving—even a finger. It was entirely possible someone was listening to their shouts but was too weak to respond.

Matt and Sam spent the best part of the next hour searching the area close to the lake where the hunters' camp-site had been—while Blair and Hazel stuck to higher ground —but the only other item they stumbled across was a badly dented, solar-powered lantern.

"Doesn't look like anyone survived," Matt said. "Retrieving the bodies is a job for search and rescue. We should call it a day and get out of here while we still can. The mountainside could be unstable."

As they turned to go, a faint cry reached Blair's ears. She stopped dead in her tracks. A bird, or was it human? For a split second, she thought she'd imagined it. But Duke's insis-tent barking indicated otherwise. "Did you hear that?" she asked, swinging around to face the others.

"I thought I heard something." Matt pressed the binocu-lars to his eyes, scanning the battered landscape as they huddled together, motionless, listening intently. After a moment or two, another muffled cry drifted their way.

Wordlessly, Sam slipped the backpack from his shoulder

and unleashed Duke. The dog took off, zeroing in on a distant target. Sam locked eyes briefly with Matt and they both followed in Duke's tracks.

Tenting her hand over her eyes, Blair watched their progress as they staggered through the mud to where Duke was waiting for them by a cluster of boulders and tangled vegetation. Instantly, both men fell to their knees, hands scrabbling at the mud.

"They've found something," Hazel said breathlessly.

Blair's thoughts tumbled together. *Please don't let this be what I think it is. Matt really doesn't need to be by another dying man's side.*

She watched apprehensively as the two men paused and appeared to assess the situation. After a moment's deliberation, Matt stood and started shoveling mud aside. Sam remained kneeling on the ground, hunched over as though talking to someone. After a few minutes, Matt tossed the shovel aside and then leaned down and reached into the debris.

Blair sucked in her breath as her husband and Sam slowly hoisted a mud-caked figure to his feet.

7

"*I* can't believe it! He's alive!" Hazel gasped.

Blair watched with morbid fascination as Matt and Sam inched their way toward them supporting the man they'd rescued. Even at this distance, he looked like some kind of monster from the deep—covered in slick, oil-colored filth from head to toe. But at least he was moving his legs, which was a good sign. It was anyone's guess what internal injuries he'd sustained after being swept away in his sleep by a torrent of mud and trees.

As the three man drew closer, Blair and Hazel trudged through the muck to meet them.

"Any obvious injuries? Is he bleeding?" Hazel asked in a clipped tone, already unzipping her medical bag.

"I think his right arm's broken," Matt said, panting from the exertion of digging the man out of the mire and half-dragging him through it.

"What's your name?" Hazel inquired as she worked to splint the injured man's arm and ease it into a sling she retrieved from her supplies.

"Rob," he rasped.

Hazel laid a hand gently on his good shoulder. "All right, Rob. We're going to take you back to the campground and check you out properly there."

"Got any ... water?" Rob's tone verged on pitiful as he looked around at them, the whites of his eyes starkly arresting against the muddy backdrop of his face.

Quashing down the random thought that she might be looking into the eyes of a killer, Blair hurriedly pulled out her water bottle from her jacket and unscrewed the cap. Sam took it from her and held it up to Rob's lips. He sucked greedily on it and then spat out a mouthful of mud, repeating the process a couple of times before swallowing the rest of the water in a few hasty gulps. His thirst quenched, he sank back in Sam's and Matt's arms, eyelids drifting half-closed.

"We need to keep him moving." Matt's voice vibrated with a heightened sense of urgency. "He's going into shock."

Blair flashed her husband a tight smile of encouragement. Despite the traumatic circumstances they'd been unexpectedly thrown into, he was holding up well and doing everything he'd been trained to do. It wasn't the first time he'd carried a wounded man to safety. This certainly hadn't been on the itinerary they'd drawn up before they'd pulled out of her father-in-law's driveway a few weeks earlier. But this was the hand they'd been dealt. Blair only hoped it didn't prove to be too big a setback on Matt's road to recovery.

The return trek to Bird Creek was woefully slow, and, more than once, Rob pleaded with them to stop so he could rest.

"No can do, buddy," Matt replied firmly. "We're going all the way. The sooner we get you to a hospital, the better."

Blair breathed out a silent sigh of relief when the campground came into view. Overhead, a hint of blue had made a weak appearance in a crack between the clouds, a welcome indication that the storm had finally moved on, and that they could pack up and leave.

Back at their trailer, they divested themselves of their outer garments and tossed everything into the bed of Matt's truck. Sam tied Duke up outside while Matt and Hazel half-carried Rob up the steps and inside the trailer. Blair threw an old blanket over the couch and helped Rob hobble over to it. Sam followed them inside and sank down in one of the captain's chairs by the door.

Blair retrieved a bottle of water from the fridge and opened it before handing it to Rob. His hand trembled as he gripped it and guzzled it down, exhaling a satisfied sigh when he was done. Blair discreetly draped another blanket around his shaking shoulders. Other than trying to keep him warm, she wasn't sure how to help him.

Hazel knelt at his side and took his pulse. "Apart from your arm, does it hurt anywhere else?"

"Everywhere." Rob groaned softly. "I'm battered head-to-toe. It was like being in an industrial-sized trash compactor with boulders, rocks, and branches smashing up against me."

"I need you to lie down so I can check you out," Hazel said. "I'll try not to hurt you, but I have to press on your abdomen and make sure nothing's swelling in there."

Rob closed his eyes and nodded his permission. Hazel prodded him carefully for several minutes and then adjusted his sling. "I don't detect any traumatic internal injuries, which is a good start," she announced with a measure of relief in her voice. She held a finger up in front of Rob's face. "Can you follow my finger?"

His eyelids popped open and he flicked his eyes obligingly left then right.

"Good," Hazel said. "No apparent sign of concussion. That in itself is a miracle considering what you went through."

"Did you … find any other survivors?" Rob asked.

Matt and Sam exchanged an uneasy look. Matt tightened his lips. "Not yet. Were you tent camping?"

Rob gave a despondent nod. "We were on a five-day hunting trip."

"How many were in your party?" Sam asked.

"Four, including myself." Rob hesitated before adding, "My brother was with us. I don't know if he got out or not. He was in a hunting blind about a half mile away scoping out bear. He spent most of the last forty-eight hours there."

Blair's stomach churned at the news that Rob might have lost a family member in the mudslide. Everything about this scenario was a nightmare.

Matt motioned to her. "Let me see your phone for a minute."

She frowned back at him, her eyes widening when it dawned on her what he was getting at. The dead man might be Rob's brother. Surely Matt wasn't planning on showing him the pictures of the body. She doubted Rob was capable of absorbing any more bad news at the moment. The last thing he needed was to see his brother's corpse. Not to mention the fact that they'd have to tell Rob he'd been murdered. And then they'd have to break the news to him that they'd left his brother's body where they'd found it—and that it might never be retrieved now.

Blair chewed on her lip. On the other hand, if she were in Rob's situation, she'd rather know her family member's fate, regardless of how dire it turned out to be. Hesitantly, she fished out her phone and clicked on the camera roll. She scrolled through to the series of pictures she'd taken of the dead man and then passed the phone to Matt.

"Rob," he began. "We stumbled on a body yesterday on the hiking trail up to the lake. Maybe you can take a look at these pictures and tell us if you recognize him. I really hope for your sake it's not your brother, but you should check just in case."

A deep furrow formed on Rob's brow. He held out a shaky hand for the phone and studied the screen for a long moment. "It's not him."

"Do you recognize him?" Sam asked.

Rob shook his head. "Never seen him before. He's not one of our hunting party." His eyes darted uncertainly around the room before settling back on Matt. "You said you found him yesterday. So, he didn't die in the mudslide?"

Blair rubbed her hands on her pants, swallowing back the dread rising in her throat. They'd come full circle to the subject of the unidentified killer.

"He was stabbed in the stomach," Matt said quietly.

Rob's jaw dropped. He took another look at the picture before handing the phone back to Matt. "So if he's not one of our hunting party, and he's not camping here with you, who is he?"

Matt folded his arms in front of his chest and leaned back against the counter, his gaze boring into Rob. "That's what we're trying to figure out. There's a camper van here that's been sitting empty ever since we got here. It's possible it's this guy's rig, but that begs the next question—who killed him?"

Rob shot another nervous glance around the room. "It wasn't one of us if that's what you're thinking. I've known the guys I hunt with for years." He rubbed a hand over his jaw contemplatively. "Come to think of it, there was another hunter in the area a couple of days ago. He stopped by our site briefly. Kind of aloof. Seemed irritated to see us. He said he was going duck hunting."

Matt locked eyes with Sam. "Maybe he owns the empty van next to you."

"So he hasn't shown up here, yet?" Rob asked.

"I haven't seen anyone, and I was the first to arrive—shortly before Sam," Hazel said. "It's possible he got caught up in that mudslide."

"It's a police matter now," Blair said. "Our first priority is to get Rob—and Sandy, of course—to a hospital. We should get to work clearing the fallen branches off the road."

Sam got to his feet. "I'll bring Harvey up to speed and see if he needs any help getting their RV ready."

Matt opened the door, hesitating at the top of the steps at the sound of a truck pulling into the campground. Duke broke into a frenzied barking fit. "Sounds like we have company." Matt reached for a hoodie hanging by the door and pulled it on before heading outside with Sam.

Moments later, Whitney and Logan sprinted into view. Blair watched as they communicated something to Matt, gesticulating wildly. Heart thumping, she called down to them. "What's wrong?"

Matt's expression was grim as he ushered Whitney and Logan up the steps and inside. Whitney's face paled at the sight of the mud-encrusted man sprawled on the couch.

"This is Rob." Matt glowered at Logan. "He was one of the hunting party camping up by the lake. We found him buried in the mud."

Logan ogled Rob with an air of distaste, not even momentarily chagrined at being introduced to a survivor he'd elected not to search for.

Blair didn't bother masking the look of contempt on her own face. Honeymoon aside, Logan was a self-centered jerk. She wasn't impressed with Whitney either—hanging on his every word instead of calling him out on his egocentric attitude.

Before Logan had a chance to say anything, Sam and Harvey appeared in the doorway. Harvey nodded to no one in particular, zeroing in on Rob with a mistrustful air. Blair wouldn't blame him if he was wondering whether Rob was the killer. The same thought had crossed her mind. But Harvey didn't know about the lone hunter still out there somewhere.

"How's Sandy doing?" Hazel asked.

"Not great. Worse, actually." Harvey cast another wary glance at Rob. "Looks like we won't be the only ones heading straight to the hospital once we pull out of here."

"No one's going anywhere anytime soon," Logan said through gritted teeth.

Harvey frowned at him. "What are you talking about?"

Logan scowled around the room. "We're trapped at Bird Creek."

8

"The mudslide took out the road leading from the campground down to the highway," Logan blurted out.

"It's washed out a huge section," Whitney added, looking every bit as distraught as she sounded.

Gasps of disbelief reverberated around the trailer, followed by a momentary stunned silence.

"How did you find out?" Sam asked, pinning an accusatory gaze on Logan, who narrowed his eyes, his posture decidedly defensive.

"Whitney and I tried to drive out of here earlier. I ... we have to get back to work or we'll lose our jobs. The road's shot. I'm telling you, we're trapped. The only way we're getting out of here any time soon is by helicopter."

Trapped! Blair fought to resist the fear that pummeled her mind. She cast a hesitant glance Rob's way. So much for getting him to the hospital today. She only hoped Hazel's initial diagnosis was right that his injuries amounted to nothing more than a broken arm. And what about Sandy? By the sound of things, she was worsening by the hour. She'd barely been outside her RV since they'd got here. Hazel might be able to set a broken bone in a pinch, but there wasn't much she could do for an advanced case of cancer. And then, of course, there was the frightening possibility that the killer was still out there. Her stomach twisted and she quickly quashed the thought.

As if reading her mind, Harvey took a step toward Logan, a half-crazed look in his eyes. "There must be some way out —some way we get around the slide."

Matt scratched the stubble on his jaw. "Did either of you get out to take a closer look at the road? Maybe we could dig around it. Even if we have to wait for a backhoe—"

"You can't—there's a gaping chasm to the valley below," Logan cut in.

Whitney threw a skittish look around as she picked at her nail polish. "Maybe we can build some kind of a bridge to walk across it."

Logan threw her a scornful look. "And how are we supposed to do that? This is a campground, not Bird Creek school of engineering. Like I said, the only way we're getting out of here is by air. It'll take months to rebuild that road."

Harvey clenched and unclenched his fists. "I need to get Sandy out of here. Today."

Hazel laid a hand on his arm. "We'll do the very best we can for her until we figure this out."

Matt folded his arms across his chest. "All right, listen up, everyone. I'll drive out to the road and evaluate the situation. I don't doubt what these guys are saying, but maybe there's something that can be done about it."

Logan snorted. "Who do you think you are, Superman?"

Matt narrowed his eyes at him. "I've been trained to get out of some pretty tight spots. I'm willing to wager you've had a pretty cushy run of life so far."

Logan scowled and took a step toward him. "What's that supposed to mean?"

Blair stepped between them, holding up her palms. This had to end now before Matt exploded. There was no knowing how far he would take it once he began to unload. Not that Logan wasn't asking for it. "Enough! Calm down, both of you! There's nothing to be gained by winding each other up. What we need to do is work together—take stock of our circumstances and assess what we're going to do next."

"I'm guessing it won't be long before search and rescue have helicopters flying over the area," Sam said. "As soon as they spot that mudslide, they'll be looking for survivors."

"What makes you think they'll spot us anytime soon?" Logan retorted. "We're in the middle of nowhere. It could be days, or possibly weeks, before the forest service comes anywhere near here."

Whitney let out a whimper and pressed her knuckles to her lips.

Matt looked daggers at Logan. "Way to go with the fear-mongering."

"Someone will call it in," Sam insisted. "Some backcountry pilot will spot the mudslide and fly low to investigate."

"And even if they don't, my family—and the other hunters' families—will alert the authorities when we don't show up tonight," Rob added. "They know the general area we were camping in."

"In the meantime, we need to figure out what we can do to help guide SAR to our location," Matt said. "The first priority is to get Sandy and Rob airlifted out of here."

Harvey drew his brows together and combed his fingers through his beard as if he was weighing something up. Blair got the distinct impression he wasn't buying into the idea of Matt taking charge and telling people what to do.

Harvey got to his feet abruptly. "I have to go check on Sandy, see if she needs anything."

"Why don't we all grab some lunch and meet back here to make a game plan, say around two?" Blair suggested.

Matt eyed the sun filtering through the clouds. "Bring your camping chairs. I'll get a fire going."

"We'll keep a close eye on you for the next twenty-four hours or so," Hazel said to Rob, as she got to her feet. "I'll check for any signs of swelling again after lunch."

After the group dispersed, Matt helped Rob into the shower while Blair found some clean clothes for him to dress in. When he reappeared a few minutes later, she scarcely recognized him. He was a large-boned man in his late fifties with ginger hair, a scruffy beard, and hands as big as paws. His forehead was badly scratched above his left eye and a nasty bruise bloomed on his right cheek. An intimidating figure by any standards. A tiny shiver crossed Blair's shoulders. Was it possible they were hosting a killer in their trailer?

Suppressing the frightening thought, for now—after all, he was incapacitated with his broken arm—she determined to treat Rob as she would any other guest. She pulled out a chopping board and set about making some ham and cheese sandwiches, careful not to turn her back on him, another safety tip she'd learned from Matt. "What can we get you to drink, Rob? Water, soda, coffee?"

"Just some water, thanks. Can't seem to quench my thirst. My throat feels ripped raw."

Matt unscrewed the cap from a bottle of water and handed it to him. "You probably swallowed some mud mixed with ash."

"I'm worried about internal injuries," Blair said, setting a paper plate with a sandwich on the couch next to Rob.

"I'm beat up, that's all," he assured her. "Sounds like Harvey's wife is in worse shape."

Blair pressed her lips together. "Her cancer's bad. Harvey told us the doctors referred them to hospice."

Rob furrowed his brow. "It's odd, I feel like I know him from somewhere, like we've met before. Maybe at another campground."

Matt gestured to the recovered backpack that Sam had left lying by the front door. "Do you recognize that?"

Rob let out a heavy sigh. "Yeah, it's my buddy, Jeff's." He lifted his sandwich and then set it back down on the plate. "Did you ... find anything else?"

Blair shook her head. "Just a broken camping lantern."

"I can't thank you guys enough for pulling me out of there. And Duke for finding me. I only hope no one else is still trapped in the mud. I've hunted with those guys for years. Salt-of-the-earth folks. I know all their wives and kids." Rob sniffed and frowned down at his sandwich. "I need to go back out there and look for my brother. I can't tell his kids I didn't even try."

Matt scratched his chin. "You're in no condition to look for anyone. We'll go back out and take another look this afternoon. First, we need to focus on assessing the damage to the road and figuring out how to alert SAR that we're here."

"I can't help wondering if that hunter who came by our site killed the man you found," Rob said quietly, almost as if he was talking to himself. "I feel bad now that we didn't question him more. He was a bit of an oddball to be honest—not the least bit friendly."

"If he died in the mudslide, it's possible we'll never know for sure," Blair mused.

Rob shot her a wary glance. "Or the killer could be alive and well—here in this campground. You don't know these people. They're all strangers."

Matt stared fixedly at him. "Which is why I keep a close eye on folks until I get the feel of them."

Rob threw a questioning look Blair's way, but she averted her eyes. Of course Matt didn't trust Rob. He didn't trust anyone. And, given the circumstances they found themselves in, she could hardly fault him.

Two o'clock rolled around, and one-by-one the other campers gathered at the blazing fire Matt had started in the pit outside their trailer with the help of a blowtorch. Rob had fallen asleep on the couch, and Matt and Blair had elected to let him rest after his ordeal. Ordinarily, a flickering camp fire had a way of stimulating good conversation of its own accord, but the atmosphere was strained and the faces reflected in the flames wore the defeated air of prisoners reeling from the sound of the gate clanging shut on their sentence. Duke was the only one who seemed contented, resting his head on his paws at Sam's feet.

"Welcome everyone," Blair began. "We're in a difficult spot and I realize nerves are raw right now. Two nights ago, a man was murdered, and last night we narrowly escaped a mudslide with our lives. We've been thrown into this mess, forced to depend on one another, and we scarcely know one another. That can be dangerous in an already stressful situation. So I suggest we take a few minutes and introduce ourselves briefly. If we're going be stuck here for the next few days, it's important to develop some level of trust."

"I couldn't agree more," Hazel piped up. "I'm a big believer in making connections. I'll kick things off. I'm divorced, fifty-six years old, and a retired nurse. After my sister died of pancreatic cancer, I wanted to do something meaningful in her memory. So I'm traveling around the country writing a book about naturopathic medicine and healing, which I'm going to dedicate to her." She laughed self-consciously. "Admittedly, it's taking me a bit longer than I'd like. I spend more time foraging for plants than actually writing."

She turned an expectant gaze on Whitney, seated on the other side of a vacant chair between them. "And you two lovebirds are on your honeymoon—you told me that when we met at the gas station—but that's all I know about you. You've been hiding out in that trailer ever since you got here."

Whitney slipped a hand through Logan's arm and glanced coyly around the circle. "Yes, Logan and I are newlyweds."

A subdued chorus of congratulations met her announcement. Blair squirmed in her seat. Despite her misgivings about Whitney and Logan, she couldn't help feeling sorry for them. This had to be about the most disastrous honeymoon imaginable.

Whitney prodded Logan in the shoulder. "You're next. Tell them something about yourself."

"I'm a computer systems analyst," he said grumpily, folding his arms in front of him to indicate that was the height of what he intended to share with the group.

After an awkward silence, Blair cleared her throat. "Matt and I have been married for five years. We decided to borrow his dad's trailer and do some traveling before we settle down and set up our landscaping business together. I'm a landscape architect."

"I'm Blair's husband, in case anyone's still trying to connect the dots," Matt said. "I got back from a tour of duty in Afghanistan a few months ago. It's been rough … assimilating."

Blair squirmed in her seat. Matt had glossed over the worst of it, but then she hardly expected him to open up to a bunch of strangers when he'd barely opened up to her about it.

Hazel inclined her head toward him. "Thank you for your service."

Matt leaned back in his chair and turned to Harvey seated next to him.

Judging by his expression, Blair surmised he'd just as soon forego the kumbaya bonding and get on with packing up and getting out of here. But he was stranded at Bird Creek like the rest of them. Isolating himself right when he needed them most wouldn't accomplish anything.

"Sandy and I are retired. She finished her latest round of chemotherapy a few weeks ago." Harvey dropped his gaze and twiddled with his hands in his lap. "We're both avid campers and we were eager to get back out on the trail. But this was a mistake. She's going downhill fast."

The crackling of logs muffled the sympathetic murmuring that followed his comments.

After a respectful moment of silence, Sam spoke up. "Seems like we all came out here to get away from something. I lost my climbing buddy in an accident a couple of months back." He rubbed Duke's head distractedly. "It's been tough to keep going and stay motivated ever since."

Blair stretched a sympathetic smile across her face. Everyone had their own story of heartbreak, except for Logan and Whitney. But they were young—it was only a matter of time before life smacked them in the teeth too. "Thanks, everyone," she said. "Now that we've broken the ice, let's brainstorm about how we can rally together while we ride out this mess."

Across the road, the door to Harvey's and Sandy's RV creaked open. Everyone craned their necks, watching with curiosity as an unsteady Sandy descended the steps and began making her way toward them.

Harvey went to get out of his chair, but Blair jumped to

her feet first. She ran across to Sandy and gently guided her to the empty camping chair next to Hazel.

"You shouldn't be out here in the cold," Harvey scolded, hurrying over to her. "Let me take you back to bed."

"I'm … fine," she replied, slurring her speech as she motioned to him with a flop of her hand to sit back down.

Blair shot a concerned look Hazel's way. Sandy sounded far from fine—more like she was dosed up on some heavy-duty pain medication.

"You're just in time," Matt said. "We were about to discuss our predicament and make a game plan going forward. Logan and Whitney informed us that a mudslide took out the road that leads from the campground to the highway. I'm going to drive out there in a few minutes and assess the situation. No harm in a second opinion. But, as it stands, we're stranded here. So we need to come up with some ideas of how we can help ourselves while we wait for rescue."

Sandy darted a confused look around the group. Her eyes looked even glassier against the backdrop of the flames.

"We could start by gathering up some boulders from the mudslide and building an SOS," Sam proposed. "Basic stuff, but it works."

Matt gave an approving nod. "Can you coordinate that?"

"Sure." Sam looked pointedly at Logan. "Maybe you can help. Like you pointed out, the only way we're getting out of here now is if we're airlifted out. We'll need to build something big enough so it can be spotted from the air."

Logan gave an offhand shrug that indicated nothing.

"These kinds of situations bring out the best and the worst in people," Matt said, directing a meaningful look at Logan. "We need to work together to get everyone out alive. We have an injured man inside, and a sick woman out here. And I don't need to remind you that the killer's still unaccounted for. We don't know that he succumbed to the mudslide. All we know for sure is that a man was murdered right outside our campground."

Sandy's head whipped toward Matt, her eyes wide like saucers. She moaned softly and then, without warning, keeled over in her chair and collapsed. Hazel darted over to her. "Quick! Someone help me get her back to the RV."

Sam swooped in ahead of Harvey and lifted Sandy's frail body into his arms. She stirred and groaned again.

Matt grabbed Duke by the collar to stop him from following Sam.

"Take her inside and I'll check her vitals," Hazel said, reaching for the medical bag she'd left by her folding chair.

"What did you have to bring the murder up for?" Harvey growled to Matt in passing. "She can't handle that kind of stress."

Still muttering under his breath, Harvey strode back over to his RV.

A couple of minutes later, Sam reappeared and joined the others by the fire. Duke licked his hand and settled back down at his feet.

"Is she all right?" Blair asked.

"I think so," Sam said. "She came around again. Hazel's making her one of her herbal tea concoctions. Harvey's making a stink about it, but Hazel's not taking no for an answer."

Matt got to his feet. "I'm going to drive out to look at that road now. I won't be long. Maybe you guys can start on the SOS when Hazel gets back."

He pulled Blair aside as he made his way over to the truck. "Whatever you do, stick with the group. I don't want you alone up there with Sam, or anyone else for that matter."

After Matt drove off, Sam looked around at the others. "Who wants to pitch in with the SOS?"

"I will," Blair said.

Whitney squirmed in her seat. "I don't have any boots with me—just these shoes and my tennis shoes."

Blair arched a brow at Logan. "What's your excuse?"

He got to his feet with a contemptuous grunt. "You can't expect me to leave my new bride on her own when there's a killer on the loose."

A stony silence prevailed as Sam and Blair watched Logan and Whitney fold up their camping chairs and walk off.

"Unbelievable," Blair muttered as soon as they were out of earshot. "I get that they're on their honeymoon and this totally sucks for them, but it's not like they'll never get a chance at a redo."

"Forget them." Sam let out an aggrieved breath. "We'll get more done without them."

The door to Harvey's RV slammed and Hazel made her way back over.

"How's Sandy doing?" Blair asked.

Hazel sank back down in her camping chair, a perturbed look on her face as she studied the flickering flames.

"What is it?" Blair pressed. "Is something wrong?"

"No," Hazel said, looking pensive. "That's just it. I don't think there's anything wrong at all. I don't think Sandy has cancer."

9

*B*lair wrinkled up her brow. "I don't understand. What do you mean you don't think she has cancer?"

"I can't figure out what's going on," Hazel admitted. "Unless it's Munchausen syndrome or something—you know, when a person acts as if they're sick to gain sympathy."

Sam frowned. "She seems pretty sick to me. What makes you think she's faking it?"

Hazel cast a lingering glance across the way at the RV. "After I checked out her vitals, I asked to use the bathroom. I wanted to take a quick look through the cabinet to check her prescriptions, to make sure she wasn't taking anything that was having an adverse effect on her. You heard her slurring her words. The weird thing is, there was nothing there other than Vicodin."

Sam shrugged. "Wouldn't that be normal? For the pain, I mean."

"Yes, but the strange thing is that I distinctly remember Harvey telling us she was on a bunch of medication."

"I bet it's in the cabinet by her bed," Blair said.

Hazel shook her head. "It's not. I checked her nightstand when I helped her into bed. And that's not all. When I went to make her a cup of herbal tea I noticed—"

She broke off abruptly as Harvey exited his RV and made his way over to them. "She's sleeping now." He scratched the back of his neck uneasily. "Thanks for your help. Didn't mean to appear ungrateful or anything. It's a ... bad situation and she won't listen to reason."

"I'm sure it's not easy," Blair sympathized.

"I can help you build that SOS," Harvey said. "I'd like to do my part."

"We appreciate that," Sam replied. "But you should probably stay here and keep an eye on Sandy. Between the three of us, we'll get it done."

"And it would be good to have someone close by in case Rob needs anything," Hazel added.

"Well, if you're sure," Harvey said, sounding uncertain.

"Absolutely, we've got it covered," Blair assured him.

He nodded and retreated across the way to his RV.

"Do you think he suspects Sandy's faking her illness?" Blair asked. "He acts like he's annoyed with her at times."

Hazel puckered her brow. "He might be in on it. The world is full of neurotic people."

"Then they're both nutcases." Sam got to his feet and doused the fire. "Right now, we've got other things to worry about. It's starting to spit rain again. Let's get to work before Matt gets back. I'm going to put Duke inside."

"I'll check on Rob. Be right out," Blair said.

When she slipped inside, Rob was still fast asleep on the couch, so she scribbled a note to let him know where they were going, and then draped a blanket over him before heading back outside to where Sam and Hazel were waiting. She felt somewhat uncomfortable about leaving a stranger alone in their trailer, but it wasn't as if there was anything worth stealing, and where was he going to go? He was stuck here like the rest of them.

BETWEEN THE THREE OF THEM, and despite the rain that grew increasingly heavy, they managed to arrange enough boulders into an SOS in under two hours. They elected to build it on the edge of the mudslide closest to Bird Creek to give anyone flying overhead the best chance of spotting the trailers. Blair was somewhat concerned that the boulders they'd used weren't large enough to be seen from the air, but she couldn't have lifted anything heavier anyway.

By the time they got back to the campground, Matt was just pulling in.

"It's not good," he said as he climbed out of his truck. "Like Whitney said, the road's completely washed out. There's no way around it." He hesitated. "At least, not in a vehicle."

Sam studied him, eyes alert. "What are you thinking?"

Matt stuffed his hands into his back pockets. "It might be possible to climb up the other side of the mountain and cross over that way on foot—bypass the section of the road that's destroyed. From what I remember, it's only about a six-mile-hike back to the main road."

"I can drive out there with you and take a look," Sam said. "I've got all my climbing gear in the trailer."

Matt nodded thoughtfully. "Let's go first thing in the morning. It's dumping rain again now, and it'll be dark here soon."

"What about searching for Rob's brother?" Sam asked.

Matt shook his head. "Not in these conditions. We can't risk getting caught in another slide. We'll have to wait until morning and hope it clears up again. In the meantime, let's get everyone back together for an update."

"I think we should inventory our supplies, as a precaution," Hazel proposed. "The most critical issue will be making sure we have enough drinking water for the next few days."

Blair nodded. "I agree. I doubt anyone was planning on staying here more than a night or two. We certainly weren't. Our plan was to stock up once we got to Black Rock."

Matt gave a grim nod. "All right, we'll gather back here after dinner for a quick meeting."

"I'll let the others know," Sam said, striding down to the road.

"Tell them to go through their supplies and figure out how many days' worth of food and water they have," Matt called after him. "We might have to start pooling our stuff."

"I should check on Rob again before I go," Hazel said.

Blair waved a hand dismissively. "He's sleeping. Leave him for now."

Matt cast a quick glance across at the unoccupied camper van next to Harvey's and Sandy's RV. "What do you guys think about moving Rob in there?"

"You mean ... break in?" Blair threw Matt a reproving look.

He shrugged. "It's an emergency. The usual rules don't apply. Besides, if it belongs to that duck hunter, he could be dead for all we know."

"I'm okay with it," Hazel said. "At least Rob would have a real bed to sleep in."

Matt contemplated the idea for a moment or two before opening up a storage compartment on the side of the trailer. He pulled out a small tool bag and checked the contents. "All right, let's take a look inside—see if it's even habitable. It's our civic responsibility to check it out anyway as the owner hasn't made an appearance yet. It doesn't bode well for him."

Hazel and Blair followed Matt over to the empty camper van. He threw down his tool bag and lifted out a screw gun.

"Before you break in, maybe we should check in case there's a window open," Blair suggested.

"There isn't," Matt replied tersely. "I walked around the van yesterday to make sure no one was inside. Don't worry, I won't damage anything. I'm only going to remove the lock."

Ten minutes later, Matt swung the door wide open. With a pang of contrition, Blair followed him and Hazel up the steps. Inside, the dingy space was permeated with a musty odor, but neat and well-organized. A man's overcoat and Carhartt cap hung on a hook just inside the door."

"I didn't expect this," Blair exclaimed. "For some reason I thought it would be trashed—neglected at least."

Hazel scanned the countertops and opened and shut a couple of kitchen cabinets. "Far from being a slob, this guy might have a touch of OCD. Do you notice how everything's lined up according to height; spices, books, even the mugs?"

Blair made her way back to the bedroom and opened an overhead cabinet. "You're right about the OCD thing. I've never seen shirts and sweaters folded this neatly before. Matt, this guy might be ex-military." She walked back out to the main area and pulled open the fridge, reeling back on her heels from the foul odor that emanated from it. "Ugh, what's that smell?"

Matt leaned over her shoulder and peeked inside. "The milk's spoiled. He reached for a Ziploc bag on the bottom shelf and studied the label on it. "Duck meat. It's dated from a week ago." He tossed the package back on the shelf.

"That's worrying," Hazel said. "I can't imagine anyone going off hunting and not coming back to their camper for a whole week."

Matt shrugged. "It's not out of the norm for a hunter. He probably has a tent with him. The real question is whether or not he survived that mudslide."

Blair locked eyes with him. "You mean whether or not he's the killer."

Matt gave a shallow nod as he tugged a hand through his wet hair. "That too."

For the next few minutes, Blair busied herself taking a quick inventory of the food inside the camper van. She estimated there was enough pasta and canned goods to last one person for a couple of days. Water was a different matter. There didn't appear to be any in the camper other than a trickle left in a plastic dispenser sitting on the counter next to the fridge. "We'll have to bring over some water," Blair commented. "But the place is clean and dry."

"All things considered, I think Rob will be very comfortable here," Hazel said.

Blair closed a cabinet door she'd left lying open. "I hope for his sake the neurotic owner doesn't show back up. I doubt he'll be too happy about sharing his perfectly ordered world with a stranger."

"Yeah, well, he isn't here to argue the point," Matt said with an edge to his voice. "And I'd rather not have a stranger sleeping in our trailer. We don't know the first thing about Rob. We don't even know if he's telling us the truth about the dead guy, or his brother, or the duck hunter he suddenly remembered he'd met. He could be playing us all like fools."

Hazel shot him a startled look. "You don't think he's the killer, do you? He seems like a pretty decent guy to me."

"I'm just saying we shouldn't take anything at face value," Matt answered with a shrug. "What evidence do we have that any of us are telling the truth?"

"For starters, you can learn a lot about a person from their environment." Blair wandered over to a shelf of books arranged by height and picked one up. "Let's see what makes this guy tick." She flipped through it before carefully replacing it and glancing at the other titles. "Check these out:

The Untold Stories of World War II, The Forgotten 500, The Illustrated World Encyclopedia of Guns, Gunsmithing Modern Firearms. Is this guy obsessed with World War II and weapons, or what?"

Hazel frowned. "That's a little unnerving. We should take a closer look around. Make sure there are no weapons lying about the place."

Blair's eyes met Matt's. "Maybe it's irresponsible of us to ask Rob to move in here. What if the owner returns in the middle of the night?"

"Any reasonable person will understand once we explain the situation," Matt responded.

"I still think we should search the place for weapons, just to be safe," Hazel said. "We can do our best to leave it as undisturbed as possible, but—"

She broke off at the sound of the door opening.

"What are you guys up to?" Sam asked, looking around the camper with an air of curiosity.

"We're thinking about moving Rob in here," Blair explained. "Looks like this guy's a bit of a gun fanatic so we need to make sure there aren't any weapons lying around first."

Sam rubbed his brow. "What if the owner comes back?"

"Then we'll explain the situation to him," Hazel said. "If he's a halfway decent human being, he'll hardly turn his back on an injured man we dragged from the mud."

With Sam's help, they conducted a cursory search of the camper van without finding any weapons, or anything else incriminating. Blair even dug through several neat stacks of paperwork to see if there were any photographs, but she found nothing linking the owner to the dead man.

Matt clapped his hands to get everyone's attention. "All right, let's wrap this up and get out of here." He turned to Sam. "Got everyone on board for our meeting?"

"Yeah. I don't know about Sandy, but everyone else is up for it."

"I'll head back over and figure out something for us to eat," Blair said, accompanying Hazel to the door.

Matt nodded. "I'm right behind you. I'll lock up here."

To Blair's surprise, Rob was sitting up at the dining table when she walked back in. She pulled off her rain gear, and hesitated by the door, wondering if she should wait for Matt, but the sight of Rob's arm balanced awkwardly on the table assured her he wouldn't be hard to incapacitate if he tried anything. She beamed at him in a bid to quell any lingering reservations. "You're awake! How are you feeling?"

"Hungry." He gave a sheepish grin. "I didn't want to help myself to your food without asking."

"I'm going to make us something to eat right now." Blair walked over to the fridge and pulled out a few items while subtly keeping a close eye on Rob. She set out some salsa and chips, and then heated up some pre-cooked lasagna she'd defrosted the day before. "We checked out that unoccupied camper van next to Harvey's and Sandy's. It's a tad musty, but clean and dry. We figured you could use it in the meantime. No one's been in there since we got here. I hate to speculate, but the odds are the owner got caught up in that mudslide and won't be coming back."

Rob shifted uncomfortably in his seat. "I keep wondering if my brother's still out there somewhere."

"I'm really sorry we weren't able to go back out and search for him." Blair gestured to the window. "The weather's not cooperating. In these conditions, there's always the risk of another slide."

Rob gave a grave nod. "He was farther back from the lake

than the rest of us—in that hunting blind. It's a long shot, but I haven't given up hope that he made it out alive."

Blair twitched her lips into a sympathetic smile. "I wouldn't give up hope either if it were my family."

She glanced up when Matt came through the door and kicked off his boots. He walked over to the sink to wash up. "I reinstalled the locking mechanism." He sat down opposite Rob and reached for a chip. "That rig is clean and neat as a new pin. You'll be comfortable there."

"Yeah, sure. Appreciate that," Rob replied.

Blair dished out the lasagna and joined the men at the table. She toyed with her food, feeling somewhat guilty about eating it—wondering if everyone else had enough, and how many days their food would have to last. They might have to start rationing.

"You're quiet. What's on your mind?" Matt asked, chewing on a mouthful of pasta.

"I'm wondering how long we'll be stuck here. I mean, I'm not worried that we're going to die of hunger or anything. I know as soon as we're spotted SAR will make a drop."

Matt nodded in agreement, but his eyes told another story.

"What?" Blair prodded. "You don't think so?"

He shrugged. "It's just that we're not in any flight paths up here in the mountains."

"He's right," Rob added quietly. "And the weather's been too rough for backcountry planes. It could be several days before anyone realizes we're here."

"Well, we're not going to starve in a matter of days," Blair said brightly.

Matt grimaced. "No. But, the killer could strike again."

10

*B*lair studied the circle of somber faces in the trailer. Judging by their expressions, it was beginning to sink in just how dire their situation was. They were essentially cut off from the outside world with a very sick woman in their midst, a guy with a broken arm—potentially with internal injuries they were unaware of—and several men with short fuses and a propensity to throw their weight around. Not to mention the fact that the killer was still unaccounted for.

Sam leaned over and muttered something to Matt before getting to his feet to address the group. "You're all aware of how serious the situation has become. Matt's confirmed that the road out of here isn't navigable. At the same time, there's no reason to panic. We just have to sit tight, pool our resources, and ration our supplies until help arrives."

He reached behind him and lifted a yellow legal pad and pen from his chair. "Let's begin by taking an inventory of our provisions. The most important thing is to make sure everyone has enough food and water for the next few days." He glanced down at his legal pad. "I've got half a case of water and enough energy bars and trail mix to last me for two or three days. I also have a large bag of dogfood so feeding Duke won't be an issue. Probably should have done a better job of stocking up, but I was only planning on staying here for a night or two." He tilted his chin in Harvey's direction. "How are you and Sandy doing for supplies?"

Harvey cleared his throat. "We've got a couple of unopened plastic water dispensers. Enough frozen food to last for the next couple of days, I reckon." He drew his brows together before continuing. "But that's not my main concern. If Sandy runs out of her medication, she might not make—" His voice wavered and broke off.

Blair winced at the pain his slouched posture conveyed. It was hard to imagine he could be a party to faking his wife's illness. And to what purpose?

Hazel fixed a penetrating look on Harvey. "What medication is Sandy on?"

He threw her a wounded look. "What difference does it make? We're stuck here and we're not gonna be able to get refills, are we?" He dropped his head into his hands with a heavy sigh.

Blair leaned across and squeezed his arm. "We're going to get Sandy out of here as soon as we possibly can. You need to stay strong for her." She frowned across at Hazel, hoping she'd take the hint and drop it. Just because Hazel hadn't found any medication during her cursory search of the RV, it wasn't conclusive proof that it didn't exist. Hazel had a tendency toward the dramatic—to be a bit of a conspiracy theorist as Matt had pointed out. She was jumping to conclusions.

"What about you and Matt, Blair?" Sam asked. "How are your supplies?"

"We have a few bottles of water left in the fridge and another case underneath the trailer. We could scrape by on food for several days. We've got canned chili, beans, and soup."

"And I've got enough frozen dinners for the next few days," Hazel piped up. "Enough water too. Although it wouldn't be a bad idea if we all start collecting rain water. Just in case."

"Good idea," Sam said. He scribbled the information down on his legal pad, before turning to Logan and Whitney. "How about you two?"

"We're out," Logan said abruptly.

Sam frowned. "*Out*, out? Or do you mean almost out?"

"What do you think I mean?" Logan scowled. "We're out of everything. Our propane tank's almost empty too."

Whitney pouted at him. "Well, we're not quite out of *everything*. We're down to our last bottle of water each, and we finished off our sandwich meat tonight. We have a few slices of bread left and a Hershey bar. Oh, and a bag of marshmallows."

Sam tightened his lips and consulted his notes. "Nothing we can do about the propane tank. You should have filled that at the gas station. But we'll get you two squared away with some more food and water."

Harvey threw Sam a disgruntled look. "Why's it up to us to feed them? It's not like they've contributed anything useful since they got here. If they want to eat, they need to get off their rear ends and do something."

"Back off, old man," Logan hissed through clenched teeth. "We brought all the food we needed for the two nights we planned on being here."

"It's not our fault we're stuck here," Whitney whined.

"And it's not my job to feed you," Harvey growled.

"All right, calm down everybody," Blair said, raising a hand to get their attention. "This isn't about punishing anyone for not stocking up enough. No one could have foreseen the mudslide. I'll fix Logan and Whitney up with food and water for tomorrow. We'll reevaluate our supplies after that and distribute more as necessary."

Harvey folded his arms across his chest, while continuing to glower at Logan and Whitney.

Matt glanced over at Rob. "We'll give you some water to take across to the camper van. There's enough food in there for a day or two."

Rob dipped his head in acknowledgment. "Sounds good."

"Moving on to another topic," Sam said. "The SOS is complete and I'm confident it can be seen from the air."

"Is there anything else we can do? Does anyone have flares?" Hazel looked around expectantly, but, one-by-one, everyone shook their head.

"We're not going to sit around and do nothing in the meantime," Matt asserted. "Sam and I are planning to drive back out to the road in the morning to assess the possibility of climbing over the mountain to reach the highway and flag down help."

"What about searching for survivors?" Rob asked.

Sam raised his brows. "If the weather cooperates, we'll try again tomorrow. That's the best we can offer you."

"We should talk about safety next," Matt said. "We still don't know who or where the killer is."

Harvey got to his feet abruptly. "I can't leave Sandy on her own any longer. This isn't getting us anywhere." Without waiting for a response, he stormed out the door.

Blair laid a hand on Matt's arm. "Maybe we should call it a night. Everyone's frazzled. You and Sam can trade off shifts again tonight. It's not like we have much else to do tomorrow anyway so we can hammer out the rest of the details then."

"All right," Matt conceded. "Get some sleep, everyone. We'll continue this back here in the morning at nine."

Blair got to her feet and proceeded to pack a paper bag

with a few water bottles, two granola bars, instant rice, beans and a small bag of grilled chicken strips. "Here you go." She handed the bag to Whitney. "That should keep you two going for now."

"Thanks," Whitney said, accepting the bag with a grateful smile. She exited the trailer and hurried down the steps to catch up with Logan, who'd left without saying goodbye to anyone and was yelling for her to hurry up.

Blair placed three plastic water bottles in a paper bag for Rob and handed it to him. "That should tide you over for tonight. You need to keep drinking plenty of water to flush out your system."

"I'll take you over to the van and help you get set up," Sam offered.

"I'll walk over with you two," Hazel said. "I want to check Rob's vitals one more time."

After they'd all left, Matt and Blair set about tidying up the trailer as best they could. The couch where Rob had been sleeping would have to be steam cleaned before they returned the trailer to Matt's dad, but it was hardly a priority at the moment. Blair rolled up the dirty blanket, stuffed it into a trash bag and put it under the bed. Matt pulled out the hand vacuum and started cleaning up the crumbs and dried mud on the carpet, while Blair turned her attention to the dishes. When she was done, she headed to the bedroom. "I'm going to turn in. I'm wiped out."

"I have the first watch and then Sam will take over," Matt said, joining her. He took her in his arms and hugged her tightly to his chest. "I know you're worried about how all this is affecting me. We'll get through this, Blair. One day, this will be nothing more than a black mark on the map that we can forget about."

She smiled wanly back at him. She hoped he was right

about that. Because the way things were going, it might be an "X" on the map that marked more than one grave.

By NINE-FIFTEEN THE NEXT MORNING, everyone had gathered back in the trailer. Except for Hazel.

Sam got to his feet. "I'll go over there and see if she slept in or something."

Blair sipped on her coffee while making small talk with Whitney. "Do you have any of your wedding pictures on your phone?"

Whitney blinked at her. "Uh, no. They're … on my computer … at work."

"Bummer, I'd love to see them. What do you work at?"

Whitney's face flushed. "I'm … a teacher's aide."

Blair tightened her grip on her mug, allowing an uncomfortable pause to unfold. She got the distinct impression she was being lied to. "What age group?"

"They're young. Preschoolers." Whitney gave a dismissive wave, her sleeve slipping halfway up her arm.

Blair's eyes widened in shock when she caught sight of the purple bruises on Whitney's wrist. "Yikes! What happened to your arm?"

Whitney stiffened, hurriedly tugging down her sleeve. She shot a quick look in Logan's direction, but he was staring at his phone, oblivious to their conversation.

"It's nothing. I tripped on my way to the outhouse in the dark and fell on the trailer hitch." She lifted her travel mug to her lips and proceeded to take a long draught.

Blair frowned down at her coffee. Surely the holding tank in Whitney's trailer couldn't be full already. But why else would she use the outhouse after dark with the possibility of a murderer at large? Unless … she knew the murderer wasn't at large. Blair pulled distractedly on her lip, contemplating the ugly bruises she'd glimpsed. Was Whitney protecting Logan? It was a terrifying prospect, but not outside the realm of possibility. If Logan was violent enough to leave bruises like that on his new wife's wrist, maybe he was violent enough to kill. His behavior had all the hallmarks of an abuser. Controlling and demeaning. And from the start, he'd kept Whitney as isolated as possible. But why would he have killed that man? What was their connection?

A moment later, Sam burst through the door, startling everyone. "Hazel's gone!"

The hair on the back of Blair's neck stood on end. "You mean ... her trailer?"

"No! I mean she's disappeared!"

---

11

*B*lair's heart thumped with fear. "How do you know she's not in her trailer? Did you go inside?"

Sam shook his head. "The door's locked. I looked in all the windows. She's definitely not in there. Maybe she went off into the forest looking for plants or something. You know what she's like."

A dark look crossed Matt's face. "I can't believe she'd be that stupid. What would possess her to take off on her own knowing there's a killer out there?"

He got to his feet and reached for his coat. "We need to find her. Everyone go grab your gear and meet me at her trailer."

Blair turned to Rob. "Wait for us in the camper van. You're too weak to be searching for anyone else right now."

After the others had dispersed, Blair pulled on her outer-wear, locked the door behind her, and hurried down the road to Hazel's trailer. Matt and Sam were already there, heads pressed to the glass as they peered through the windows. Blair tented her hands over her eyes and joined them, her gaze sweeping the interior, searching for any clues as to where Hazel might have gone. She made her way around to the back of the trailer and looked in through the large bedroom window that doubled as a fire escape. The bed was unmade, which seemed to fit with the theory that Hazel had spent the night there and gone out early this morning. But that didn't explain why she hadn't returned.

Blair was about to walk back around to the front of the trailer to join the others when she noticed a small dent in the window frame. Tucking her fingers under it, she easily pried the window open. It struck her as odd that Hazel hadn't locked it on the inside. Her hand brushed against the screen and she sucked in a sudden breath when it gave beneath the light pressure. Taking a closer look, she realized the screen had been slit on three sides and taped back to the frame with duct tape. "Matt! Sam!" she yelled, unable to stem the panic in her voice.

Seconds later, the two men came running up to her.

"What is it? Did you see someone?" Matt demanded, scanning the forest behind them.

"Something's not right," Blair said, motioning to the window.

Sam inspected it, a grim look on his face. "It's not torn. This was deliberate. Someone took a knife to the screen, and then tried to cover it up afterward."

The knot in Blair's stomach tightened. Her thoughts went straight to the body they'd found. "It must have been the killer!"

"Don't say that!" Matt cautioned her. "You'll freak everyone out. No one's going to want to help us look for Hazel if they think the killer's stalking us."

"But I'm right, aren't I?" Blair's voice quivered with fear. "We know the killer used a knife, and Hazel's screen was cut with a precision blade."

YOU WILL NEVER LEAVE

"Everyone here has knives," Matt said dismissively. "Let's not jump to conclusions. We have to keep this to ourselves, at least for now. We need everyone on board to help search for Hazel."

Sam looked uncomfortable. "Don't we have a moral obligation to tell them? What if one of them is next?"

"We will tell them," Matt snapped. "But not yet. The screen was taped up from the inside. Maybe Hazel cut it for some reason and then taped it back up. Maybe she really is out there looking for plants and lost track of time." He thrust his hands into his hair and paced in front of the window. "If we can't find her within the next hour, then—"

He broke off at the sound of voices approaching. "Remember, not a word to the others, yet."

They walked around to the door of the trailer just as Logan, Whitney, and Harvey came walking up from the road.

Matt nodded to them. "Thanks for coming to help with the search."

"Are you sure Sandy will be all right on her own?" Blair asked Harvey.

He gave a tentative nod. "She's sleeping. I left her a note to let her know Rob was in the camper van next door if she needed anything."

Blair swallowed back her trepidation at the thought of leaving Sandy—as sick as she was—to the mercy of a stranger. Logically, she reassured herself, Rob couldn't possibly have managed to cut out the screen on Hazel's trailer with a broken arm. It stood to reason he wasn't the killer—or kidnapper—whatever the case might be.

"We'll go in pairs," Matt said. "Stick together at all times. Blair and I will head into the woods behind the trailer. Sam, you and Harvey search along the hiking trail up to the mudslide. Logan and Whitney, take your truck and head down the road as far as the washed-out section. We'll meet back here in one hour."

Blair's pulse drummed in her temples as she and Matt set off through the dense undergrowth behind Hazel's trailer. It was cool and dark among the trees, a shadowy kaleidoscope of greenery and dappled sunlight—all of her senses heightened as she quietly cataloged the sounds of the forest; the rustling of rodents running along the forest floor, and the chirping of birds calling to one another. Ordinarily, she found the familiar sounds comforting, but in her elevated state of fear, everything had become an ominous purveyor of doom.

Matt threw her a harried glance. "Are you all right?"

"No. I'm scared out of my wits. I just want to go home. I can't believe this is happening. I'm beginning to feel like I'm on the set of a Stephen King movie."

"Like it or not, it's happening. And if Hazel's in trouble, we have to find her."

Blair winced at the brush that scratched at her face and hands as she clambered after him through the undergrowth. She was grateful that despite Matt's initial reservations about Hazel, he was willing to do whatever it took to find her. But what if they were too late? What if the killer had struck again?

"You're falling behind." Matt rested one foot on a log as he waited for her to catch up. "We need to stick together."

"What if she's dead?" Blair asked, coming to a halt next to him. "What if we find her body somewhere? I don't think I could bear it."

"We're not going down that path yet," Matt said firmly, placing his hands on her shoulders. "I need you to stay strong —for me. I can't have you falling apart. You're the only person here I can really trust."

Blair sniffed and wiped the back of her hand across her eyes. "That reminds me of something. Whitney has some bad bruising on her wrist. I noticed it this morning in the trailer. When I asked her about it, she told me she tripped going to the outhouse and landed on the trailer hitch—which is about the stupidest explanation ever."

The expression on Matt's face hardened. "Do you think Logan did it?"

"I'm sure of it. She even shot him a look before she answered me. She's afraid of him. You've seen how controlling he is—he's pretty much kept her shut up in that trailer since they got here. I realize they're on their honeymoon, but she never ventures anywhere without him, and when he calls, she jumps."

"Harvey's much the same way with Sandy," Matt mused. "We've scarcely set eyes on her."

"He is controlling," Blair admitted. "But that's a different situation. It's pretty obvious Sandy is ill and out of it. Someone has to be her advocate. But if I'm right about Logan, he's violent. What if he did something to Hazel too?"

Matt gave a dismissive grunt. "It doesn't add up. Why would he harm her? No. I've seen Logan's type before. Puny little wannabe gangster beats up on his girlfriend. Bet he'd be too scared to take on any man in this camp." He gestured toward the forest. "We need to keep looking."

They continued their search through the woods, periodically calling out Hazel's name. Blair was beginning to despair of ever finding her alive. She couldn't imagine Hazel taking off on her own to look for plants, not after everything that had happened—it was far too dangerous. And it was unlikely she'd been kidnapped. How could someone have dragged her out of her trailer without any signs of a struggle? As terrifying a thought as it was, it was entirely possible the killer had struck again and strangled Hazel in her bed before removing her lifeless body. She couldn't weigh more than ninety pounds—she wouldn't have had a chance against an average-sized man.

"We should turn around now," Matt said, glancing at his watch.

"Can't we search just a little longer?" Blair pleaded. "I know Hazel wouldn't give up if one of us was missing."

"We're not giving up," Matt assured her. "But we need to get back to the others like we arranged, or they'll think something's happened to us too. Maybe Hazel's shown back up by now. Logan and Whitney might have picked her up in the truck, or Sam and Harvey could have found her foraging along the hiking trail."

The words rang hollow, bouncing off Blair like pebbles off a tin roof. Granted, Hazel had some free-spirited tendencies, but she would never have blown off the meeting to root around for a few plants—not with everything that was at stake.

BLAIR AND MATT were the first to arrive back at Hazel's trailer.

"Odd that Logan and Whitney aren't back yet," Matt commented, scanning up and down the road.

Blair rolled her eyes. "They're probably making out in their truck somewhere. I'd be surprised if they even made it as far as the mudslide. Logan's a self-centered jerk."

"Let's go next door and take a quick look at their trailer," Matt suggested, cocking a brow for Blair's blessing.

She tightened her lips and cast a nervous glance around. "Okay, but we'd better make it quick before they come rolling back in."

They darted across to the adjacent campsite where Whitney's and Logan's trailer was parked. Matt walked up to the front door and tried the handle. "Locked. No surprise there."

Blair walked around to the dining room window and peered inside. "It's a mess in there. And I'm willing to bet Logan was lying about their food supplies, judging by the bag of cookies and soda cans on the table."

"He's exactly the kind of selfish scumbag you hope and pray your platoon never gets saddled with, for everyone's sake," Matt growled.

"Let's take a look in the rear," Blair said, leading the way to the back of the trailer. All the blinds were pulled tight on the bedroom windows.

"Guess they don't want anyone looking in on their love nest," Matt muttered.

"You know what's weird about that," Blair said, lowering her voice. "I asked Whitney to show me some of her wedding pictures, and she didn't have a single photo on her phone."

Matt threw Blair a confused look. "Why's that weird?"

She let out a frustrated sigh. "Really, Matt? A young couple, newlyweds, and she doesn't even have one picture of her wedding on her phone to show people. I'm surprised it wasn't her screensaver."

Matt shrugged. "Like you said, they're young. Maybe they couldn't afford a white wedding. Perhaps they got married in a registry office and she was too embarrassed to tell you."

"That's not the only thing bugging me," Blair went on. "Why are they so desperate to get back to work? To tell you the truth, I'm not even sure Whitney has a job. I think she was lying to me about being a teacher's aide. Did you notice that Logan started to say *he* had to get back to work and then he corrected himself and changed it to *we*? And who takes only a three-day honeymoon, anyway?"

"Military," Matt replied with an abashed shrug.

Before Blair could respond, a truck came hurtling around the corner and pulled up behind them.

Logan jumped out and narrowed his eyes at them. "What are you doing here?"

"You're late," Matt said pointedly. "We decided to search the other campsites for Hazel." His eyes flicked to Whitney. "In case she tripped on a trailer hitch or something."

*W*hitney's face flushed and she tugged self-consciously at her sleeve. Logan flashed her an icy glare that made her stiffen before turning on Matt. "You got a problem?"

Blair laid a restraining hand on her husband's arm. "We should all head back over to Hazel's trailer. Sam and Harvey will be wondering where we're at."

Without waiting for an answer, she slipped her hand into Matt's and led the way, thankful when Logan and Whitney fell in behind them.

Minutes after they arrived back, Sam and Harvey showed up.

"Sorry we're late," Sam said. "We stopped off to check on Sandy and Rob. They're both asleep."

"No sign of Hazel, I take it?" Blair asked.

Sam twisted his lips. "Not a trace."

Matt gave a grim nod. "At this point, I think we can assume foul play. That window definitely wasn't damaged when Hazel showed Blair and me around her trailer."

"So … the killer's still out there," Whitney whispered, a tremor in her voice.

"We don't know that," Blair countered, even though her heart told her differently.

Matt cast an appraising look around. "Maybe the killer was never out there to begin with."

An uneasy silence descended over them.

Harvey pulled his bristly brows together indignantly. "What's that supposed to mean?"

"It means the killer could be standing right here." Matt widened his stance as he surveyed the disconcerted group a second time. "The hunter posing with the prey. Let's face it. How well do we really know each other?"

Logan let out a caustic laugh. "You're about as paranoid as they come, soldier boy. I bet you still hear bombs going off in your brain."

In a flash, Matt's arm shot out, scrunching up Logan's collar in his white-knuckled fist. "I've had about all I can take of you and your loose lips and cocky attitude. I don't know what your game is, or what sewer you crawled up from, but judging by the way you like to knock that new wife of yours around, I wouldn't put it past you to kill a man."

Without warning, he released Logan with a disgusted shove. Whitney reached for him as he stumbled backward, but he shook her off and strode right back over to Matt, sticking his face up to his. "I hate to be the one to break it to you, but you're not in charge here and we're not your platoon. Touch me again and you'll regret it."

A shiver of trepidation crossed Blair's shoulders. Logan was no match for Matt in a fist fight, but she didn't like the menacing undertones in his threat. As conniving as he was, he might find a way to get back at Matt that wouldn't be reliant on brute strength.

"Easy!" Sam interjected. "Lay off the threats. We're all just trying to figure this thing out. Somebody killed a man, and now Hazel's missing. Everyone's scared half to death."

Logan continued to stare Matt down. "Funny thing is, you're the only one here who's actually done any killing, isn't that right, *Sergeant?*"

"You tell me," Matt spat back. "Are you capable of strangling a man?"

Before Logan had a chance to respond, Blair yelled, "Enough! Everyone just take a breath and calm down. This isn't helping us find Hazel. And that's what we need to be focusing on."

"Forget her!" Logan hurled back. "She's history. We should be talking about how we're going to protect ourselves from the raving lunatic out there. What if one of us is next?"

"Do you ever think about anyone other than yourself?" Harvey growled.

"Look, we can't go on like this," Blair said, raising her voice again. "We either work together, or we call it quits and go our separate ways."

Matt and Logan continued to size each other up, narrowed eyes glinting their mutual dislike.

"Please, Logan," Whitney pleaded. "We need to stick together. I'm scared."

He scowled, clenching his hand into a fist at his side. "Tell that to Rambo over there."

Blair threw Matt a warning look, begging him not to retaliate.

Harvey cleared his throat, cutting through the tension in the air. "I say we forget our differences and start pulling together—concentrate on finding Hazel and working out a plan to keep everyone safe going forward."

Matt folded his arms in front of him and gave a conciliatory nod. "Fair enough. We should start by searching Hazel's trailer. Maybe we'll find something that will give us a clue to her whereabouts."

Sam frowned. "We can't just go around breaking into people's trailers."

"The woman's missing," Matt shot back. "Do you want to help find her, or arrest me?"

Sam gave a discomfited shrug.

"How are we going to get in?" Whitney asked.

"Matt can take the lock off," Blair explained.

"It would be quicker if you climbed through the damaged window," Matt said. "Come on, I'll give you a leg up."

They disappeared around the back of the trailer and, a moment later, Blair opened the door from the inside.

"Try not to trash the place," she warned, as they filed in. "But search it thoroughly. Anything could be a potential clue, so don't dismiss things outright."

"Wouldn't surprise me if she turned out to be the killer." Logan snorted. "The witch and her herbal brews."

Whitney smothered a laugh. "You're so mean! She could be injured or dead for all you know."

Blair shot Whitney a look of disgust. Her reaction indicated she was more amused than dismayed at Logan's juvenile behavior. She was almost as annoying as him—in a different way. Even her high-pitched voice was beginning to grate on Blair.

Matt signaled for everyone's attention. "All right, listen up. Whitney, you search the bathroom. Sam, you and Logan take the main area. Harvey can focus on the kitchen. Blair and I will tackle the bedroom area."

As they dispersed throughout the trailer and got to work, Blair couldn't help feeling somewhat disconcerted at the thought of rummaging through a stranger's possessions. Then again, she scarcely knew the other campers either. She hoped none of them pocketed anything that didn't belong to them—not that it would matter much if Hazel was dead. Her stomach lurched at the thought.

"Her coat and boots are still here by the door," Sam called back to them.

Blair and Matt exchanged a grave look. It didn't bode well for Hazel's fate. She'd hardly have ventured into the forest of her own accord without donning her outerwear.

"Let's get this comforter off the bed and check for clues," Matt said.

After a thorough search of the sheets, underneath the mattress, and even in the storage compartment beneath the bed, Matt and Blair turned their attention to the bedside cabinets. Blair knelt and opened the one on the right. She rummaged through a small wicker basket of miscellaneous reading materials—crime fiction, for the most part, which surprised her. She'd expected to see a naturopathic hand-book or something. She replaced the basket inside the cabinet and was about to get to her feet when she noticed a piece of paper wedged between the edge of the mattress and the bedside cabinet. Slipping her fingers into the small gap, she gingerly tugged out a scrap of lined paper.

"Find something?" Matt tilted his chin at her questioningly.

Blair frowned as she studied the words scrawled on the page amid a menagerie of random scribbles.

Mug/face
9?

She passed the sheet across to Matt. "Doodling, mostly. And a couple of obscure notes that I can't make sense of."

Matt let out a confounded grunt. "No clue what that's supposed to mean. It probably doesn't have anything to do with what's going on. It could have fallen down the side of the mattress months ago." He scrunched it up and threw it on the nightstand. Blair reached for it and pocketed it. It might not be significant, but until she knew for sure, she wasn't about to leave it behind.

Whitney stuck her head into the room. "I didn't find anything in the bathroom, except for Hazel's purse—it was sitting on the counter." She held up a small brown leather satchel. "I feel kind of funny about going through it."

Matt motioned impatiently to her to hand it over. "Give it here. The woman's missing for crying out loud. We need to find out who she is and where she lives."

Whitney gave a miffed shrug and tossed the purse to him. She hung back in the doorway, eying him curiously as he pulled out Hazel's keys and passed them to Blair. "Hold on to those." He dug around inside the purse and retrieved a slim, black wallet. Flicking it open, he studied the license briefly before partially sliding each of the credit cards out in turn. All of a sudden, he inhaled a sharp breath.

Blair frowned at him. "What?"

He held out a laminated white card to her. "Concealed carry permit. Odd choice for a hippie homeopathic author, don't you think?"

Blair shrugged. "Not really. She's a single woman traveling around remote parts of the country on her own. Makes sense to me."

Matt's eyes narrowed. "So you're okay with her having a gun for protection, but you didn't want us traveling with one?"

The atmosphere in the room instantly ignited. But Blair wasn't about to take the bait. She took a quick calming breath before answering. "That's different and you know it. Let's not go back and rehash that again."

"What did you say about a gun?" Whitney interrupted, stepping into the room.

Before Blair had a chance to answer, the others appeared in the doorway, eyes zigzagging around the space.

"Did you guys find a gun?" Sam asked.

Matt held the card aloft between two fingers. "A concealed carry permit."

Harvey scratched his forehead. "If Hazel has a gun, how was the killer able to abduct her?"

"Maybe because that's not what happened," Logan said, a crust of smugness forming on his face.

"What's that supposed to mean?" Sam asked.

"Hazel could have damaged the window herself to throw us off the trail," Logan suggested.

Blair threw him a bewildered look. "What trail?"

"Maybe she's not the quack she portrays herself to be, at all. She might be the killer. It's a genius move—faking her own abduction."

Muttered protests echoed back and forth.

"Not likely," Sam responded. "She's not strong enough to strangle a man."

"And why wouldn't she have just shot him?" Matt added.

"Because someone from the campground could have heard it," Logan said.

Harvey folded his arms in front of him and grunted. "Wouldn't matter. We'd have put it down to the hunters."

"It makes absolutely no sense whatsoever," Blair protested. "Hazel's a healer, not a killer—you saw how she treated Rob and Sandy. Anyway, like Sam said, she doesn't have the strength to overpower a man."

Logan sniggered. "Maybe she gave him one of her potions first and knocked him out."

Blair glowered at him. "What's wrong with you? This isn't a joking matter."

Harvey stroked his beard, a perturbed look settling in his furrowed face. "Logan could be on to something. Hazel was here before the rest of us arrived. We have only her word that the camper van was vacant when she got here. It's possible she killed the guy."

Logan turned to Whitney with a triumphant gleam in his eyes. "I told you there was something off about that old hag when we ran into her at the gas station. Asking a bunch of questions, insisting we check this place out."

"It doesn't explain why she disappeared," Matt countered. "It's not like any of us suspected her of murdering that man."

"Once a killer, always a killer," Logan said in a loaded tone. "Maybe she's hunting for her next victim. Can't help herself."

"You're sick, you know that!" Matt sputtered.

Logan shrugged. "I don't hear you coming up with a better theory."

To Blair's relief, Matt let Logan's jibe slide and turned instead to Harvey. "Did you notice anything out of place in the kitchen?"

Harvey shook his head. "Not that I could tell."

"Sam, how about the living area?" Matt went on.

"All the usual stuff; books, cards, board games, blankets. She has a high-end Canon camera with a telephoto zoom lens that I'm more than a little jealous of. It would be great to take on climbing expeditions."

Blair frowned. "Where is it? Let's take a look."

They all trooped back into the living area and Sam retrieved the camera from a cabinet above the couch.

"Did you go through the pictures?" Blair asked.

A furrow formed on Sam's brow. "That's a bit personal. Didn't know we were getting that nitty-gritty. Like I said, this whole search doesn't feel right to me."

Matt grunted. "You'll feel differently if it helps us find Hazel." He took the camera from Sam and pressed a few random buttons, looking increasingly frustrated.

"Give it here." Blair thrust out her hand for the camera. "You'll never figure it out. You barely know how to take a picture with your phone."

She clicked swiftly through to the photo stream and began scrolling through the pictures. Her heart drummed a slow, ominous beat. She could scarcely believe what she was seeing.

"*B*lair!" Matt gestured urgently for the camera. "Let me see that!"

A cold sweat broke out over the back of her neck. She darted an uneasy look in Logan's direction before passing the camera to Matt. Her brain scrambled to find an explanation for the startling string of photos Hazel had taken of Logan and Whitney. Some of them were innocuous—the pair going in and out of their trailer, fetching something from their truck, or walking down to the road, arms entwined. But many of the pictures crossed a line of privacy. Evidently, they'd been taken with the zoom lens through the windows of Logan's and Whitney's trailer. Granted, none of them were in the bedroom area due to the blinds being closed. But Hazel had shot countless photos of them at their dining table, opening the refrigerator, playing cards, in the throes of an argument, even kissing on the couch. Every conceivable move had been captured. Blair bit her lip, at a loss as to why Hazel was spying on the honeymooning couple in the neighboring campsite.

Matt looked up from the camera and met her gaze. She

knew he had all the same questions that were flitting around inside her head. What had Hazel been up to? And was this somehow connected to her disappearance?

"Pass the camera around!" Whitney clamored.

"Hurry up!" Sam reiterated. With an air of reluctance, Matt handed him the camera. The rest of the group clustered around, their faces slackening with shock as Sam began clicking through the surveillance-type pictures.

"That crazy cow!" Logan fumed, thrusting his hands into his hair. "I knew she was up to no good. She gave me the creeps from the get-go! Talking it up with Whitney at the gas station. Luring us here. All this time, she's been snapping pictures of our every move—stalking us. She's a predator!"

Whitney pressed her palms to her cheeks, her face chalk-white with fear. "She … she was going to kill us next. That's what this means, doesn't it? Why else was she taking those photos of us?" She cast a terrified glance around the room as though seeking confirmation.

Sam shook his head in disbelief. "I'm not buying it. Hazel's not a killer. I never got that kind of vibe from her."

Harvey moved his jaw slowly side-to-side. "Come to think of it, she was bound and determined to get inside my RV and sniff around."

Blair frowned, contemplating his words. Hazel had been eager to accompany Sandy into the RV—pushy even. And she'd admitted to snooping around in the bathroom, purportedly looking for Sandy's prescriptions. Had Hazel lied about not finding any, other than Vicodin? A shiver ran down Blair's spine when another thought occurred to her. Hazel had insisted on making Sandy some herbal tea, despite Harvey's protests. She could have put anything in it.

Was it possible they were trapped in this campground with a crazed female serial killer—one they'd unwittingly entertained? Blair rubbed her arms, mulling the idea over.

Was Hazel going to methodically pick them off? It wouldn't be hard if she had a gun. Suddenly, Blair wished with all her heart that she hadn't talked Matt out of bringing his weapon with them on this trip. What had made so much sense at the time now seemed like a reckless call that could cost them their lives.

"What are we going to do?" Logan spat out. "If she's the killer, we've no way of defending ourselves." His unsettling look slid from one person to the next. "Unless one of you has a gun?"

Blair shot Matt an abashed look. "We didn't bring ours."

Harvey let out a heavy sigh. "Sandy's always been dead set against weapons."

"I don't own a gun either," Sam said.

Logan narrowed his eyes, shooting suspicious looks around. "I don't know if I believe any of you. Maybe you're all armed and lying through your teeth about it."

"Wait a minute!" Blair held up her palms in protest. "Why would you assume any of us are lying? Maybe you're the one who's lying. How about we put this issue to bed once and for all and search everyone's trailer? If we've nothing to hide, then it won't be a problem." She cocked a challenging brow at Logan.

"What for?" he scoffed. "Do you think one of us has got Hazel stuffed in a closet or something?"

"The point is, we don't know what you might be hiding," Matt replied, fixing a piercing gaze on him. "You keep crying about wanting to feel safer. How about everyone throws down their cards and opens up their rigs for inspection?" He looked intently around at the others. "Unless one of you has something to hide?"

Sam blinked rapidly, looking extremely uncomfortable. "It's a bit intrusive, going through each other's trailers. I'm not sure we need to take it to that extreme."

"I agree," Harvey said. "The last thing Sandy needs right now is you lot traipsing through our RV."

Matt folded his arms across his chest. "Like Blair said earlier, we either pull together or go our separate ways. I like to know who I'm working with. I say we search the trailers. Let's vote on it."

Whitney gave a non-committal shrug. "Fine with me. If we can't trust each other, then it only adds to the danger we're in."

"Are we all in agreement then?" Blair asked.

Sam frowned. "I think it's taking things a step too far."

Harvey pressed his lips together. "I'm with Sam. I'm against the idea."

"That's three yesses and two no's so far," Matt said.

They all turned to Logan who sputtered in indignation. "No way! Too invasive and a total waste of time. We should be figuring out how to defend ourselves in case that lunatic strikes again." He turned and took a step toward the door, but Matt grabbed him by the arm. "Hold up! Where do you think you're going?"

Logan wrenched his arm out of Matt's grasp and took a swing at him, but Matt easily sidestepped him. Logan scowled and turned on his heel. "I'm heading back to my trailer." He pinned an accusatory gaze on Whitney. "Are you coming or what?"

"We're not done here yet," Matt cut in. "We're in the middle of a vote."

"Voting's closed." A cocky grin danced across Logan's lips. "Three in favor, three against. A tie means we aren't searching the trailers."

"I disagree. A tie means we need another voter," Blair said.

"How about we ask Rob to break the tie?" Sam suggested.

"Why should he have a vote?" Harvey protested. "He won't care either way—it's not his trailer he's bunking in."

"I think Sandy should cast the deciding vote," Blair said.

Harvey frowned. "I can tell you what she'd say. You really think, as sick as she is, she'd want you lot piling into the RV and going through all her stuff."

"That's Sandy's decision to make," Matt replied. "Let's take one last look around here before we leave. Now that we know Hazel has a concealed carry permit, it's possible she has a safe in the trailer somewhere. Keep an eye out for any cabinets with a false panel."

"She might have her gun hidden in a fake book," Whitney piped up. "I saw that on TV one time."

Blair turned away to mask her frustration.

"Only an amateur would do that," Matt said.

"Oh, so now she's gone from being a missing person to a professional hit woman." Logan curled his lip. "You're so full of it."

Before Matt could retaliate, Blair spoke up. "Get busy! If there's a gun here, we need to find it. And if there's an empty gun safe, we need to know about it."

She returned to the bedroom with Matt and began checking all the panels at the back of the overhead cabinets. Next, they pulled up the bed and searched the storage area beneath it again carefully, looking for a removable panel that might conceal a hiding place for a weapon. "There's nothing here," Matt said, pushing the bed back down on its hinges. He opened the bedside cabinet nearest to him and got down on his knees to peer inside. Turning on his pocket flashlight, he tapped on the panel at the back. "Check the cabinet on the other side," he called to Blair.

"Nothing," she confirmed.

After straightening up the covers on the bed, they went back out to the living area.

"Find anything?" Matt asked, looking around hopefully.

Sam shook his head. "I pulled out the sleeper sofa and

searched behind it, and underneath, and all around. No hiding places that I could see."

"Nothing in the kitchen either," Harvey said.

"Or the bathroom," Whitney added.

"All right," Matt conceded. "We've done all we can for now. Let's lock up here. If Sandy's up to the task, we'll have her cast the final vote on whether or not we search the other rigs."

The atmosphere was decidedly frosty—a Cold War of sorts—as the group wound their way to the RV, darting furtive looks at one another along the way. The whole situation was confusing to Blair. She was torn between believing Hazel was a victim and wondering if she could possibly be the killer. Or was it Logan? He could be hiding a whole lot more than just the fact that he was an abusive husband. Was that why he didn't want them searching his trailer? Or could the killer be the elusive duck hunter? Blair traced her fingertips across her throbbing forehead. Everyone was hiding secrets. The only thing she knew for sure was that Bird Creek had become a hunting ground, and their unknown predator was extremely dangerous. It was time they formulated a plan to defend themselves.

When they arrived at the RV, Harvey went up the steps and unlocked the door.

"If Sandy's sleeping, don't disturb her," Blair said. "We can always go to plan "B" and have Rob vote."

Harvey nodded. "Wait here. I just need a few minutes to explain to her what's going on."

A moment later, his desolate cry for help echoed throughout the RV.

*W*ithout a moment's hesitation, Blair flung open the RV door and darted back to the bedroom. Harvey was hunched over, a dazed expression on his face. Blair fastened a horror-stricken gaze on Sandy who was lying motionless in the bed. "Is ... is she—"

"She's dead," Harvey rasped. He brushed a shaking hand over his wife's pallid forehead. "She's gone. Sandy's gone."

Blair checked for a pulse and then turned to the others, who'd followed her inside. She tightened her lips and gave a subtle shake of her head.

Whitney let out a whimper of fear. She clung to Logan who wore a look of bored indifference.

Matt's eyes clouded over. He laid a hand on Harvey's arm to get his attention. "Do you mind if I check to make sure?"

Harvey gestured dispassionately for him to go ahead. He appeared stupefied, as if he could barely grasp what was happening.

Blair stepped back and joined the others huddled by the doorway, their faces taut with shock. The unrelenting stress of the past couple of hours was engraved in their eyes, along with the burning question: *Had the killer struck again?*

Matt straightened up after a moment or two. "I can't detect a pulse. I'm so sorry, Harvey."

"How ... did she die?" Whitney asked, her eyes flitting from Matt to Harvey. "I mean ... was it the cancer?"

"I don't see any apparent injuries," Matt said, his face betraying nothing. "It appears she passed away peacefully in her sleep."

Harvey gave a rueful shake of his head. "If only I'd been able to get her to a hospital yesterday. This wouldn't have happened. We shouldn't have stopped off here. I tried to tell her this place was too remote, but she was a stubborn one."

"It isn't your fault, Harvey. Don't blame yourself," Blair soothed. "There probably wasn't much more the hospital could have done to help her."

"Would you like some time alone?" Matt asked.

Harvey gave a tentative nod. "I ... think that would be good." He sank down on the edge of the bed, folding in on himself like a deflated balloon.

Matt and Blair discreetly exited the bedroom and motioned to the others to follow them.

Back outside the RV, they congregated around the picnic table.

"Please tell me this wasn't the work of the killer." Whitney's voice trailed off on a note of despair.

Matt scrubbed his hands over his face. "I don't see any injuries," he said in a low tone. "Or blood. She definitely wasn't strangled or shot."

"But?" Sam prompted.

Matt exhaled a heavy breath. "I'm not a medical professional. I can't say for sure how she died."

"It doesn't take a rocket scientist to figure it out," Logan said derisively. "The woman had stage four cancer. She barely made it through the last round of chemo—she was the walking dead. Hardly a shocker."

Matt grimaced. "Heck of a coincidence, though."

Sam raised his brows. "Are you suggesting the killer might have struck again?"

"I don't know." Matt gave a helpless shrug. "I just don't know. And that's what bothers me."

"Could Sandy have been suffocated—smothered with a pillow in her sleep or something?" Whitney asked. "That wouldn't leave any apparent injuries."

"It isn't how serial killers operate," Sam replied. "They usually have a pattern, commonalities to their crimes. They wouldn't strangle one victim along a hiking trail, and then smother another one in their bed." He shook his head as if to convince himself. "It doesn't fit."

"What do you know about it?" Logan scoffed. "Are you some kind of FBI profiler now? I thought you climbed rocks for a living. Or did you give that up after your little *accident*?"

A flash of anger ricocheted across Sam's face, shocking Blair in its intensity. He took a step in Logan's direction, but Matt barred his way.

"Knock it off, Logan," Matt barked. "We might be depending on Sam's climbing skills to reach help if someone doesn't find us soon. In the meantime, let's stay focused on the issue at hand."

"There's no indication the RV was broken into," Blair said. "We can't rule out the possibility that Sandy overdosed on her pain medication. Only an autopsy could determine that."

Logan pursed his lips. "She'd have been foaming at the mouth if she'd OD'd."

"She could have been poisoned with something that isn't so easily detected," Matt said, tucking his hands into his armpits. "Any one of us could have done it."

Whitney frowned. "How? We were all over at Hazel's trailer."

"Except for Rob," Sam pointed out. "But I can't imagine he would have any reason to harm her."

"You keep talking like serial killers are rational beings." Logan threw up his hands in frustration and began pacing between the picnic table and the fire pit. "They're not. They're raving lunatics."

Blair eyed him warily. His own words were condemning him. And the bruising on Whitney's arm proved he had a violent streak. She couldn't shake the notion that Logan might be the killer. At the very least, he wasn't to be trusted.

"Sandy might not have ingested the poison today," Whitney piped up. "Hazel made her herbal tea yesterday, remember?"

Blair flattened her lips. She wasn't the only one entertaining that suspicion.

All at once, the door to the camper van opened, and Rob stuck his head out. "Did you find Hazel?"

Matt groaned, and muttered, "We'd better bring him up to speed on everything that's happened."

They made their way over to the adjacent campsite and filed into the camper van.

"I feel terrible," Rob said, passing a trembling hand over his forehead after Blair broke the news to him about Sandy. "I checked on her an hour or so ago. I meant to go back over, but I fell asleep on the couch. I only just woke up at the sound of your voices outside."

Matt raised his brows a fraction. "You were in Sandy's RV an hour ago?"

Rob nodded. "Harvey wanted me to check up on her while he was gone. He left a spare key." Rob fumbled in his pocket and handed it to Matt. "Maybe you can return it for me."

Matt and Blair exchanged a guarded look. It seemed odd —out of character—that Harvey would trust a virtual stranger to look in on his sick wife. Up until now, he'd been more intent on keeping people out of his RV.

Whitney frowned. "Was she alive when you checked on her?"

"Yes," Rob answered emphatically. "She was sleeping— definitely breathing. I saw the covers moving up and down. I asked her if she wanted any water, but she didn't respond."

"You didn't happen to see anyone else go into the RV at all today?" Blair inquired.

"No. No one other than Harvey." Rob's eyes scanned the expectant faces turned toward him. "Why? Is there something suspicious about her death?"

"Nothing obvious," Blair responded. "Just … the timing of it."

Rob opened his mouth to speak and then hesitated, as though bracing himself for more bad news. "What about Hazel?"

Logan scowled and rested an ankle over his knee. "No trace of her anywhere. But we searched her trailer and we did find out some interesting things about the self-appointed camp medicine woman."

A befuddled look passed over Rob's face. "I don't understand."

"She's a retired nurse and she's writing a book about homeopathic medicine," Whitney explained. "Or so she told us."

"Turns out she's not the earth-loving, hippy-dippy natu- ralist she wanted us to believe she is," Logan went on. "In fact, she's a gun-toting pervert."

Rob looked helplessly around the room. "Are we talking about the same woman—the one who fixed up my arm?"

"Yeah, that's her," Matt affirmed. "We don't know for sure if she has a gun, but we found a concealed carry permit in her purse."

"And she was spying on Logan and me," Whitney added vehemently. "She had some kind of high-powered zoom lens on her camera. She'd taken dozens and dozens of photographs of us inside our trailer." Whitney reached for Logan's hand and interlaced her fingers with his. "I think she was planning on killing us next." Her lip trembled and she swallowed back a small sob.

"That's a bold assumption," Sam cut in. "Let's not go there. She's not here to explain herself."

"The truth is, we don't know what her game was," Blair said. "The gun could have been for protection—traveling around on her own as a single woman."

"We didn't find it in her trailer, and, trust me, we looked everywhere. What does that tell you?" Logan ranted. "She's the killer, that's what! She wasn't abducted!"

Rob scratched at his beard with his good hand. "So you think she's out there somewhere now with a gun?"

"It's more complicated than that," Sam responded. "The back bedroom window on her trailer was forced open from the outside and the screen was cut."

Rob's eyes widened at the news. "Sure sounds like someone took her against her will. If that's the case, they might have her gun too."

"It would have been tough to abduct her without waking her and risking someone hearing her scream," Matt said. "But if the killer forced the window open earlier in the day, it's feasible he came back and strangled her in her bed while she was sleeping."

Whitney sucked in a sharp breath and buried her head in Logan's flannel shirt.

Sam blew a strand of hair out of his eyes. "Why would the killer take her body instead of leaving it there? It's just making work for himself."

"There's only one reason I can think of," Matt said grimly. "To make us think that Hazel's the killer."

15

*M*att's ominous words hung in the air between them. It was the theory that made the most sense, but in many ways it was also the most disturbing. Not only was there a killer out there, but apparently now he was playing mind games with them, pitting them against one another while he picked them off one-by-one.

Deep down, Blair didn't believe for one minute that Hazel was the killer. Granted, she was a tad eccentric, and it was disturbing to think she'd been snapping countless pictures of Logan and Whitney since their arrival. Still, a female Peeping Tom was not in the same class-A category as a murderer.

Matt turned to Rob. "We need you to settle an issue for us. We were going to ask Sandy but …" His voice trailed off and he cleared his throat.

Logan looked aghast. "You're not seriously still going on about searching the trailers, are you?"

Matt locked a piercing glare on him. "After everything that's gone down, I'd say it's more important than ever that everyone's cards are on the table."

Rob gave a one-shouldered shrug, careful not to disturb the sling on his other arm. "Ask away, whatever you need."

"The truth is," Blair continued, picking up from where Matt had left off, "none of us really knows what's going on, and none of us really knows or trusts each other. We have a killer at large, possibly with a gun at his disposal. It's not in Hazel's trailer, so the logical conclusion is that the killer got his hands on it." She frowned to herself, searching for the right words. "I'm just going to come right out and say this. Any one of us sitting here could be the killer."

Rob blinked rapidly, clearly taken aback at her words.

"We need to be sure we know who we're dealing with," Matt said, regaining his composure. "Blair proposed that we go through each other's trailers together—to clear the air, so to speak."

"If we're going to band together and help protect each other, we can't have any more surprises," Blair hastened to add.

"Like Hazel—she certainly wasn't who we thought she was," Whitney chimed in. "She had no right—"

"It's a stupid idea," Logan interrupted, glaring at Whitney. "I don't want a bunch of strangers trekking through my trailer, trashing the place like they did Hazel's."

"Bet you're glad we went through her rig now," Matt interjected. "You'd never have found out what she was doing if we hadn't." He tilted a chin accusingly at Logan. "Maybe she's not the only one with something to hide."

"Let's just get on with the vote," Sam cut in. "I'm sick of you two jumping at each other's throats every five seconds. I happen to agree with Logan that it's overkill, but I'll go along with the majority."

"What do you say, Rob?" Blair prodded. "You get to break the tie."

He glanced nervously around the group. "I don't want to start a camp war here."

"You won't," Blair assured him. "We'll abide by your vote."

Rob gave a cautious nod. "In that case, my gut says go for it. We're a bunch of strangers in survival mode, and if anyone's hiding anything, it's best that the rest of us know about it."

Matt slapped his thighs and stood. "That settles it. Where should we start?"

"How about the camper van?" Rob asked, glancing around. "If you're searching all the trailers, you might as well start here."

Logan groaned. "Forget it! The guy's dead, washed away in the mudslide."

"You don't know that," Matt said. "He could still be out there somewhere—he could even be the killer."

Sam scratched the back of his neck. "We can't make any assumptions that could cost us down the line. If this is the killer's van, we might be able to find out some valuable information about him."

"Have you looked around it at all, Rob?" Blair asked.

He shook his head. "To be honest, I've been asleep most of the time."

"All right," Matt said, springing into action. "Let's get busy. Stick to the same area you searched in Hazel's trailer. We've got a good system going, let's keep things simple. And try and leave the place like you found it. Rob, you can sit tight for now."

Matt and Blair left the others to their respective zones and headed to the bedroom area.

"Let's start with the cabinets and work our way down," Blair proposed. She removed the contents of an overhead cabinet and set the items on the bed while Matt began methodically going through a pile of neatly folded clothes. Blair watched out of the corner of her eye as he shook out each item in turn, making sure nothing was hidden inside, before rolling it back up. If the owner returned, he wouldn't be too impressed to discover his highly organized wardrobe had been rifled through and reconfigured, but it was the least of Blair's concerns at present.

As she worked, her mind kept going back to Sandy's sudden passing. The thought that Hazel might have had something to do with her demise nagged at her. Hazel had made a point of brewing one of her tea concoctions for Sandy. What if she'd poisoned her? Or could Harvey have asked her to give Sandy something to end her pain and suffering? And then gotten rid of Hazel afterward? It all seemed too outrageous. And how was any of this connected to the man they'd found strangled on the trail?

After going through all the overhead bins, Blair moved on to the bedside cabinets. She pulled out a dog-eared composition notebook, flicked it open and began to read. Goosebumps prickled her skin. "Check this out," she said, passing the book to Matt.

He turned a few pages and let out a low whistle. "Yikes! This guy's full on anti-government."

"In other words, he could be dangerous," Blair said. "Possibly unstable in light of his obsessive interest in weapons."

"He could also be dead," Matt said, tossing the notebook back to her. "But in the event he's not, you'd better put that back where you found it."

After going through the remainder of the cabinets, and finding nothing else of interest, they lifted up the bed to examine the storage area beneath it.

"Bingo!" Matt lowered his voice to a whisper. "He has a gun safe in here." He rattled the combination lock for good measure. "Doesn't do us any good if we can't get into it though."

Blair stared at the built-in safe beneath the foot of the bed. "Can't you get your tool bag and open it?"

Matt let out a snort. "I didn't bring my power tools. Why are you so keen to open it anyway? You're the one who insisted I leave my gun behind." He avoided her gaze, the bitter note in his voice serving as sufficient condemnation.

"I made the best decision I could based on the facts at hand. How was I supposed to know we were going to end up in this mess?"

"That's why you always bring a gun," Matt hissed. "To be prepared for anything—a bear, a killer, a mudslide."

Blair shrank back from the dark look he shot her. They'd all been under an enormous amount of stress in the past forty-eight hours. It wouldn't take much more to make Matt snap. She bit back the retort on the tip of her tongue. Having the last word, even if she was right about the decision they'd made, wasn't worth risking stoking the fire of his frustration any further.

He cast a wary look toward the bedroom door, and then tugged at the lock on the safe one more time. "The only good thing is that the others can't open it either. Supposedly none of them even own a gun. The last thing we need is untrained civilians arming themselves, especially as we don't know who the killer—"

"Well, what do we have here?" Logan drawled, slinking into the room. "Were you intending on keeping that a secret from the rest of us? So much for laying all our cards on the table."

"Is that a safe?" Whitney questioned, peering around the doorframe.

"A gun safe," Logan corrected her. "Not sure Matt was planning on telling us about it though."

Before Matt had a chance to respond, Sam and Rob stepped into the room to take a closer look.

Rob stroked his beard thoughtfully. "Makes me think this rig belongs to that duck hunter I met."

"Any idea how we can open it?" Sam asked.

"No," Blair responded. "And it's probably better that way."

"I don't know about that," Rob said. "I'd rather have a weapon than not. I can shoot one-handed, if that's what you're worried about."

"It's a moot point. We can't open it." Matt looked around. "Anyone turn up anything else?"

"Nothing other than more books about war and guns," Sam replied.

Matt pushed the bed back down and got to his feet.

"If we're done here, we should go check on Harvey," Blair suggested.

"You go, and give him back his key." Matt pulled it out of his pocket and handed it to her. "We'll finish up here. If Harvey's having a rough time of it, he might not want us all piling into his RV just yet."

BLAIR FOUND Harvey sitting on the couch clutching a mug of black coffee. He eyed her warily when she knocked on the door and peeked inside. "Can I come in for a minute?"

He made a disgruntled noise, which she took as a reluctant invitation. "How are you doing?" she asked, sinking into the captain's chair opposite him.

He waved his mug vaguely at her. "So-so. Find anything next door?"

Blair nodded. "Turns out your mysterious neighbor has a small library of books about war and weapons, not to mention a gun safe in the storage area beneath his bed. I suppose that's hardly surprising if he's a hunter."

Harvey stared at her raptly, eyes that seconds earlier were

glassy and unfocused, suddenly remarkably alert. "Were you able to get it open?"

She shook her head. "No. It might be empty anyway for all we know. If he took off hunting, it stands to reason he would have taken his gun with him."

Harvey set down his mug, looking thoughtful. "I'm willing to bet he has more than one gun in that safe."

Blair cast a discreet glance down the hallway. The door to the bedroom was closed. "Do you need anything, Harvey? Is there anything we can do for you?"

He rumpled his brow. "I ... need to do something with the body."

Blair swallowed, unsettled by the distance Harvey had injected into his words. His *wife* had transitioned to *the body* in an astonishingly short space of time. A shiver ran down her spine. No doubt, it was a defense mechanism—putting space between himself and the stark reality that his wife was dead. Still, it irked her.

"We can help you move Sandy's body into the back of our truck, if you want," she offered.

Harvey frowned down at the carpet and drew a heavy breath. "Or we could bury her."

Blair threw him an alarmed look. "I don't think ... I mean ... help will be here in a matter of days. Don't you want to take Sandy home to your family—have a proper funeral and burial? Besides, there's bound to be an autopsy, under the circumstances."

"What circumstances?" Harvey took a long swig of his coffee. "She was dying of cancer. It's not a matter of how she died. It was only ever a matter of when."

"I realize that," Blair said, looking intently at him. "But we can't bury her until the police get here. Two people are dead, and a woman is missing. Like it or not, the campground's a crime scene now."

16

*B*ack in the camper van, Blair shared with everyone the gist of her conversation with Harvey. She didn't bother mentioning the fact that she hadn't returned his spare key. Her fingers had curled around it a time or two in her pocket while they'd been talking so she couldn't honestly say she'd forgotten about it—but some sixth sense had told her to hold on to it.

"I mean, I realize Harvey's grieving, but he's not thinking straight—talking about burying Sandy here," she concluded. "There has to be an autopsy, under the circumstances."

"You can't blame the man for wanting to bury her." Logan shuddered. "There's no way I'd sleep in that RV with a dead body. And I wouldn't put it in the truck either. It won't take but a day before it starts to stink."

"We have to put it somewhere. We can't leave her body outside," Sam said. "It will attract wild animals and then—" His voice tapered off at Whitney's sharp intake of breath.

"It's starting to rain again too," Blair pointed out. "Outside's definitely not an option."

"I have a cover for my truck bed," Matt said. "We can

wrap Sandy's body in a tarp and put it in there for tonight. If we're trapped here for too much longer, we might have to figure out an alternative—move her to the outhouse or something."

"We won't be able to keep the critters out of there," Sam said, sounding dubious.

"And we'll need to use the outhouse once our holding tanks are full," Blair pointed out.

"Can't we put her in a big cooler or something?" Whitney asked.

Blair arched a brow at her. It was hard to tell if Whitney was actually that much of an airhead or if she played into the role for the attention it brought. "She won't fit in a cooler. Not once rigor mortis sets in."

Whitney pressed a fist to her mouth, a horrified look spreading across her face.

"Changing the subject," Blair said. "It's time we got on with searching the rest of the trailers. You're up next, Logan and Whitney."

Rob got to his feet. "I'll come with you. I could do with some fresh air."

"I'll meet you over there," Sam said, making a beeline for the door. "I need to let Duke out for a quick sniff around first before it really starts dumping."

Logan scowled as he got to his feet. "I don't know why we're still going through with this."

"Because it's paying off. We've discovered some pretty serious discrepancies in everyone's story so far," Matt retorted. "Not to mention secret weapon stashes. You wouldn't happen to have anything to declare, would you, Logan?"

"Let's just cut the jabs and get this over with," Blair said exiting the camper van.

A sullen Logan led the way to his campsite and unlocked

his trailer. "You trash it, you clean it up," he warned them as he held the door open to let them in.

"You and Whitney can wait outside under the awning if you want," Blair suggested. "It might be easier if you don't have to watch us going through your things."

"Not gonna happen," Logan growled. "We'll be right here making sure no one walks off with any of our stuff."

Whitney followed them into the trailer and reached for a camel-colored leather purse on the counter. She rummaged around in it and pulled out a lip gloss, casually applying a layer as she sank down on the couch.

Blair held out a hand for the purse. "I'll need to take a look inside that too."

"Don't be ridiculous!" Whitney cried.

"It's called being thorough," Blair replied sharply. "The contents of Hazel's purse proved to be very revealing."

"Yeah, but unlike Hazel, Whitney's not a killer," Logan snapped. "You've no right to look through her purse. Just get on with what you came here to do and then get out."

In a flash, Matt shot out an arm and snatched the purse from Whitney's hands.

"Hey! Give that back!" she yelled, jumping to her feet.

Blair shoved her back down on the couch. "We're not playing games here. This is a matter of life and death. Everyone needs to prove they are who they say they are. No exceptions."

To Blair's surprise, Whitney's eyes filled with tears. "I need my purse back."

"You'll get it back, just as soon as we search it," Blair said. "Stop being so dramatic and pull yourself together."

Silently, Matt passed the purse to Blair. She unzipped it and tipped the contents onto the dining table. Miscellaneous make-up items, a hairbrush, a small planner, a pack of tissues, a tube of Burt's Bee lip balm, and a pink Juicy

Couture wallet. Blair reached for the wallet, furtively observing the agitated look Whitney fired in Logan's direction. Something was off with them. They had been cagey from the get-go. She'd put it down to the fact that they were on their honeymoon, but was there more to it than that? Maybe Hazel had noticed something was going on too. She might have realized early on that Logan was abusing Whitney—even as far back as when they'd first met at the gas station. That might have been why she was taking all those photographs, documenting everything.

Blair opened the wallet in her hands, surprised to see no credit cards inside—only a single debit card. She pulled out the driver's license and studied it for a moment before reading the details aloud. "Whitney Dolliver, 207 Creekside, Ketchum, Idaho. Pretty town to be from." She scrutinized the birthdate on the license for a moment, frowning in confusion. That couldn't be right. She recalculated, and then whipped her head around to stare at Whitney. The look in the girl's eyes told her everything.

"You're only *sixteen*-years-old?" Blair said in an incredulous tone.

After a tense moment, Whitney gave a defeated nod, tears sliding in quick succession down her cheeks.

"You scumbag!" Matt hissed at Logan. "And don't try and tell me you're only sixteen too, 'cause I know you're lying. Show me your license."

"I don't have to show you anything," Logan spat back. "Get out of my trailer, now! All of you!"

Matt lunged at him, pinning him to the couch in an instant. "Search his pockets!" he called over his shoulder.

Sam sprang into action and, seconds later, plucked a brown leather wallet from Logan's back pocket. He flicked it open and slid out the driver's license. "Logan Hutchins, 1611 Bedford Place, Ketchum, Idaho." He hesitated, a look of disgust on his face as he tossed the wallet on the dining table. "He's twenty-four-years old."

Blair let out a dismayed gasp.

"You're a sorry excuse for a man," Rob said, shaking his head in disbelief.

Blair turned to Whitney. "Do your parents know you're here with Logan?"

She shook her head, keeping her eyes downcast, her face blotchy from crying. "I told them I was going on a trip to celebrate my girlfriend's birthday with the rest of her family."

"So the honeymoon story was a bunch of baloney—I take it you two aren't married at all?" Blair said.

Whitney threw Logan a furtive look, sniffing back tears.

Exasperated, Blair snatched up Logan's wallet. One-by-one, she pulled out all the cards and tossed them onto the table. Tucked in the last slot was a photo of a little boy around two-years-old. Blair held it up in front of Logan's face. "Is this your kid?"

He curled his lip contemptuously and looked away.

"That's ... Gavin," Whitney stammered. "I'm ... I'm his babysitter."

Sam shook his head incredulously at Logan. "Let me guess, you're already married."

Logan's shameless sneer in response said it all.

"Guys like you disgust me. You give the rest of us a bad name," Sam growled.

"Worse than that—he's a criminal," Rob added. "Whitney's a minor and he took advantage of her when she was in his house looking after his kid."

"Now I think I know what Hazel was doing," Blair said. "I'm guessing Logan's wife hired her. She probably had her suspicions that he was a philanderer, and boy was she ever right."

Matt reached for Logan by the collar. "What did you do to Hazel?"

"Get your hands off me, you raving lunatic!" Logan yelled back.

"Let him go, Matt," Blair urged, sensing he was dancing on the edge of the danger zone, oblivious to everyone around him, fixated on the enemy in front of him.

"What ... did ... you ... do ... to ... her?" Matt shouted, shaking Logan with every breath.

"Let him go, man," Sam said, wrestling his way between them. Rob took a step toward them too and then hesitated, as if belatedly remembering his broken arm.

Matt glared over Sam's shoulder at Logan for a long moment, before finally releasing him with a shove and stepping back.

Whitney sat sobbing helplessly into her hands, unable to meet anyone's gaze.

Matt's expression was pasted into the kind of battle-ready grim determination that Blair knew only too well. She would have her work cut out for her to talk him down now.

"We're not leaving here until you tell us what happened to Hazel," Matt said through gritted teeth.

"I don't know what happened to her," Logan insisted. "I didn't lay a hand on her."

"Do you know where she is?" Blair asked.

"I don't know, and I don't care. I hope the killer got her."

"That's ironic, coming from you." Matt folded his arms across his chest. "I think I know how things might have gone down. You damaged her bedroom window and slit the screen, and then you knocked on her door to let her know you'd seen a suspicious figure at her campsite. Afterward, you accompanied her on a quick search around the trailer where you "discovered" the damage. And that's when you killed her."

"You're out of your mind! I didn't even know she was taking those stupid pictures until Sam found the camera."

"He has a point," Rob interjected. "What motive did he have to hurt Hazel?"

"We only have his word for it that he didn't know what she was up to," Blair said. "And his word's worth nothing. There's a good chance he caught her shooting photos of the trailer and put two and two together."

Blair fastened a circumspect gaze on Whitney who was dabbing her mascara-rimmed eyes with a tissue. "Did you know what Hazel was doing?"

"No." Whitney sniffed and let out a weary sigh. "My parents are going to be so mad. I really want to go home."

Blair rolled her eyes. "We all want to go home."

"At this rate, we're not all going to get out of here alive," Sam said grimly.

"Then we need to do everything in our power to tip the odds in our favor," Matt replied."

Sam rubbed his jaw. "What are you suggesting?"

Matt gestured to Logan. "Root out the bad apples. I say we begin by tying this punk up until he starts talking."

17

"You can't do that. You're not in charge around here." Logan narrowed his eyes to slits as Sam and Matt closed in on him. "That's unlawful detention."

"In case you haven't noticed, we're a law unto ourselves with a murderer on the loose," Matt replied. "Someone needs to take the reins. And it sure isn't going to be you as long as I have a say in it." He gestured to Rob. "Block the doorway."

"Wait! You can't tie him up!" Whitney pleaded, brushing away tears. "He didn't kidnap me. I agreed to go with him on this trip."

"Was beating you up one of the perks he promised you?" Blair asked. "Because that's illegal. You can have him prosecuted for abuse."

Whitney gaped at her, eyes glistening. "He didn't mean to do it. He said he was sorry."

"Is that what he's planning to tell his wife too when he gets back home?" Blair shook her head in disgust. "His apology isn't worth the breath it took to launch it from his lying lips."

Whitney opened her mouth to respond but seemed to think better of it. She threw Logan a tentative look while twisting the sodden tissue between her fingers.

"I'll grab some zip ties and rope from our trailer while you guys keep an eye on him," Blair said, throwing up her hood.

As she made her way back through the rain to their campsite, she toyed with the possibility that Logan had done something to Hazel. She wouldn't put it past him. He'd certainly proven he was capable of violence—abusing Whitney, and only too eager to raise a fist to Matt or anyone else who challenged him. If he'd caught Hazel spying on them, he might have erupted and lashed out in a moment of fury—inadvertently killed her and then panicked and hidden the body. The only other feasible alternative was that it had gone down more or less like Matt had described, with premeditation and cold calculation. Wherever the truth lay, Logan couldn't be trusted.

Armed with a bag of zip ties and a coil of rope she retrieved from the storage compartment, she hurried back to Logan's and Whitney's trailer.

"You can make this as easy or difficult for yourself as you want," Matt said, taking a step toward Logan. "Now, turn around slowly and put your hands behind your back."

Without warning, Logan bolted for the door, elbowing Rob aside as he reached for the handle. Before he could wrench it open, Matt and Sam tackled him to the floor and secured his arms while he kicked and screamed and swore at them. "You're gonna pay for this. I'll hire a lawyer and sue you for everything you've got."

"All in good time," Matt responded, sounding unfazed as he and Sam hoisted Logan to his feet and half-dragged him across to the door. Rob cut him an icy glare before stepping aside.

"Where are you taking him?" Whitney whined.

Sam threw her a look of pained sympathy. "He can't stay here, that's for sure."

"Put him in with me if you want," Rob proposed.

"You don't want to listen to him ranting," Matt said. "We'll park him in Hazel's trailer, for now."

Whitney sniffed. "Why can't he stay here?"

"Because," Blair responded in an overly patient tone. "You're only sixteen years old, and he's a predator. We can't trust him not to talk you into freeing him as soon as we're out of here. He's done a good job of manipulating you so far."

Whitney's face crumpled. "I don't want to stay here on my own. What if the killer returns?"

"You can sleep on our couch if you like," Blair offered. "Either way, we're moving Logan next door, so you don't have any unsupervised contact with him."

Matt and Sam hauled a resistant Logan out the door and down the steps. Rob and Blair followed, leaving a forlorn-looking Whitney alone on the couch.

"Are you coming or what?" Blair asked, peering back over her shoulder.

Whitney blew her nose. "I need a few minutes."

"Bring your sleeping bag, and lock the trailer door behind us," Blair cautioned her as she walked away. "We'll be right next door if you need us."

INSIDE HAZEL'S TRAILER, Matt fastened another zip tie around Logan's ankles, while Sam tied the rope around his waist and secured it to the oven door, leaving him just enough slack to hobble into the bathroom.

"What do I do if the killer comes back?" Logan yelled after them as they all tripped back out of the trailer. "How am I supposed to defend myself? If I die, it'll be on your heads."

"We'll take our chances," Matt retorted as he locked the door behind them. They convened in a huddle at the bottom of the steps, shivering in the rain.

"He seems genuinely scared of the killer," Rob said, a concerned expression on his face. "If he isn't behind Hazel's disappearance, then we're putting him in a vulnerable position."

Matt snorted. "Don't forget, he's a good actor. Let him sweat it out for a bit. We'll figure out something later."

"Whose rig do we want to tackle next?" Blair questioned, stuffing her hands deep into her pockets to keep warm. "The secrets just keep coming."

Matt tilted his chin in Sam's direction. "You're up."

Sam gave a non-committal shrug. "Let's do it. We still need to ride out to the road and assess the climb."

"What about searching for my brother this morning?" Rob suggested.

An awkward silence ensued before Matt spoke up. "We can't risk it in this rain. Not with a chance of another slide. Sorry, man."

Rob pressed his lips together and gave a tight nod. "Maybe it will ease off in a bit."

Inside Sam's trailer, Duke jumped down from the couch and eyed them warily. Rob walked straight over to him and rubbed his neck. "How's my favorite canine ever?"

Discreetly keeping her distance from the dog, Blair looked around the interior curiously. It had the air of a well-lived in bachelor pad and smelled a bit like a kennel. Not much care had been taken with the decor, but there was evidence of Sam's passion everywhere—in the maps that plastered the walls, the dog-eared books on climbing, stickers from sponsorship companies on the cabinet doors—not to mention climbing gear stashed in every corner of the room. An empty box of performance energy bars was folded flat by the door next to a bag of garbage.

"Have at it. We'll be outside whenever you're done," Sam said, letting the door slam behind him and Duke.

"It's pouring out there," Blair called after him, but he didn't respond. She peered through the window and watched as he pulled out a camping chair from beneath the trailer and slumped down in it under the awning. He folded his hands behind his head and stared up at the iron-cast sky and the rain sliding off the awning in sheets. Duke settled down at his feet and rested his head on his paws, seemingly as indifferent to the cold as his master.

"Where did he go?" Rob asked.

"He's sitting out there beneath the awning in a camping chair," Blair said. "I'm afraid he'll freeze to death."

"He's used to the outdoors," Rob said. "He'll be fine."

"All right, let's get busy," Matt said. "Blair, you concentrate on this main area. I'll take the bedroom, Rob you search the bathroom."

Blair began working her way through the shelves in the kitchen and then moved on to the cabinets above the couch. By now, she was over her initial awkwardness when it came to rifling through strangers' possessions. The first few searches had turned up a lot of valuable information about their fellow campers, which more than justified what they were doing as far as she was concerned. As she poked around in Sam's belongings, her thoughts pivoted back to Harvey, alone and grieving in the RV next door. Could they really barge in there and demand to search it next, under the circumstances? Maybe they should give him some more time.

She only hoped they were rescued from this wretched campground soon. She dreaded to think what they would do with a decaying body on their hands. Despite her earlier speculation, odds were an autopsy wouldn't reveal anything untoward in Sandy's death. It was tragic that she'd died at the campground, but maybe she would have chosen it over dying in a hospital bed hooked up to a bunch of machines. After all, she and Harvey had spent a good deal of their lives camping and loved the outdoors. Blair doubted Harvey would continue RVing after this. It was a shame Sandy had contracted cancer while he was still fit and strong—they could have had many more years of traveling around the country together.

"No shortage of climbing gear in this rig, that's for sure," Matt called from the bedroom. Blair glanced up and saw that he was digging through the storage area beneath the bed.

"That's not the half of it," Rob said, coming out of the bathroom. "He has more tubs under the trailer too. I've seen him rooting around in it, coiling up ropes and stuff."

"We'll take a look in the storage compartments afterward," Matt said. "We might need to use some of that gear anyway if we decide to try and climb around the washed-out section of the road."

Blair flipped through a few dog-eared technical climbing instruction manuals that were stashed on a shelf above the couch. "*Crack Climbing: An Engineer's Approach*," she read aloud. "Way too thrilling for my taste."

Rob shook his head in bewilderment. "Guaranteed way to end up dead. These extreme athletes are nutcases."

Blair reached up to replace the manuals on the shelf. A folded piece of paper fluttered out of one of them and landed at her feet. She leaned down and picked it up. After straightening it out, she glanced at the headline. *Death of elite climber under investigation.*

"What's that?" Rob asked, gesturing to the paper in her hand.

"It's a newspaper article." Blair furrowed her brow, studying it. "It must be about Sam's friend, the one who died."

Matt leaned against the bedroom doorframe. "What does it say?"

Blair perched on the edge of the couch and began to read aloud.

"Acclaimed free solo climber, Andy Schipper, fell three-hundred meters to his death Wednesday while attempting to rappel down the side of a popular route known as El Sendero Luminoso in Mexico. Fellow American climber Sam Hunter, who was climbing with him, landed on a ledge and fractured his wrist. Hunter told members of law enforcement and rescuers that something had gone wrong with their ropes. Investigating authorities are calling the accident suspicious and detained Mr. Hunter for questioning after an initial examination indicated that the ropes had allegedly been tampered with."

Matt let out a long, low whistle. "Does it say anything else?"

Blair shook her head. "That's it. It's only part of an article torn from a newspaper." She pulled out her phone and took a quick picture of it.

"I'll ask Sam about it," Rob said, heading for the door. "I'm done searching the bathroom."

"Wait! I'm not so sure that's a good idea," Matt replied, rubbing his brow. "Let's think this through. Why didn't Sam mention this?"

"To be fair, he did tell us his friend died in a climbing accident," Blair said.

Matt scowled. "Yeah, he just left out the part about the accident being under investigation."

"Can't say I blame the guy," Rob said. "Why would he tell a bunch of strangers that?"

Matt squared his jaw. "Maybe he's guilty. Who else could have tampered with the equipment but him?"

For a long moment no one spoke, and then Blair said, "If he was guilty, he would have been arrested by now."

"Not necessarily," Rob said. "Not unless they have sufficient evidence to prove it. Otherwise it's a circumstantial case."

"He could be on the run," Matt suggested. "I knew there was something off about him the first time I set eyes on him."

"That's ridiculous! I can't believe Sam had anything to do with it," Blair protested. "He's gutted about his friend's death. And I don't blame him for not wanting to talk about the grisly details. Being accused of having had a hand in it must have been devastating. It's no wonder he took off in his trailer by himself. And it explains why he's so protective of his privacy. I wouldn't trust people either if they accused me of killing my friend."

Matt rubbed a hand over his jaw. "I think it's best if we don't mention that we found the article, for now. We've got enough on our hands with Logan to deal with. The last thing I want to do is make an enemy of Sam too, or make him think we suspect he's the killer."

Blair arched a brow at him. "Well, we don't, do we?"

Before Matt had a chance to answer, the door opened and Whitney entered the trailer. Her flushed face had been scrubbed clean of makeup and she wore a look of chastened resignation. "I'm here to help with the search."

"We're just wrapping up in here," Blair said brightly. "We're heading over to our trailer next. Why don't you let Sam know we'll be right out."

Whitney nodded and dutifully trekked back down the steps.

"So we're in agreement?" Matt said in a low tone, his gaze flitting from Rob to Blair. "We keep this to ourselves for now."

Blair gave an affirming nod.

Rob shrugged. "Fine with me."

Matt switched off the lights and headed to the door. "Let's see what he's got stored underneath the trailer."

"IT'S JUST CLIMBING GEAR. Why do you need to pull it all out in the rain?" Sam growled, getting to his feet. He folded up his camping chair and tossed it angrily into the open storage compartment. "I don't like anyone messing with it. I've got it organized just the way I need it."

Duke pricked up his ears observing the interaction closely.

"All part of the search," Matt said abruptly. He pulled out a tub and started rummaging through the contents: lanterns, mosquito nets, a camping stove. Rob hunkered down next to him and attempted to help. Whitney stood off to one side rubbing her arms distractedly. Blair cast a discreet look at Sam as she reached for another tub, searching for any trace of guilt in his expression. Was it possible his friend's climbing accident hadn't been an accident at all? At the end of the day, who would ever really know what happened hundreds of feet up on a cliff face? It would be the perfect way to kill someone.

Blair dumped the tub unceremoniously at her feet. It was heavier than she'd anticipated. Unlatching the lid, she saw that it was filled with climbing harnesses and miscellaneous gear. She lifted out a couple of coils of rope and then froze, paralyzed by the sight of a knife lying in one corner of the tub. A fluttering feeling swirled around in her gut as she tried in vain not to make the connection that was forcing its way into her brain.

She desperately wanted to pull out her phone and check the photograph she'd taken of the murdered man. Her rational self knew it was common for climbers to carry knives. It was a safety feature in case you needed to cut a rope at any point.

But there was no getting around what her eyes were telling her—the knife in the corner of Sam's tub looked exactly like the one protruding from the dead man's belly.

18

*B*lair stood welded to the spot, staring down at the knife, her blood thudding in her temples.

"Everything all right?" Matt asked, walking over to her.

She gestured emphatically to the tub, not wanting Sam to overhear anything.

Matt followed her gaze, his expression hardening as he reached in and lifted out the knife. He turned it over and studied the brand name on the handle.

Blair's heart knocked against her ribs. What was Matt doing? He wasn't even trying to be discreet about it.

"Petzl. Nice knife," he commented, holding it aloft for Sam to see. "Is this a specialty climber's knife or something?"

"Yeah, it is," Sam said, walking over. He took the knife from Matt's hands and pointed to the odd-looking hole in the handle. "The carabiner hole is so you can attach it to a harness. It's a super lightweight knife—ideal for climbing."

Or killing. Blair squeezed her hands slowly into fists, mulling over the frightening possibility. Coincidentally, Sam had been the one to find the body. And it had been him who'd sounded the alarm by banging on their door in the early hours. A chill fingered its way down her spine. Isn't that what murderers did to throw the police off the scent? Report the crime themselves, or call in a tip? She swallowed down the bile seeping up her throat. Matt was right to be paranoid about their fellow campers. Any one of these strangers they were stuck here with could be a killer. Even Duke was far from harmless. She was fairly certain the dog would willingly attack any one of them given the command. A wave of panic hit. She desperately wanted to get out of this place. Gritting her teeth, she averted her eyes, determined to quash her burgeoning fears before she fell apart. Now was not the time to lose it, not when the killer was still an unknown entity.

With a casual flick of his wrist, Sam tossed the knife back into the tub. Blair snapped the lid back in place and returned the tub to the storage compartment. "We're all done here," she said, trying hard to hold her voice steady. "Let's head over to our trailer and wrap this up."

"I'm starving," Sam exclaimed. How about we take fifteen and grab something to eat first?"

"I could go for that," Rob agreed.

Matt gave an approving grunt.

"What about Logan?" Whitney asked.

"You can make him a sandwich and bring it back here," Blair said. "One of us will take it to him."

Inside their trailer, Matt threw himself down on the couch and rubbed the bridge of his nose between his thumb and forefinger. "Now you know why I don't trust people, especially when I don't know them."

"That's exactly what the killer wants," Blair said quietly.

Matt frowned. "What do you mean?"

"I've been thinking it through. He wants us to turn on one another. It makes us weaker."

"What choice do we have?" Matt threw up his hands. "Everyone's lying to us—like Logan, for instance. *On his honeymoon.* With his kid's babysitter! What a loser."

"I still can't believe Whitney's only sixteen," Blair commented. "Her parents must be worried sick by now."

"That could be a good thing," Matt mused. "If the police are looking for her, they might be checking CCTV footage."

"But even if they manage to track her here, they can't navigate the road in to Bird Creek."

"No, they'll have to enlist the help of search and rescue. Until then, we're on our own with an unidentified killer."

Blair shivered. "I still think it could be the duck hunter stalking us. It's a game to him, picking us off one-by-one."

Matt clenched his teeth. "Then we won't make it easy for him. If it's a game of last man standing, I intend to win."

Blair blew out a frustrated breath. "You can't fight against a gun. We're defenseless if he strikes again."

Matt walked over to the refrigerator and started pulling out condiments and sandwich fixings. "We don't have to be defenseless. We can set up a watch, arm ourselves with knives—"

"The knife!" Blair blurted out, jumping to her feet. She fumbled for her phone and quickly scrolled through the pictures until she came to the ones she'd taken of the body. After enlarging a photo of the knife in the man's belly, she studied the brand name on the handle. "Petzl!" she announced with a triumphant air. "I knew it! It was a climbing knife in the victim's belly. A hunter wouldn't use a knife like that. And the body was found a lot closer to our campground than to the hunters' campsite anyway."

"All of which points to Sam." Matt frowned as he slathered mayonnaise on the sandwich bread he'd laid out on the counter. "I was right to be wary of him from the get-go."

Blair pulled at her lip. "It doesn't necessarily mean Sam

had anything to do with the murder. He never locks any of the compartments under his trailer. Anyone could have pulled the knife out of there to set him up and make him look guilty."

Matt screwed the lid back on the mayonnaise. "Why didn't Sam notice it was a climbing knife in the man's belly?"

Blair shrugged. "He was too distraught to give the body more than a passing glance. I think finding Andy at the bottom of the mountain messed him up."

Matt finished making the sandwiches and carried them over to the dining table on paper plates. Blair grabbed a bag of chips and two bottles of water and joined him. "We're going to have to do something about the water situation. If we're stuck here for much longer, we'll have to start collecting spring water and filtering it."

Matt swallowed a mouthful of sandwich. "We'll worry about that tomorrow. We need to start putting together a plan to get out of here. I'll drive Sam out to the road after this and let him assess the climb."

Blair stopped chewing and stared at Matt incredulously. "You can't drive out there alone with him. What if he really is the killer?"

Matt took a swig of water and set the bottle down on the table, a contemplative look in his eyes. "I'll take someone else along too." He reached for a handful of chips and dropped them on his plate. "From now on, we need to go everywhere in groups of three. No one goes anywhere alone with anyone else."

They glanced up at a knock on the door.

Matt squared his jaw and reached for the paper plates to clear the table. "Brace yourself. Here comes the search party."

"Come on in!" Blair called out.

Sam entered and kicked off his boots, munching on a

granola bar. "I knocked on Harvey's door. He's going to join us."

"How's he doing?" Matt asked.

Sam shrugged. "Just the same. He's in shock. It will be good for him to get out of the RV for a bit."

The door opened again, and Rob appeared, followed by a haggard-looking Harvey. Glancing around, he gave a tense nod and then seated himself in the chair closest to the door.

Blair locked eyes with him. "Are you doing all right, Harvey?"

He scratched his chin, frowning. "I just need some fresh air for a few minutes." He threw her an uneasy look. "You know, with the body being in there and all."

"Once we've finished searching, we can talk about what to do with Sandy's body," Blair promised him.

"No sign of Whitney?" Matt asked.

"Not yet," Sam replied.

"Why don't you guys get started?" Matt said. "Blair and I will be right here if you need us."

He patted a spot on the couch for Blair and she sank down next to him while Sam, Harvey, and Rob set about searching the trailer. Blair picked up her book from where she'd stashed it down the side of the couch and pretended to read, all the while monitoring the search proceedings out of the corner of her eye. It wasn't that she was afraid they might discover something in their trailer. But she was half afraid they might leave something behind. What if Sam tried to plant one of his climbing knives on them? Or if Harvey stashed Sandy's prescription drugs in a cabinet? Or what if Rob had managed to open the gun safe in the camper van and planted a weapon in their trailer? She knew her thoughts were running amok, painting increasingly far-fetched scenarios for her brain to worry over, but the truth was, there was either a killer stalking them, or walking among them. And at this point, she didn't trust her fellow campers any more than Matt did.

After what seemed like forever, Sam finally announced that they were done. Blair breathed out a silent sigh of relief.

"All right, let's talk about what we can do to get out of here," Matt said. "One of the options is to try to find a way around the section of the road that's washed out. It would require climbing up and over the mountain so Sam will have to assess it to see if it's even possible."

"The other issue we need to address is safety," Blair went on. "We don't know who the killer is, and we don't know who took Hazel. We're assuming that someone is stalking the campground, but we don't know that for a fact." She hesitated, clearing her throat before continuing. "Like I've said before, the killer could be any one of us."

The others shifted uncomfortably, casting awkward sideways glances at one another.

"For that reason, it would be best if we went everywhere in groups of three from now on," Blair continued. "So when Matt and Sam drive out to the road, they'll take a third person with them and leave three of us here. For now, Logan's out of the equation. He stays right where he's at, for everyone's sake."

"Makes sense to me," Rob agreed. "Safety in numbers and all that."

Matt looked around for approval. "Everyone in agreement?"

The others nodded in unison.

"I need to do something with ... Sandy's body," Harvey said, his voice fading away.

Matt puckered his brow. "Yeah, I was getting to that next. If it's all right with you, I'm going to suggest we wrap her body in a tarp and lock it in the back of my truck."

Harvey blinked solemnly back at him and then gave a hesitant nod.

"Why don't you use Logan's truck instead?" Sam suggested. "He has a cover too, and he won't be driving anywhere any time soon."

Blair frowned. "Speaking of Logan, where's Whitney?"

a hint of suspicion hardened in Matt's face. "Whitney had better not be trying to figure out a way to free Logan. It shouldn't take that long to make a couple of sandwiches."

"We have the key to Hazel's trailer," Blair reminded him. "Whitney can't get in."

Sam frowned. "Something might have happened to her."

Matt strode to the door. "Blair and I will go check on her. The rest of you wait here in case she shows up."

A steady downpour of rain flailed them as they hurried off down the road in the direction of Logan's and Whitney's trailer.

"I really hope she's okay," Blair said, pulling her hood down tighter over her face. "You don't think the killer could have struck again, do you?"

Matt grunted. "I'm more worried Whitney might be trying to help the killer escape. As far as I'm concerned, Logan's still our number one suspect."

By the time they reached the other campsite, the rain had turned it into a hopscotch of mud puddles. They picked their way gingerly over to the trailer and Blair rattled the handle before banging loudly on the door. "Whitney! Are you in there?" She waited for a moment or two and then tried again.

Matt peered through the nearest window. "She's got all the blinds drawn. I can't see in anywhere."

Blair walked around to the other side of the trailer and tented her hands over her eyes as she tried to peer through a tiny crack in the blinds. She didn't detect any shadowy figures moving around inside, but it was hard to see much. She rejoined Matt who was jiggling the door handle again.

"It's not going to miraculously open," Blair said. "If Whitney's in there, she's deliberately ignoring us."

Matt thumped his fist on the door in frustration before turning on his heel. "We'll come back. Let's check Hazel's trailer and make sure Logan's still secure."

With a sinking feeling, Blair followed him over to the adjacent campsite. They should never have left Whitney alone, not even for a minute. She was vulnerable and couldn't be trusted—a dangerous combo.

At Hazel's trailer, Matt reached for the front door handle, his breath catching when the door swung open. "Brace yourself, this doesn't look good," he muttered. Blair hurried up the steps after him and came to a screeching halt in the doorway. Her jaw dropped. The rope that had secured Logan lay limp on the floor, one end still tied to the oven door. The severed zip ties that had secured his wrists and ankles had been tossed on the couch.

"Figured as much," Matt said through gritted teeth. He strode into the bedroom at the back and called to Blair. "Looks like our enterprising teen climbed in through the damaged window. Probably stood on a camping chair or something."

"Logan put her up to this," Blair replied. "He knows exactly how to manipulate her. They must be holed up in their trailer. Where else would they go in this weather? I just hope Logan's not holding Whitney against her will."

"He's got another thing coming if he thinks he can hide in there like a rat. It won't take much to break in if that's what it takes to flush him out."

After retracing their steps, Matt and Blair took turns hammering insistently on Whitney's and Logan's door. This time, they didn't let up until they heard Whitney's voice through a small slider window to the left of the door. "What do you want?"

"We know Logan's in there with you," Blair answered, positioning herself directly below the window. "Open up and let us in."

"I can't."

Blair and Matt exchanged a quick look. "Can't or won't?" Blair asked, her heart racing.

There was no immediate response from Whitney, but Blair could hear the urgent murmuring of voices in the background. "Logan's in there," she mouthed to Matt. "He's telling her what to say."

"Whitney!" Matt called out. "Open the door now or I'm gonna break it down."

"No!" Whitney yelled back. "We have knives!"

"That confirms it," Matt growled. "He's in there with her."

Blair tensed. "You don't think Logan would hurt her if we break down the door, do you?"

Matt rubbed a hand across his jaw. "He's hurt her before. We can't take that chance."

"Whitney, is Logan threatening you?" Blair asked.

After a protracted silence, Whitney gave a high-pitched laugh that sounded almost hysterical. "You're an interfering cow, you know that. Go back to your trailer and leave us alone."

Matt scowled and strode over to the window where Blair was standing.

"I know you can hear me, Logan, so listen up," he shouted. "If you as much as lay a hand on Whitney, I'll make sure it's the last time you hurt anyone."

The window snapped shut cutting off all communication.

"Worthless coward!" Matt pounded a fist on the window in frustration. "Getting a sixteen-year-old girl to negotiate for him."

"We can't risk confronting him like this," Blair said. "He's a loose cannon. If we break in, he could put a knife to Whitney's neck and use her as a hostage."

Matt squared his jaw and gave a curt nod of agreement. "We'll give them some space for now. Lull them into a false sense of security. But the minute we get a chance, we need to get Whitney away from him. She has no idea how dangerous he might be. And neither do we."

BACK AT THEIR TRAILER, they filled the others in on what had unfolded.

Harvey moved his jaw side-to-side. "I don't like it one bit —leaving that girl alone with Logan. Her life's at risk. Even if he's not the killer, he's got a violent streak."

"I agree," Matt said. "I still think he had something to do with Hazel's disappearance. But we can't just charge the trailer and break the door down. They've armed themselves with knives. Someone could get hurt."

Rob gave a worried shake of his head. "We need to get Whitney out of there somehow. She's fooling herself thinking she's safe with him."

"We'll have to wait until night to strike—when they're asleep," Matt said. "That'll give us the element of surprise."

"And there's more of us than them," Sam added. "That counts for something."

Harvey frowned. "We'll need to arm ourselves."

"If we go in there with knives too, it'll only end up in a bloodbath," Rob said. "Knife fights never end well. I say we figure out a way to open the gun safe in the camper van. Staring down the barrel of a gun will soon change Logan's mind."

Matt got to his feet. "First things first. Sam, Blair, and I are going to drive out to the road and see if there's any possible way to climb over the mountain and get help."

Rob and Harvey exchanged uncertain looks as they got to their feet.

"Stay in your trailers until we get back and keep your doors locked," Blair warned them. "Logan's bound to hear our truck pulling out. We can't trust him not to take advantage of the situation."

"I'll leave Duke in my trailer," Sam offered. "If you hear him barking, it's a good indication someone's sneaking about the place or heading your way."

Blair laid a hand on Harvey's arm as he was exiting the trailer. "We'll take care of Sandy when we get back, I promise."

He gave a stiff nod but said nothing as he descended the steps.

A few minutes later, Matt, Blair, and Sam piled into the truck.

"Do you seriously think Logan's the killer?" Sam asked as they drove out of the campground, wipers on full speed.

Blair leaned forward to join in the conversation from the back seat, "He did have a motive to harm Hazel."

Sam rubbed his brow. "It's possible we're dealing with two separate incidents. The body we found might have nothing to do with Hazel's disappearance."

"I've been wondering about that too," Matt mused. "None of us even knew him. I think the guy who owns the camper van killed him. That's the only explanation that makes any sense to me."

"One of the hunters could have killed him. We've only got Rob's word for it that they were all on good terms," Sam said. "And we can't trust anyone's word around here."

Matt threw him a sidelong look. "You got that right."

Blair prodded him discreetly from behind.

"What's that supposed to mean?" Sam questioned, narrowing his eyes.

"I know about your friend's climbing accident," Matt said. "The one you're under investigation for. We found a newspaper cutting in your trailer."

Blair clenched her hands into fists. What was Matt thinking? They couldn't do this now. They needed Sam on their side if they were ever going to figure out a way to get out of here.

Sam turned and stared out his window for a long moment. "Andy was my best friend. I had nothing to gain from his death. I'd give my right arm to have him back."

Blair's heart lurched at the choked-up agony in his voice. Surely, he couldn't be faking that.

"Why did the cops say the ropes had been tampered with?" Matt asked.

Sam gave a despondent shake of his head. "I don't know. I never got to examine them afterward. I was distraught when the paramedics and cops arrived. My only concern was Andy, and how I was going to tell his family he was gone. The cops confiscated everything as evidence." He let out a deep sigh. "Andy didn't have any enemies that I know of. He was well respected in the climbing community—we both were." His voice trailed off. "That's all changed. I even lost my sponsorship. I don't know if I'll ever be out from under this cloud of suspicion now. Once a rumor like that starts, it's hard to shake it."

Matt rolled to a stop a few feet from where the mudslide had ripped out the road. He gripped the steering wheel and stared straight ahead of him. "I want to believe you, Sam. But I'll be honest, I'm having a hard time trusting anyone right now."

Sam nodded knowingly. "That's what I love about free climbing. You only ever have to trust yourself." A flicker of grief crossed his face. "Or your climbing partner." Without another word, he opened the truck door, jumped out into the rain, and walked over to the washed-out section of the road where he stood appraising the imposing wall of granite he'd have to scale in order to climb around the slide.

"You shouldn't have brought it up," Blair grumbled, as Matt undid his seatbelt.

"Why not? I needed to hear what he had to say about it."

"And?" Blair pressed.

"I don't think he had anything to do with his buddy's death. And I don't think he's the killer either—he doesn't have the stomach for it."

"But it was a climbing knife in that guy's belly."

Matt tapped his fingers on the steering wheel. "Like you said before, anyone could have taken it out of Sam's tub."

"Hey! Are you two coming or what?" Sam yelled, signaling to them to join him.

They hurriedly threw up their hoods, clambered out, and made their way over to where he was standing.

"What's the verdict?" Matt asked.

"Hard to say for sure until I get into the climb," Sam replied, gazing up at the rock face. "But I'm optimistic there are enough cracks and handholds for me to scale it."

Matt scratched his jaw, looking unconvinced. "What happens if you get stuck halfway up?"

Sam gave a rueful grin. "Unless you're offering to come and get me, my only option will be up and over at that point."

"You don't have to do this," Blair said. "It's more dangerous with the rock being so wet."

"I need to try," Sam replied. "We've got an unsolved murder, a dead body, a missing woman, and a potential killer on our hands. If we hang around here much longer, no one's getting out alive."

"Up to you, man," Matt said. "I don't want you risking your life if you're getting in over your head."

Sam smoothed a hand over his jaw. "I think it's doable. I'll get my gear ready tonight and tackle it in the morning. The light will start fading soon."

Matt started up the engine and they retraced their route to the campground.

"I'll fill Rob and Harvey in on the plan," Blair said when they pulled up outside their trailer. She crossed the road to the camper van and rapped on the door, then peered through the window when no one answered.

She tried the door handle, and the door swung wide. Blair pressed her lips together in disapproval. So much for Matt warning everyone to keep their doors locked.

"Rob? Are you sleeping?" She stuck her head into the bedroom and bathroom but there was no sign of him.

Just as she was about to exit the camper van, her eye fell on a note on the kitchen table.

20

*W*ith a growing sense of foreboding, Blair reached for the note and read it.

Gone to look for my brother.

Her stomach plummeted. She scrunched up her eyes in disbelief and groaned out loud. What an idiot! Now they were going to have to go out in the pouring rain and look for him—with only two hours of daylight left, at best.

With a resigned sigh, she returned to her trailer and handed the note to Matt. He read it aloud to Sam and then crumpled it in his fist. "Forget it! We're not going after him. We already pulled him out of the mud once. This is on his head."

"We did promise we'd help him look for his brother today," Sam pointed out.

"Only if the weather cooperated," Matt shot back. "And so far, it hasn't. He's lost his mind heading out there in the rain in his condition."

"I suppose we can hardly blame him for wanting to look for his brother," Blair piped up.

"We don't even know if he has a brother," Matt growled.

"What if Rob's the killer? Or what if he and his brother are both in on it? Those gashes and scratches on Rob's face could just as easily have come from wrestling with the guy he strangled for all we know."

"Now you're being ridiculous," Blair scolded.

"I have to agree. Rob doesn't strike me as the killer type," Sam added.

Matt tossed the note into the sink. "You can't take anything at face value. Anyone's capable of killing given the right set of circumstances."

They glanced up at the sound of someone outside the trailer.

"It's Harvey," Blair said, peeking out the window before opening the door to him.

He pulled down his hood and nodded to them, water dripping from his rain gear onto the floor. "Thought I heard you come back."

"Rob's taken off to look for his brother," Blair said.

Harvey let out a grunt of disapproval. "Doubt we'll see him again in that case. He'll never survive out there tonight." He frowned and scratched his head as if something had just occurred to him. "He still has my spare key."

Blair's fingers instinctively pressed against the cold metal in her pocket. She wasn't sure why she hadn't returned the key—maybe because they hadn't had a chance to search Harvey's RV, yet. Or maybe because she felt obligated to Hazel to follow up on her suspicions.

"What's the verdict on the climb?" Harvey asked.

"I think it can be done," Sam answered. "I won't know for sure until I get into it. I'm going to make the attempt tomorrow."

Harvey gave a grim nod, his eyes darting around the group. "I could use some help in the meantime." He hesitated, tugging on his beard before continuing. "We talked about moving Sandy's body to Logan's truck, but I suppose there's not much chance of that now that he's barricaded himself in his trailer."

"We're going to force our way in tonight and get Whitney away from him," Matt said. "As soon as we have the keys to his truck, we can move Sandy's body."

"It's just that … it can't wait." Harvey cleared his throat. "The smell … you know."

Blair traced her fingers lightly across her brow, her stomach roiling. "We can move her to our truck until we have a better option."

Matt frowned at her, but she shot him back a defiant look. "Why don't you and Sam help Harvey take care of that right now?"

Masking his initial irritation, Matt accompanied Sam and Harvey across the road while Blair sank down on the couch, exhausted from their ongoing ordeal. It was an unending mental game of survival. A maze of uncertainty and indecision. Not knowing was the hardest part—not knowing if Hazel was dead or alive, not knowing if anyone knew they were trapped at Bird Creek, not knowing the killer's identity, or whether he was still out there or not. And now there was Rob with his broken arm wandering around in the rain searching for his brother—another thing to worry about, thanks to her mother-hen instincts. Doubtless, it would be another long, restless night.

She got up and made her way into the bathroom, her mood plummeting when she noticed the holding tank was registering full. Using the outhouse was a minor inconvenience in the grand scheme of things, but not one that she relished from either a sanitary or safety point of view at present.

She filled the kettle to boil some water for a cup of tea, watching discreetly out the window as Matt unlocked their truck, and Sam and Harvey carefully slid Sandy's tarp-draped body into the covered bed. Guilt pricked at her. This had to be especially rough for Matt—triggering painful memories of loading his buddies' bodies into an armored truck to bring them back to the base. She moved away from the window before the men caught her watching them. A moment later, the door opened, and a drenched Matt trudged inside.

"Is Harvey doing all right?" she asked, filling her mug with hot water.

"Yeah, I think so. He's not the touchy, feely sort, so he's not saying much." Matt eyed the kettle. "I'll take a tea if you've got one going." He let out a weary sigh and slumped into a chair. "It's been a long day and I barely slept last night."

"No surprise there." Blair retorted. Matt still struggled with insomnia, wrestling well into the early hours to fall asleep. On several occasions, she'd woken up and found him pacing the room, or standing guard in the doorway like a sentry. The chronic lack of sleep and paranoia had become a vicious cycle, one feeding into the other. "Are we still planning on breaking into Logan's trailer tonight?" she asked, handing him a steaming mug.

Matt slurped his tea with satisfaction. "Yeah, I told Harvey and Sam to meet us at my truck at 2.00 AM. We can't leave a sixteen-year-old at Logan's mercy. Not after he left those bruises on her. It wouldn't take much for him to choke a lightweight like Whitney in a fit of rage."

Blair shivered and interlaced her fingers around her mug. "Maybe we shouldn't wait until tonight."

"Breaking in while they're asleep is the best chance we've got of making sure no one gets hurt."

"They're bound to wake up," Blair objected.

"We're not literally going to smash the door down," Matt

responded. "I can remove the lock quietly while they're asleep at the other end of the trailer."

"Where should we put Logan this time? We can't put him back in Hazel's trailer as long as that window's broken."

Matt drew his brows together and thought about it for a moment. "We'll move him into the camper van. If Rob shows back up, he can bunk in Hazel's trailer."

Blair nodded and sipped her tea. After a moment of silence, she asked, "How are you holding up?"

Matt threw her a sharp look. "Are you afraid I'm going to crash and burn?"

Blair gave a helpless shrug. "You can hardly blame me. This is the worst possible scenario, the very thing we planned this trip to get away from—death, high-octane, adrenaline-charged missions, invisible enemies."

Matt set down his mug and ran his fingers through his hair. "Things happen for a reason. Maybe I was meant to be here. I need to stay strong for the others. This isn't about me anymore."

Blair smiled across at him, biting back tears. She was immensely proud of Matt, but the selfish part of her was loath to sacrifice her husband's mental wellbeing to save any more lives than he already had.

THE 2:00 am alarm shot through Blair like a bolt of electricity. She sat straight up in bed, forgetting momentarily where she was and what she was doing.

Matt was standing by the door with his coat zipped up, tool bag in hand. They'd both gone to bed fully clothed, so it only took a moment for Blair to pull on her wool cap, jacket, and boots and declare herself ready. After locking the door behind them, they joined Harvey and Sam who were waiting by the truck.

"Any sign of Rob?" Blair asked.

Sam shook his head. "I took a quick peek in the camper van before I came over. He hasn't been back."

"Chances are he won't be," Harvey muttered. "In his condition, he's liable to succumb to the elements."

"Let's dispense with the gloomy predictions and get busy doing what we're here to do," Matt said.

Aided by their flashlights, they wound their way along the road and waited in the trees at the edge of Logan's and Whitney's campsite for a few minutes to make sure there were no lights on, or signs of activity inside the trailer.

"Looks like they're out for the count," Matt said. He picked up his tool bag and was about to make a move toward the trailer when the door opened. Whitney stepped out, the collar of her jacket pulled up tight around her mouth. She threw an apprehensive look around the shadows before turning on a flashlight and scuttling off down the road in the direction of the outhouse.

"This is our chance to get inside," Blair whispered to the others. "She left it unlocked."

Matt gave a grim nod. "Harvey, wait by the road and intercept Whitney on her way back. Make sure she doesn't get past you until we have Logan under control."

Blair's blood thundered in her veins as she and Sam crept toward the trailer, following in Matt's footsteps. She had no idea what lay ahead of them. Logan could be awake and armed—waiting just inside the door, for all they knew. But there was also a chance he was snoring his head off, oblivious to the danger Whitney had put herself in by venturing to the outhouse on her own.

Turning off his flashlight, Matt quietly depressed the handle and pushed open the door. He slipped inside, motioning to Blair and Sam to follow. Single file, they padded silently to the back of the trailer where a figure lay sprawled in the shadows. Without a moment's hesitation, Matt and Sam easily overpowered the sleeping Logan. In a flurry of limbs, they made swift work of zip tying his wrists and ankles—his enraged screams piercing the air when he came to and realized this wasn't a dream.

After a cursory search, Matt retrieved Logan's truck keys from the bedside cabinet and pocketed them.

With Sam's help, he hoisted Logan to his feet and dragged him down the steps of the trailer, and out into the rain. Whitney's wails reached their ears from the road below where she was wrestling with Harvey who was keeping a firm grip on her arms. No doubt, she was afraid of Logan's reaction once he found out that she'd left the door unlocked. Blair felt a pang of remorse at the obvious distress in the girl's voice. Her initial judgment of Whitney's immaturity had been based on the assumption that she was a young woman in her mid-twenties. She jogged down to the road and put an arm around the girl's shaking shoulders. "It's all right. Everything's going to be okay."

"You can't do this," Whitney blubbered. "You can't just trespass in people's trailers whenever you feel like it."

"It's for your own safety," Blair soothed. "Logan hurt you once. He could do it again, and with more serious consequences next time. You can stay with us tonight. We'll wait here for you while you grab your things from your trailer."

"Don't listen to them, Whit!" Logan yelled. "They're trying to tear us apart."

Whitney sniffed and wiped the back of her hand across her eyes. She cast a wary look in Logan's direction before trudging back up to the campsite and into her trailer.

A few minutes later, she reappeared with a small duffel bag slung over her shoulder.

All the way to the camper van, Logan carried on, yelling at Whitney to do something. But to her credit, she kept her eyes forward and refrained from answering him. While Matt and Sam escorted him inside the camper van, Blair took Whitney by the elbow and gently guided her across the road to their trailer.

"You must be exhausted," Blair said, pulling out the sofa bed. She grabbed a pillow and blankets from the closet and proceeded to make up the bed. Whitney flashed her a wan smile of thanks as she crawled in, promptly falling asleep.

Blair opened the refrigerator and lifted out a bottle of water before sitting down at the table to wait for Matt.

It was a good half hour later before she heard the sound of his key in the lock. "I was beginning to get worried. What kept you?"

"We were transferring Sandy's body to Logan's truck. We'll need ours to drive out to the road tomorrow." He gestured to the couch and whispered, "How's Whitney holding up?"

"She's shattered—poor thing." After a beat of silence, Blair let out a soft sigh. "I bet she regrets lying to her parents now."

"I'm not so sure she regrets anything," Matt replied. "She's pretty devious if you ask me. But she won't be able to free Logan a second time. I'm keeping the camper van key on me."

BLAIR WOKE SHORTLY before five a.m. with a full bladder. She squirmed uncomfortably in her sleeping bag. For once, Matt was sleeping soundly and she was reluctant to disturb him, or Whitney either, for that matter. But she wasn't going to last for much longer. At 5:35 she unzipped her bag and tiptoed to the trailer door. She reached for Matt's oversized jacket and pulled it on. He would have a fit if he knew she was heading out to the outhouse alone, but it would be light out soon—not the preferred hunting hour for predators.

Still, she grabbed a kitchen knife and stashed it inside the jacket just in case.

After locking the trailer door behind her, she switched on her flashlight and made a beeline for the outhouse, shivering in the chilly morning air but thankful for a break in the rain, however brief. Safely inside, she slid the bolt across and breathed a little easier. A new day had dawned. Today was the beginning of the end. Sam would climb out of here in a few short hours and hike down to the highway. Then it was only a matter of flagging down a car. Once they had a signal, they would notify the authorities. Search and rescue would helicopter them out of here—possibly as early as this afternoon. As for her father-in-law's trailer, it would be stuck here until the road was repaired, which could be months down the line. But it was less of a concern than getting out of here alive.

Buoyed with renewed hope, she exited the outhouse, and stopped dead in her tracks. Sucking in a hard breath, she watched in horror as a shadowy figure skulked away from the dumpster and into the trees.

21

*B*lair remained frozen in place, her eyes twitching from left to right, searching the shadowy shapes of the trees for any sign of a figure lurking among them. She hadn't imagined it, had she? No! Someone had slunk away from the dumpster when she'd exited the outhouse. Was it the killer? It couldn't have been Hazel—the figure was too tall and broad. Definitely a man. Perhaps Rob had returned.

She swallowed hard, remembering Matt's warning not to take anything at face value. Maybe Rob and his brother were both here, closing in on the campground. Fear ricocheted through her. Had they spotted her? She was beginning to understand why Matt had returned from war so paranoid about everything and everyone. This kind of situation messed with your mind until you couldn't tell if you were upside down or right side up.

Instinctively, her fingers wrapped around the handle of the knife inside her husband's oversized jacket. Matt had shared some self-defense tips with her over the years, but she'd never actually used any of them. She wasn't sure she remembered anything he'd painstakingly drilled into her head. It was all a blur in her confused mind.

After what seemed like an eternity of silence, she took a couple of tentative steps away from the outhouse in the direction of her trailer. She didn't dare turn on her flashlight in case she alerted anyone watching from behind the cover of the trees that surrounded the campsites. Gingerly, she made her way back down the dirt road casting furtive glances over her shoulder every so often. All of a sudden, she felt the cold steel of a barrel pressed to the side of her head. Her eyes bulged, every nerve ending tingling with instant fear. She hadn't heard her attacker approach, not even the slightest crunch of a footstep, not the smallest hint of his breath on the back of her neck. She began to shake. "Please—"

"Blair?" Matt's urgent whisper sounded equal parts relieved and shocked. A beam of yellow light appeared as a flashlight clicked on.

Blair exhaled slowly as the cold circle of steel abruptly withdrew from her skull. Her mind whirled with unanswered questions. What was Matt up to out here? Was that really a gun he'd pressed to her head? He must have managed to open the safe in the camper van. But why hadn't he told her?

"What are you doing out here all by yourself?" Matt's tone was clipped but it didn't hide the tremor that ran through it. Before Blair could answer a word, he crushed her to his chest, resting his chin on top of her head. "I was scared sick. I woke up and you were gone."

"I needed the outhouse," she said sheepishly. "I didn't want to wake you. That's the only time you've slept properly in the past three nights."

"What were you thinking?" Matt groaned. "You know better than to come out here alone. You can't trust anyone. We've been over this enough times already."

"I know, it was stupid. I didn't think it would be quite so dark out." She sucked in a hard breath. "Matt, was that a gun you were holding to my head?"

He grabbed her by the hand. "Come on, let's get back to the trailer. We'll talk there. It's not safe out here."

"I saw someone darting away from the dumpster when I exited the outhouse. I couldn't see who it was, but it was obvious they were trying to make sure no one saw them."

"What?" Matt threw her a look of alarm and then panned the flashlight around them. "Man or woman?"

"A man—I think. He was tall."

Matt quickened his pace, tugging her along with him. "I don't like the sound of it. If the killer's stalking the campground, then he's getting ready to strike."

WHEN THEY OPENED the trailer door, Whitney stirred on the sleeper sofa and propped herself up on one elbow. A look of confusion crossed her face before she remembered where she was.

"Go back to sleep," Blair said. "I was just using the outhouse."

Whitney yawned, eyelids drooping, and obediently laid back down without a word.

Matt and Blair made their way to the bedroom and closed the door behind them. They sank down on their bed and stared across at one another.

"Matt," Blair began.

He held up a hand to silence her and then reached into his waistband and pulled out a gun from his concealed carry holster. "Is this what you want to ask me about?"

Blair stared at it for a brief moment and then met Matt's gaze. "It's yours, isn't it? You lied to me. You brought it after all."

Matt rubbed a hand across his jaw. "You gave me no choice. You were so insistent. You wouldn't budge. But you were wrong about this. It wasn't safe to head out on this trip without a gun."

Blair took a couple of shallow breaths. She felt as if she was hyperventilating. She didn't know whether to laugh or cry, slap Matt or hug him. She was equal parts incensed that he'd deceived her, but relieved at the same time to know that they had a gun at their disposal now. "You lied to the others too," she said. "You told them we didn't have a gun when they asked if anyone had a weapon."

A nerve twitched in Matt's neck. "We can't trust them, Blair. I'm not going to admit to a bunch of strangers that I have a gun—especially not when one of them might be the killer."

"But they're not! Someone's stalking the campground—we know that now. It's more important than ever that we trust one another and work together to get through this." Blair shook her head despairingly. "What if someone finds out about the gun? They're going to think you're the killer."

Matt's lips flattened into a determined line. "No one can find out. This has to be our secret. It's our only chance of maintaining the upper hand if the killer strikes again."

Blair dropped her head into her hands. "I just want to go home. This whole ordeal is terrifying. Everyone's hiding secrets and we're all lying to each other."

Matt frowned. "What are you lying about?"

Blair threw him a reproving look. "I'm covering for you, aren't I? I'm part of your lies now. And it doesn't feel right. We're breaking their trust."

"I wanted to trust them, Blair. But I can't. None of them are who they said they were."

Blair bit her lip. "Neither are we for that matter. We lied to them too. They all think we're traveling for fun for a few months before we set up our landscape design business. They don't know this is make or break for us. That you walk around like a zombie some nights because you can't sleep. That you struggle with PTSD and anger management. That you're not supposed to be around weapons—for your own safety, and the safety of others, including our future family." She shook her head. "How can I trust you now?"

Matt hissed out an exasperated breath and got to his feet. "What's your gut telling you?" He replaced the gun in his holster and pulled his hoodie down over it. "I'm going to make some coffee." Without another word, he exited the bedroom and began opening and slamming cabinet doors. Moments later, Blair heard the sound of Whitney folding up the sleeper sofa. No surprise there. She couldn't possibly sleep through the racket Matt was making. Blair smoothed a shaking hand over her hair. She'd touched a nerve by steering the conversation back to the ultimatum she'd given him in therapy. She wasn't prepared to have children with a man who could lash out in anger in a split second. But perhaps it wasn't fair of her to bring that up now. These were extraordinary circumstances they found themselves in. The kind of circumstances akin to war—when you had to rely on your instincts, trust your gut, and draw on your training to survive. Matt was doing what he knew best. And right now they needed his skills.

With a resolute sigh, she tidied up the bed and made her way out to the living area. Whitney was seated at the dining table, resting her chin in her hands. She blinked tentatively at Blair, her eyes still somewhat swollen from all the tears she'd shed the previous day.

"How did you sleep?" Blair asked, joining her.

"Okay, I guess."

"Would you like some coffee?" Matt asked her.

Whitney nodded. "Yes, please."

Matt carried three mugs over to the table and slid in next to Blair. He took a swig of his coffee and looked pointedly at Whitney. "Does anyone else know about your relationship with Logan?"

Whitney flushed and shook her head. "My parents are going to kill me when they find out."

Matt grunted. "They're more likely to want to kill Logan. I'm sure they're worried sick about you."

Whitney frowned. "Do you really think the police are searching for me?"

Blair sipped her coffee and nodded. "Without a doubt. You're a minor. They might even know the general area you're in if they've tracked down the CCTV footage of the last gas station you visited."

Matt drained his mug and took it over to the sink where he washed it out and stacked it upside down on the dish rack. "I'm going to take the trash over to the dumpster now that it's light out." He directed a meaningful look at Blair.

She got to her feet and dumped the contents of her mug down the sink. "I'll come with you. I could use some fresh air." She turned to Whitney. "Will you be all right here by yourself for a few minutes?"

Whitney peered over her mug at her. "Can I ... talk to Logan?"

"I'll take you over there later. For now, you either need to stay here or come with us."

"I'll wait here," Whitney said. "I need to wash up and clean my teeth."

"Lock the door behind us," Blair warned. "And don't open it for anyone, do you understand me? Not even Sam or Harvey."

Whitney gave a glum nod. "Okay."

Blair and Matt made their way from their campsite down to the road just as Sam and Duke were walking by.

"You two are up early." Sam jerked his chin in the direction of the trailer. "Is Whitney doing all right?"

Blair shrugged. "As well as can be expected. She's traumatized and upset."

Matt cast a furtive glance up and down the road to make sure no one was coming. "You didn't see anyone snooping around the campground earlier this morning, did you?"

Sam frowned. "No, why? Did you hear something?"

"I spotted someone skulking away from the dumpster when I was at the outhouse," Blair said. "Around six or so. I'm pretty sure it was a man."

Sam's expression hardened. "Do you think it was Rob?"

"I don't know. But Matt and I are going to take a quick look around the dumpster. See if we can find any clues—footprints or whatever."

"I'll come with you," Sam said, falling into step with them. "If the killer's stalking the campground, it makes me nervous about leaving the others here while we attempt the climb this morning."

Matt nodded thoughtfully. "I was thinking the same thing. Which is why I want to do a little investigating now before we head out."

They made their way past the outhouse to the dumpster and examined the soft ground around it for footprints.

"It's impossible to make out anything distinct," Sam said. "Everyone's been here at one point or another."

Matt turned to Blair. "Did you see which direction the figure came from?"

She frowned in concentration. "No, they were darting away from the dumpster into the trees when I spotted them."

"I wonder why. Maybe they threw something in." Sam walked over to the dumpster and raised the lid. "Stinks in here. But we could check the bags on top at least."

Blair made a face. "Have at it. I don't want to touch anyone else's trash."

Sam pulled out a couple of bags and tossed one to Matt.

Blair watched from a respectable distance as Matt untied the bag and gingerly fished around inside it. "Cookie containers and soda cans for the most part. This looks like Whitney's and Logan's trash."

"Well we know for sure that neither of them were out and about in the early hours," Blair said. "What's in the other bag, Sam?"

"General kitchen trash," he replied. "Wait a minute! That's odd." He dug around in the bag and held up a pair of black tennis shoes. "These appear to be in good condition."

Blair walked over to him and turned the shoes over to inspect them. "No holes in the soles either. Whose trash is this?"

Sam rifled around some more in the plastic bag and pulled out a pill bottle. "Vicodin. That's what Sandy was taking, wasn't it? I'm guessing this is Harvey's trash."

Blair flipped over the tongue of one of the tennis shoes. "Size nine." She frowned, her gaze flitting from Matt to Sam. "Don't you think it's kind of strange that Harvey's throwing away Sandy's stuff already?"

*M*att reached for the tennis shoes and examined them more closely. "Are you sure these are Sandy's?"

Blair arched a brow. "Who else could they belong to? Harvey's a big guy—he's got to be at least a size twelve or thirteen."

"They look kind of manly to me," Matt said dubiously.

Sam shrugged. "I'd call them practical."

Blair frowned as something struck her. "Remember that note we found in Hazel's trailer?"

Matt stared at her blankly.

"The one she was doodling on," Blair added impatiently. "The one I found stuffed between the mattress and the bedside cabinet."

"Yeah, what about it?"

"She wrote the number nine followed by a question mark." Blair looked expectantly from Matt to Sam. "Maybe she noticed the shoes when she was snooping around in Harvey's RV and wondered about them too."

"Probably a coincidence," Sam said, sounding skeptical. "I doubt her note had anything to do with the tennis shoes."

"Was it also a coincidence that Hazel was in the RV helping Sandy the day before she disappeared?" Blair persisted.

Matt blew out a frustrated breath. "This kind of speculation isn't getting us anywhere."

"It's not speculation, it's a reasonable theory. Sandy was a small, frail woman," Blair countered, a growing sense of conviction swirling in her gut. "There's no way she wore a size nine."

A cold silence fell over them as the implication sank in. If neither Harvey nor Sandy wore a size nine, then the shoes must have belonged to someone else.

Blair rubbed her throat with shaking fingertips. "Maybe there's a third person in the RV. Harvey and Sandy could have been hiding someone. We never actually searched it, what with Sandy dying and all."

"Now you're really beginning to sound irrational. Why would they be hiding someone?" Matt asked.

Blair gave a helpless shrug. "I don't know. I'm only thinking out loud. A grown kid with issues maybe, or something like that. It's just that Harvey was very reluctant for anyone to go inside."

"Issues?" Sam echoed, scratching his forehead.

Matt stared intently at Blair, a gleam of understanding in his eyes. "Sociopathic tendencies. Is that what you're hinting at?"

She gave a despairing shake of her head. "No, you're right. It's too far-fetched. There's nowhere to hide anyone for days on end anyway. We'd have spotted them by now."

A collective silence fell over them as they eyed the shoes in Matt's hands.

After a moment, Sam let out a sigh. "They were likely left

in the RV by a friend or a family member. Harvey's just clearing out."

Matt shot a quick glance up and down the road. "Let's get this trash back in the dumpster before anyone sees us."

Blair snatched the shoes out of his hands and stashed them inside her coat. "I'll hold on to these in the meantime—in case there's more to it."

Matt shrugged. "Whatever."

They tossed the trash bags back into the dumpster and turned to go just as angry shouts drifted their way.

"Is that Logan?" Blair asked, her eyes darting to Matt.

His expression hardened. "Sounds like him, but I don't recognize the other man's voice. It doesn't—"

A piercing scream cut him off mid-sentence.

"Whitney!" Sam yelled.

Terror and confusion melded as one in Blair's rib cage as she pounded down the road after Sam and Matt. A series of random questions fired in rapid succession in her brain. Had Logan escaped again? Was he holding a knife to Whitney's throat? And who was the other man they'd heard? Maybe Rob had returned with his brother. They might be holding the others at gunpoint.

They tore around the corner and came to a screeching halt at the sight that greeted them. Twenty feet away, a tall, lean, wiry-haired man with an unkempt beard dressed in camo from head-to-toe stood in the middle of the road pointing a rifle at Logan who was on his knees, hands still zip-tied behind his back. A few feet from them, Whitney was sobbing and screaming hysterically, knuckles pressed to her mouth.

Blair's stomach lurched. There was no sign of Harvey anywhere. Had the stranger already killed him? It appeared Logan was next in line unless they did something, and quickly. This must be the tall figure she'd seen skulking from the dumpster earlier. A wave of guilt crashed over her. They'd suspected all along that Logan was the killer, or at least that he'd had something to do with Hazel's disappearance. They'd tied him up and left him vulnerable, at the mercy of this unhinged individual—the killer they'd lived in fear of for the past two days.

Her eyes slid to Matt who was reaching for the gun concealed beneath his jacket.

Whitney darted over to them, shrieking frantically. "Do something! He's going to kill Logan!"

Matt faced the stranger, legs astride. "Who are you and what do you want?"

The stranger's nose twitched as he scrutinized Matt, silently weighing him up. Blair wondered if he could tell that Matt had a concealed weapon beneath his jacket.

"How about I ask the questions?" the stranger growled. "Why was this man tied up in my camper?"

Blair's heart slugged against her chest. The elusive owner of the camper van had finally returned. Of course, they only had his word for it, but why else would he have made a beeline for the camper van and not any of the other trailers?

"Sorry, man," Matt said. "We thought it was abandoned."

"We were camping here when the mudslide happened," Blair explained. "No one had been near the van for days. We thought perhaps—"

She broke off, deciding against going so far as to say they'd assumed the owner had died in the mudslide. She cast a furtive look at Matt, trying to gauge his intentions. His hand was still inside his jacket, ready to pull out his gun the instant things started to go south.

"Do you think he's the killer?" Sam muttered under his breath.

"He looks deranged enough," Blair whispered back.

The stranger eyed them with a mixture of suspicion and

aggravation. "You still haven't answered my question. Why's this man tied up?"

"Because he hurt his girlfriend," Blair replied. She turned to Whitney. "Show him."

Whitney's eyes widened and she shrank back.

"*I said, show him,*" Blair repeated, enunciating every word in an unequivocal manner. Under her breath, she added, "Do you want to get out of this alive or not?"

Whitney swallowed hard and then gave a tentative nod before tugging up her sleeves and inching toward the stranger. Shaking, she held out her wrists to him.

His frown deepened and he aimed the rifle at Logan's head.

"No!" Whitney screamed, dropping to her knees and attempting to cover Logan with her body.

"Easy man!" Matt took a step toward the stranger. "We've got this under control. We'll get him out of your hair right now. We can accommodate him elsewhere. Not a problem."

Blair darted over to Whitney and hauled her upright.

The stranger prodded Logan with the muzzle of his rifle. "You heard the man! On your feet! Go!"

Logan rose unsteadily. He shot Matt a look of loathing before trudging over to him.

Matt squared his jaw and addressed the stranger once more. "I'm Matt Dawson. This is my wife, Blair, and my … friend, Sam. What's your name, sir?"

The stranger stared back unabashedly for an uncomfortable length of time, his expression oddly devoid of any emotion.

Just as he opened his mouth to respond, Harvey came walking into view. "Thought I heard—"

He came to an abrupt stop, shock swirling over his face at the sight of the armed stranger in their midst. His eyes darted around the group as he quickly tried to assess the situation and the danger they were in.

The stranger took a step toward Harvey, his rifle pointed directly at him. "Do you know this guy?" he called out to no one in particular.

"Yes! It's okay," Sam responded. "Harvey's with us. He's in the RV next to you."

The stranger motioned with his gun for Harvey to join the others.

Logan took the opportunity to sidle up next to Matt who greeted him with a cursory nod. "Are you all right?"

Logan fixed a lizard-like gaze on him. "You almost got me a bullet in the brain from our neighborhood serial killer. You're going down for this, as soon as I get out of here."

"Not now," Blair urged, tugging on Matt's arm. "Ignore him. We've got bigger problems to deal with."

She turned to address Harvey. "This gentleman owns the camper van. We were just explaining to him why we put Logan in there."

Harvey pursed his lips and cast a shrewd look at the stranger. Blair hoped he wouldn't try anything stupid or make any sudden moves. Harvey was a big man, but the stranger had the upper hand with a weapon at his disposal. The last thing Blair wanted was for Matt to have to draw his gun in what was certain to become a blood bath.

"You were about to tell us your name," she prompted the stranger, forcing a smile.

He blinked solemnly at her. "Billie Reed Henderson. You can call me Reed."

"Again, we apologize for inconveniencing you," Blair said. "It's just that we needed to separate Logan and his girlfriend, for her own protection, at least for as long as it takes for us to figure out a way out of here."

Reed adjusted the brim of his cap. "What do you mean?"

Blair's eyes widened. "You don't know about the road?"

A look of irritation crossed Reed's face. "All I know is that the mountain caved with all the rain. Took me three days to get around the slide and back to camp."

"It washed out the access road into Bird Creek too," Matt explained. "We're trapped here until search and rescue locate us."

Reed's jaw slackened as if trying to digest the improbable news.

Blair silently observed his reaction. If she had to hazard a guess, his shock seemed genuine. And if he really had been making his way back to the campground for the past three days, that ruled him out as the killer. But Matt's warning not to take anything at face value was still ringing in her ears. She'd harbored high hopes that this camping trip around the States would be an exercise in learning to trust again for Matt. Instead, it had become a cautionary tale for her to trust no one.

"Is this everyone camping here?" Reed asked, looking around.

"Yes," Whitney blurted out. "Well, there's Hazel but—"

Blair shot her a belated look of warning.

Reed's expression darkened, his grip on his rifle tightening again. "Who's Hazel?" When no one answered, he raised his gun and slowly panned the group. "Where's this Hazel woman?"

"We don't know," Sam responded. "She disappeared from her trailer yesterday."

"They blamed Logan!" Whitney added indignantly. "They're acting like he's the killer."

"Shhh!" Blair hissed in her ear. "What if it's Reed?"

Whitney threw her a horrified look before clamping her lips closed.

Reed's posture tensed, suspicion written all over his face. "I thought you said Hazel disappeared."

"She did," Matt cut in. "We don't know what happened to her."

Undeterred, Reed continued to stare at Whitney. "You said, *killer*. Why?"

Whitney's bottom lip trembled. "I ... I didn't mean to say that. What I meant was—"

"She meant to say killer, all right," Logan cut in. He turned around and looked at the others with a triumphant sneer on his face. "I'd say that guy with a knife sticking out of his belly was definitely murdered, wouldn't you?" He swung back around to face Reed. "They didn't tell you there's a killer stalking the campground, did they? That's because they think it's *you*! You can't trust them. Look what they did to me."

"Don't listen to—" Matt began.

"Enough! I've heard your side of things!" A thunderous look crossed Reed's face. He jerked his chin in Harvey's direction. "You're awfully quiet. What do you have to say about all this?"

Harvey slid a wary gaze from Reed to Matt.

"He just lost his wife ... recently," Blair blurted out, praying Reed wouldn't probe any further. She didn't relish the idea of explaining that there was yet another body in the campground.

Harvey cleared his throat. "It's like Logan said. We found the man lying in the brush off to the side of the hiking trail that leads up to the lake—he'd been stabbed in the stomach." He smoothed a hand over his beard. "We figured maybe someone from the hunting party got into an argument, but—"

"Someone tried to make it look like a stabbing after the fact," Blair cut in, afraid Harvey was going to bring up Rob's name—another unexplained missing person. If they weren't careful, Reed might start to think they were part of some cult that was knocking people off or something. Judging by the notebook they'd found in his van, he was susceptible to bizarre conspiracy theories. "Hazel was the one who noticed that the man had actually been strangled," she added.

A deep trench formed on Reed's brow. "And that's when Hazel disappeared?"

Harvey narrowed his eyes and gestured to Logan. "We think she was a private investigator, hired by Logan's wife to find out if he was cheating on her—which, it turns out, he was, with his sixteen-year-old babysitter, no less. I'd say that might have a lot more to do with Hazel's sudden disappearance than anything else."

"That's the other reason we tied Logan up," Matt said, taking him by the elbow. "We suspect he might have done something to Hazel, and we need to get to the bottom of it. I'll move him into my trailer for now."

"I can't let you do that," Reed said, a chilling calmness solidifying in his voice. "Not until I figure out exactly what's going on here and who I can believe. In the meantime, I'm going to need a hostage." A thin-lipped smile deepened the hollows of his cheeks as he turned to Logan. "Guess you're going to be bunking with me after all."

23

*R*eed marched a loudly-protesting Logan at gunpoint back to the camper van while Whitney whimpered in the background. Blair's stomach knotted when the two men disappeared inside, and the door slammed shut behind them. Had they just sent Logan to his death?

Harvey scrubbed a hand over his jaw. "I reckon we found our killer."

"You mean he found us," Sam corrected him.

"I'm not so sure," Matt said. "There's no question Reed's an oddball, but that's not enough to make him a killer. Why would he suddenly show up here if he's been stalking our campground? I think he's telling the truth about getting cut off by the mudslide."

Blair cast a worried look at Whitney, standing off to one side, hugging herself. "Do you think Logan's safe?" she whispered to Matt.

He squared his jaw. "I don't honestly know. But I'm not opposed to someone else babysitting him for a change."

"I need to feed Duke and get my gear ready in case the

climb's still a go," Sam said, glancing up at the darkening sky. "Although it looks like the weather's turning again."

Matt nodded. "We should all get something to eat. We can figure out our next move after that."

Blair gave a relieved nod. She was hungry, soaked through, and she needed to get rid of these tennis shoes inside her jacket. She would hide them in Matt's truck for now. She couldn't risk anyone seeing them and asking questions—least of all, Harvey.

BLAIR AND MATT sat down to eat breakfast at the dining table, quietly exchanging a helpless look. The minute they'd come inside, Whitney had collapsed on the couch, weeping, and was refusing to join them.

"You can't really blame her for being mad at us," Blair whispered, picking at her toast. "We put Logan in this situation."

"No, Logan put himself in this situation," Matt muttered back.

"It's not his fault he was in the camper van," Whitney piped up, pulling herself into a sitting position and glaring at them, eyes glistening with tears. "He didn't do anything to Hazel, and he doesn't deserve this. Reed's crazy. Anyone can see that."

Blair wiped a hand across her brow. She couldn't appease Whitney's fears on that count. Undeniably, there was an air of unpredictability about the man. And that strange grin of his was particularly disturbing. She didn't envy Logan being all alone with him and completely at his mercy. A shiver went down her spine. They had to get out of here before it was too late for all of them.

The plopping of raindrops on the roof startled her out of her reverie. She shot Matt a perturbed look. "Here comes the rain again. I wonder if Rob's okay out there—if he's found any trace of his brother."

Matt squeezed his fingers into a fist on the table. "He's not our problem anymore. We can't keep people alive if they won't listen to reason. We told everyone to stick together, to go everywhere in groups from now on. He chose his own fate, as far as I'm concerned."

"Are we ever going to get out of here?" Whitney whined.

Matt pushed his plate aside and contemplated the blubbering girl for a moment. "Of course we will. Sam can make the climb today, if the rain doesn't get any heavier. Once he's over the other side of the mountain, it won't take him long to hike down to the main road and hitch a ride. After that, it's only a matter of waiting for a search and rescue helicopter to find us. Worst case scenario, we'll be out of here by tomorrow."

Whitney swallowed back a sob. "Tomorrow's my seventeenth birthday. I'm supposed to be having a party with all my friends."

"You can still have a party," Blair said, softening her tone. "You might just have to postpone it for a couple of days." She got up from the table and put the kettle back on the stove. "Anyone want more coffee?"

The words had scarcely left her lips before the distant thrumming of a helicopter reached their ears.

Whitney's eyes darted between Matt and Blair. "Is that SAR?"

"Could be," Matt said, springing to his feet.

With one accord, they tore out of the trailer and raced down to the road, heedless of the rain.

Blair's pulse thundered in her ears. Peering up into the clouds, she spotted a helicopter circling over the SOS they'd built.

"It's the sheriffs," Matt announced, tenting a hand over his eyes. "They must be looking for you, Whitney. You just got the best birthday present ever."

She let out an ear-piercing shriek and began jumping up and down on the road, flailing her hands wildly.

Matt let out a snort. "Forget it! They can't see you from up there."

Moments later, Sam and Harvey joined them, bundled up in their rain gear.

"Took them long enough to find us," Sam said, the relief in his voice evident.

Blair grinned at him. "Guess you won't have to attempt that climb after all."

"Should we go up the hiking trail and wait by the SOS?" Whitney asked, chewing nervously on her nails.

Sam shook his head. "No, they'll be gone by the time we get up there. Don't worry, we're safe now. The sheriffs will notify search and rescue and they'll take it from here. They'll helicopter us out of here as soon as they deem it safe."

"They might decide to assess the damage to the road and see if they can bring us out that way," Harvey suggested.

Matt shook his head. "Not gonna happen. It's a major rebuild."

"Does this mean we're getting out of here today?" Whitney asked, a hopeful lilt in her voice.

"I wouldn't count on it," Matt said. "Visibility's not great. And the rain's getting heavier by the minute."

They fell silent as, moments later, the helicopter ascended and disappeared off to the east over the mountains.

"Don't expect a rescue attempt in this weather," Sam warned. "The best we can hope for today is that SAR makes a drop with supplies and radios. I think we should drive out to the road again too and see if there's anything going on. They might have sent out a crew by now."

Whitney looked dubious. "What about Logan? We can't leave him here alone with Reed."

"That's exactly what we're going to do," Matt replied firmly. "If the killer comes back, he won't get past Reed with his rifle."

"But what if Reed's the killer?" Whitney protested.

Matt furrowed his brow. "I'm not buying it. He didn't even know the mudslide had taken out the road. Which tells me he hasn't been anywhere near here in almost a week."

Whitney shook her head incredulously. "You don't know that. You're just saying that because you don't care what happens to Logan."

Matt pressed his lips tightly together. "Trust me, if I thought that idiot boyfriend of yours was in any real danger, I'd intervene. He's a whole lot safer with Reed than hanging out in a trailer on his own." Matt nodded to the others. "All right, let's jump in my truck and drive out to the road."

He held the passenger door open for Blair, while Harvey, Sam and Whitney all piled into the back.

"I need to stop by my trailer and pick up my other shoes on the way back," Whitney said, as they drove out of the campground. "These ones are soaked." She squirmed around on the seat and then reached down and lifted something onto her lap. "Hey, maybe these will work!"

Blair froze, staring straight ahead, the hairs prickling on the back of her neck. She'd forgotten that she'd tossed the tennis shoes into the back of the truck before breakfast, fully intending to retrieve them later. Too late now. She had to think fast. She couldn't pretend the shoes were hers. Harvey would know she was lying.

"Are these yours, Blair?" Whitney asked, angling them to take a better look. "They seem big."

Casting a casual glance over her shoulder, Blair eyed the tennis shoes and chuckled. "Oh, those. I found them in the dumpster. They're still in pretty good shape. Too bad they're nines." She arched an eyebrow and looked inquiringly from Harvey to Sam. "Either of you guys throw them out?"

Sam shifted uneasily under her knowing stare. "Nope. Not my style."

Harvey frowned at the tennis shoes. "I tossed a bag of garbage out that had some shoes in it, but I didn't pay much attention to them. I figured Sandy must have wanted to get rid of them."

"Okay if I have them then?" Whitney asked.

"Sure." Harvey gave a disinterested shrug and turned to stare out the window at the rain that was now coming down in sheets.

Blair forced herself not to look across at Matt. She was fairly certain Harvey was lying about the shoes, although she had no idea why, or if it was even important. But she had a hunch Hazel had thought so. There had to be something she was missing. She leaned her head against the glass, listening to the raindrops pelting the window. She couldn't untangle all the subterfuge around her. She just wanted out of this mess before they all ended up dead. It was like a live game of Clue with a cast of untrustworthy characters replete with baggage, weapons, and motives, moving among trailers instead of rooms. Except they couldn't put everything back in the box afterward and pretend none of this had happened.

The sound of heavy equipment and drilling reached them long before they came upon the washed-out section of the road. A jolt of excitement shot through Blair's veins. They weren't alone anymore. Help had arrived. They weren't condemned to stay in Bird Creek until an unidentified serial killer picked them off one-by-one.

Matt rammed the shifter into park and switched off the engine. They clambered out and stood in the rain listening to the welcome sounds of diesel engines and backhoes scraping up rocks, just out of sight around the bend. It was impossible to make out any voices over the sound of the rain and the machinery, but it was heartwarming knowing that only a few hundred feet around the corner the road crew was already hard at work. Now that the sheriffs' helicopter had spotted the SOS signal, rescue was imminent. All they had to do until then was stay alive.

After a few more minutes, they piled back into the truck. There was nothing to be accomplished by standing in the rain. The road crew would be forced to call it quits before too much longer.

When they pulled back into Bird Creek a few minutes later, Matt parked alongside the road and left the engine running while Whitney ran to her trailer to pick up her things. Blair peered anxiously through the window at the downpour. The wind was whipping up and she feared they might be imprisoned at the campground for several more days if conditions deteriorated again. It was not a heart-warming proposition. Another day, another body—or another missing person.

She was lost in her morbid thoughts when a thunderous crack jolted her back to her senses. She bolted upright in her seat and gasped in disbelief as a Ponderosa pine toppled over onto Whitney's trailer.

24

$\mathscr{I}$t seemed as if everyone was moving in slow motion as all four doors on the truck opened at once and Blair and the others stumbled out into the rain. Oblivious to everyone else around her, Blair dashed from the road up to Whitney's campsite, fear gripping her innards and squeezing like a fist. Just when hope was on the horizon, nature had dealt a low blow. She'd been feeling guilt-stricken and protective of Whitney—acting like a surrogate mother of sorts—ever since discovering how young she was. More than anything, Blair dreaded finding her knocked unconscious, crushed beneath the weight of the tree inside her trailer, or writhing around in pain. Rage at Logan's selfishness and recklessness welled up inside her. He was the one who'd brought Whitney to this death camp. Her blood would be on his hands if anything happened to her.

Sam was the first one to reach the mangled door. The tree had fallen lengthwise, squishing the entire trailer like a sandwich, and shrinking the entryway to a fraction of its natural size.

"Whitney!" Sam hollered, ducking down and crawling

inside without a second's hesitation. Blair followed him, shutting down the voice in her head that warned her of the danger of the roof collapsing entirely and trapping them too. Inside, the trailer looked like a dumpster had exploded, spewing its contents everywhere in reckless abandon. How could anyone have survived this? It seemed nature was conspiring with the killer to tighten the cords around them, ensuring no one would get out of the campground alive.

And then a groan reached her ears.

"We're coming, Whitney," she yelled frantically. On gloved hands and knees, she gingerly made her way over shards of glass, miscellaneous debris, and splintered particle board, following Sam's path to the back of the trailer. Her eyes widened in horror at the sight that greeted them in the bedroom. Whitney lay trapped beneath the cabinetry and a section of the roof that had collapsed under the weight of the tree bearing down on it.

"Help me!" she moaned, shivering in the rain now freely pouring through the demolished roof.

"We can't get her out this way," Sam muttered. "We're going to have to figure out how to move the tree off the trailer. You stay with her and I'll go back out and tell Matt and Harvey what we're dealing with."

He slid past her, and Blair inched her way through the waterlogged wreckage on the floor toward Whitney. She reached for her hand. "You're going to be okay. We'll get you out of here, I promise. Can you breathe all right?"

"Yes." Whitney let out a heart-wrenching sob. "I want to go home."

Blair squeezed her hand. "You'll be going home real soon —we all will. Just hang in there a little longer. Stay strong."

Whitney bit her lip. "My legs are trapped."

Blair reached for some broken pieces of particle board and jiggled them out of the way to try and get a better look.

She swallowed back the fear surging up her throat when she saw that Whitney's legs were buried beneath the debris locked in place by the tree. It was impossible to tell how badly injured she might be.

"Can you feel your legs?" Blair asked anxiously.

"Yes. I can wiggle my toes. That's a good sign, isn't it?"

Blair gave a reassuring nod. "Are you in pain at all?"

A tear trickled down Whitney's face. "Something's jabbing into my back. It hurts."

Blair immediately began digging through the rubble with her torn gloves, wincing when a splinter pierced the tender skin beneath her nails. After locating the jagged piece of wood causing Whitney's discomfort, she wrangled it out and tossed it aside. "Better?"

"Yes," Whitney croaked. "I'm going to die here, aren't I? This is my fault for lying to my parents."

Blair brushed her hand softly over the girl's forehead. "No, it's not. It was a random accident—caused by a storm— it could've happened to any one of us."

More tears slid down Whitney's cheeks. "Sonia trusted me."

Blair wrinkled her brow. "Who's Sonia? Is that Logan's wife?"

Whitney's voice dropped an octave. "Yes. She's always been kind to me. And I liked babysitting Gavin. She's never going to let me see him again after this. I feel so ashamed."

Blair exhaled a long breath, weighing her response. "What you did was wrong, but this is mostly on Logan's head. He's the adult here, and a married man."

Whitney sniffed into her sleeve. "I shouldn't have encouraged him."

"Now's not the time to beat yourself up. Let's just concentrate on getting you out of here. I'm going to leave you for just one minute while I go outside to see what the plan is. I'll be right back."

Whitney gave a shaky nod.

Blair crawled slowly back to the opening that was once the trailer door, doing her best to avoid the shards of glass. Her gloves were nicked in several places from crawling through the wreckage earlier and offered no guarantee of protection.

Back outside, she joined Matt, Sam, and Harvey who were huddled around the back end of the trailer viewing the roof and assessing the damage.

"What's the verdict?" Blair asked, pulling the drawstring on her hood tighter in a futile effort to stay dry.

"We don't have any equipment to move the tree," Matt said. "We're thinking we'll have more luck if we try to get her out from underneath the trailer."

Blair raised her brows. "You mean cut a hole in the floor?"

"There's already a gaping hole in the floor," Sam replied. "I crawled underneath to take a look. If we can enlarge it, we can extricate her that way."

Matt gave an approving nod. "I'll go back to my trailer and pick up my tool bag."

"I'll walk with you," Harvey said. "I need to put on my waterproof pants. I didn't think we'd be out in this rain."

They strode off, and Blair turned to Sam. "I'd better go back inside and let Whitney know what's happening."

"Holler if you need me," he responded. "I'll be right here."

She locked her gaze on him. "Thanks for your help through all of this—offering to attempt that risky climb and all. I'm sorry for what Matt said about Andy's accident. He doesn't find it easy to trust people, but I think he trusts you now."

"I get it. It's hard to trust when you've been betrayed," Sam said. "A lot of people in the climbing community turned against me when the news story broke—people I'd known for years. Trust's a fickle thing."

Blair nodded. "True, but like I keep telling Matt, you won't heal until you take the risk to trust again."

Sam's expression was unreadable as he wordlessly ducked down and crawled beneath the trailer.

Blair's heart jolted when she went back inside and saw that Whitney's eyes were shut. "Whitney!" She shook her gently. "Wake up! I'm back!"

After a moment, Whitney's eyelids fluttered open. "I'm so cold. Can they get me out of here?"

Blair nodded. "Absolutely. Matt's gone to get his tool bag. There's a hole in the bottom of the trailer. They're going to try and enlarge the opening and slide you out through it. They can't lift the tree off without the proper equipment."

"I thought I heard a helicopter," Whitney said. "Was I dreaming?"

Blair smiled sympathetically. "Maybe, but I'm sure they'll be here soon. Even if they can't attempt a rescue in these conditions, Sam thinks they'll make a drop with radios and supplies. We won't be here for too much longer."

Whitney thought about it for a moment. "What if I can't walk to the helicopter?"

"We'll carry you if need be," Blair reassured her. "Don't worry, Matt's a soldier. No one gets left behind."

"Not even Logan?"

Blair grimaced. "Not even Logan."

For a moment or two there was silence between them and then Whitney asked, "Who do you think the killer is?"

Blair sighed wearily. "I don't know. Every time I think I've figured it out, I change my mind."

"Did you ever think it might be me?"

Blair let out a sudden breath, somewhere between a snort and a chuckle. "No, I can honestly say I never thought it was you. Although, I've suspected almost everyone else at one point or another."

Whitney wrinkled her brow. "Even your husband?"

"Matt?" Blair raised her brows and shook her head. "No, of course not."

Whitney let out a shallow breath. "Logan thinks it's him. He says Matt's the only one here who we know for sure is actually capable of killing a human being."

Blair squirmed uncomfortably. "That's different. What he did in wartime has no bearing on what happened here."

"But he lied about the gun, didn't he?" Whitney said.

25

"*H*ow ... how do you know about the gun?" Blair sputtered.

Whitney sighed and scrunched her eyes shut. "I heard you two arguing about it when you got back from the outhouse last night."

Blair bit down on her lip, berating herself for not being more careful. She'd assumed Whitney had fallen right back to sleep. And she'd forgotten that a sixteen-year-old's ears could pick up just about anything.

"*This has to be our secret, Blair!*" Whitney twisted her lips. "Apparently Matt has his fair share of secrets—PTSD, anger issues, insomnia, paranoia. And he's the one calling Logan dangerous. How do you know Matt didn't snap and kill that guy?"

Blair let out an indignant gasp. "Don't be ridiculous! That's not possible!"

Whitney flashed her a tight smile, her eyes conveying equal measures of understanding and condemnation beyond her years. "You're defending him just like I defended Logan. You don't want to believe something so awful about your husband could possibly be true. But the fact is, you don't know for sure—"

"Blair! You in there?" Matt's voice boomed.

She startled and scrambled onto all fours. "I'll be right back," she muttered to Whitney before crawling to the trailer door and clambering out into the rain.

"We need you out of there now," Matt explained. "We're going to start expanding the hole so we can't have any extra weight on the floor in case the whole thing gives way."

"Are you sure this is safe?" Blair asked dubiously.

Matt reached for a pair of pliers from his tool bag. "It's safer than going up on the roof and messing with that tree."

Harvey opened up a beat-up metal toolbox and pulled out a claw hammer.

"Is Whitney doing all right?" Matt asked.

"I think so. She's not in any pain." Blair couldn't meet his eyes. Whitney's words were still ringing in her ears. *But he lied about the gun, didn't he?* Was it possible her husband had lied to her about other things too? Could he have had some kind of psychotic break and strangled a man when he'd encountered him on one of his insomnia-driven night hikes? Maybe he didn't even realize what he'd done. Blair shook her head free of her increasingly macabre thoughts. It was unthinkable. She was becoming the paranoid one.

Sam crouched down to wriggle under the trailer just as the distant sound of an engine reached their ears. Blair tilted her head, frowning in concentration. "Do you guys hear that? I think it's a helicopter."

They stood stock-still, breath on hold, as the unmistakable whir of helicopter blades grew louder.

"That must be SAR," Sam said excitedly.

"I can head up to the SOS point and wait for the drop while you get Whitney out," Blair said, her heart fluttering with excitement at the thought of finally making contact with their rescuers.

"No! I'll go." Harvey tossed his hammer back into his tool-box. "Whitney needs you here. And it's easier for Matt and Sam to crawl under that trailer than an old geezer like me. I'll hike up the trail and wait for the drop."

Matt gave a nod of agreement. "We'll get to work here and meet you back at our trailer when we're done—unless they make a landing. In that case, lead them here and have them bring a stretcher for Whitney, just in case."

Harvey turned and trudged off down the road, disappearing into the downpour.

Blair shivered inside her coat as Sam helped himself to Harvey's tools.

"There's not much point in you standing here in the rain watching us," Matt said. "Why don't you go back to the trailer and get warmed up? Make some coffee or something."

Blair's teeth chattered. "Yeah, I might do that. I can bring you guys a thermos if you want."

"Thanks," Sam said. "But we'll be on our bellies in the dirt for the next while. We'll grab a cup when we get back with Whitney."

Blair watched as the two men hunkered down and crawled beneath the trailer, before turning and making her way down the road to the other end of the campground. Her fingers tightened around the key in her pocket. She had no intention of holing up inside her trailer and brewing coffee. This was her opportunity to snoop around inside Harvey's RV. Whitney's words had disturbed her. *But he lied about the gun, didn't he?* She had to eliminate Matt as a suspect. Everyone else's secrets had been exposed, but the mystery of the tennis shoes still bugged her. Harvey had played it down as inconsequential, but a sixth sense told Blair there more to the shoes than that. After thinking it over, she was convinced it wasn't Reed she'd seen skulking away from the dumpster—the figure had been more broad-shouldered, like Harvey. Why would he have been tossing the trash out so early in the morning when no one was out and about if he had nothing to hide? Everyone here was hiding secrets. Harvey was no exception.

When she reached the RV, she quickly scanned her surroundings and then pulled out the key and turned it in the lock. Her heart thudded loudly in the silence that greeted her inside. A deathly pall hung over the space, almost as though Sandy's presence was there with her. What would she say if she could speak now? Had she tried to tell Hazel something?

Blair wound her way back to the bedroom and stood staring at the bed where Sandy had died. A natural death, or something more ominous? Blair's mind was stuck on Hazel's insistence that something wasn't right about the situation in the RV. Why would a terminally ill cancer patient not bring any medication with her on a camping trip?

Blair's shoulders sagged as another thought occurred to her. It was possible Harvey had brought Sandy to this isolated campground to let her die in peace. Maybe they'd had a pact. A mercy killing of sorts. Blair sucked on her bottom lip, considering this angle. He wouldn't get away with it, of course, even if Sandy had been on board with the idea. There would be an autopsy. If Harvey had given her some kind of Vicodin overdose, he'd be prosecuted for it.

Willing herself into action, Blair began her search of the RV by opening the bedroom cabinets and rifling through them one by one, careful to leave everything the way she found it. Most of the cabinets were filled with Sandy's cloth- ing. It appeared nothing had been tossed out other than the tennis shoes.

Finding little of interest in the bedroom, Blair returned to the main living area and began looking through the reading materials stacked on the shelves above the couch—house-keeping and yachting magazines, a few innocuous romance novels, a handbook on gold prospecting. She cast a glance over the kitchen appliances, frowning as her mind went back to Hazel's note. *Size 9.* She'd written something else on the note too. Something about a mug—a mug and a face to be exact. Maybe she'd noticed something while she'd been making Sandy's tea. It was a long shot, but Blair owed it to Hazel to test her theory.

She opened and shut several cabinet doors in quick succession until she found a shelf of miscellaneous coffee mugs. Looping her fingers through several handles at once, she lifted down a cluster of mugs and began examining them. A delicate sprig of roses adorned a matching pair. An over-sized mug sported a Chihuahua in a heart, and another boasted an overweight bulldog. Blair pushed them to one side on the counter and then padded quietly over to the door to make sure there was no sign of Harvey returning. Logically, she knew it would take him a while to hike up to the SOS and back, but she didn't want to take the chance of him returning early for some reason and finding her here.

Continuing her search in the kitchen, she dug out several chipped white Christmas mugs embossed with snowflakes, and a potbellied clay mug—handmade judging by the stamp on the underside. She reached to the back of the shelf for the remaining three mugs and placed them on the counter. Two were nondescript, mass-produced novelty coffee mugs. The third one had a personalized photograph—a bride and groom on their wedding day. Blair glanced at the names beneath the beaming couple. *Sandy and Harvey, June 11, 1979.* Blair studied the photograph, a smile playing on her lips. They looked like a couple who were very much in love. They were barely recognizable to her which was hardly surprising given that the picture was taken forty years ago. But something about it nagged at her. There was something wrong with the image.

A noise at the door startled her. Heart thundering in her chest, she hurriedly began replacing the mugs on the shelf. The door suddenly swung open and, in her haste to cover up what she was doing, she knocked one of the Christmas mugs to the floor where it smashed with a deafening crash that seemed to echo around the RV. Her mind raced, trying to patch together a reasonable excuse. *She was returning the key, she was—*

She sucked in a shocked breath when Reed stepped into the RV and fixed a piercing stare on her. Even without his gun, he made an intimidating figure in his camo attire. Blinking across at him, she was momentarily stunned into silence.

"You … startled me," she blurted out as she knelt and began picking up the broken ceramic pieces. "I suppose you heard the helicopter overhead. Harvey went to see if search and rescue is going to attempt a landing, or at least make a drop." She opened the cabinet beneath the sink and tore off a plastic trash bag from a roll with shaking fingers.

"They won't land in this weather," Reed said, continuing to stare unnervingly at her. "What are you doing in here?"

She got to her feet and tossed him what she hoped was an indignant look, reminding herself that this wasn't his RV. She didn't owe him an explanation. "Not that it's any of your business, but I'm waiting for the others." It was close enough to the truth. She didn't bother clarifying that they were actually meeting across the way at her trailer.

Reed folded his arms across his chest. "Got some kind of get-together going on that I should know about?"

"Yes. Harvey's going to brief us when he gets back."

"Did your husband go with him?"

"No. He and Sam are with Whitney. A tree fell on her

trailer and trapped her inside. They're in the process of getting her out. They'll meet me back here."

Reed drew his brows together. "Were you planning on inviting me to this meeting?"

Blair shrugged, her pulse drumming so loudly she feared he could hear it. "I didn't get the impression you wanted anything to do with us."

Reed curled his lip in contempt. "I don't have much choice. I had this campground to myself before I left. I come back and you lot are here—a man's been murdered, a woman's missing, a young girl's been beat up on, and now I find you nosing around in Harvey's RV." His cold gaze hardened like granite. "What are you really up to?"

Blair gave a careless shrug. "Like I told you already, I'm just waiting on everyone to get back."

Reed leaned against the counter without taking his eyes off her. "Maybe Logan was right about you."

"Right about what?" Blair wrinkled her brow.

"That I shouldn't trust you. That you're a pack of liars."

"That's rich!" Blair retorted. "He came here with his kid's sixteen-year-old babysitter pretending they were on their honeymoon. He's a married man. He's the one who can't be trusted."

Reed uncrossed his ankles and took a step toward Blair. "So why are you hiding a body in the back of his truck?"

26

"*L*ogan tells me you're trying to frame him for murder," Reed said, taking another step toward Blair.

"What?" she gasped. "That's outrageous! You can't believe anything he tells you. He's a manipulative, pathological liar. Harvey's wife, Sandy, passed away yesterday—she had terminal cancer—we had to move her body out of the RV. We only put her in Logan's truck because we've been using ours to drive out to the road to check for any sign of a rescue crew."

Reed surveyed her for a long, uncomfortable moment. "So by my reckoning, that makes two dead bodies, one missing woman, and one abused teen so far. Anything else you want to add to that? Any other camp secrets I should know about?"

Blair hesitated, then shook her head. Technically, there was also a missing man, if you counted Rob, but until she knew for sure that Reed wasn't the killer, she had no intention of letting him know of Rob's existence. "I'm not hiding anything," she asserted. "Are you?"

"Everybody's hiding something," Reed replied. "What's important is whether it's a dangerous secret or not—whether it impacts anyone else." His expression softened briefly. "My struggles are my own."

Blair's thoughts flitted to his camper van and the OCD streak in evidence throughout. By all accounts, Reed spent a considerable amount of time on his own. Maybe he had some kind of social aversion disorder. But it wasn't enough to convince her that he was harmless. Not after he'd threatened them with a gun.

She reached for the trash bag with the broken mug and stepped past him. "Guess I'll see you at the meeting."

Reed frowned. "It's not here?"

Blair shrugged. "Here, or at my trailer. We'll figure it out when the others get back. I'm going to lock up here for now."

Heart pulsing in her throat, she exited the RV and waited for Reed to follow. After locking the door behind him, she replaced the key in her pocket and watched as he strolled back toward his camper van. With a bit of luck, Reed wouldn't mention to Harvey that she'd been in his RV.

She made her way down to the road, speeding up her pace to get back as quickly as possible, certain Reed's eyes were burning into her back as she went. He wasn't a man she felt safe around, but then she hadn't given him any reason to trust her either.

Safely inside her trailer, she sank down on the couch and closed her eyes until her breathing slowed to a more regular pace. Even the very sight of Reed struck fear in her heart, but was it justified? She tried to put herself in his shoes for a moment. He had every reason to be wary of them. Obviously, he preferred his own company. After all, he'd come to a remote campground for a solitary hunting trip. But he'd returned to discover Bird Creek full of strangers in-fighting among themselves, one of whom might be a murderer. She could hardly blame Reed for being highly suspicious of what had gone on in his absence. How was he supposed to know who to believe or trust?

Weary and cold to the bone, Blair hauled herself to her feet and filled the kettle to make some coffee. Moments later, she was about to pour the boiling water over the grounds in the French press, when she heard voices outside. Peering through the window, she exhaled in relief at the sight of Matt supporting Whitney as they wound their way toward the trailer. She flung open the door and helped him ferry her up the steps and across the floor to the couch.

"Are you hurt?" Blair asked, anxiously cataloging the cuts and scrapes on Whitney's face and hands.

She shook her head. "Just bruised. Nothing broken, as far as I can tell." She looked up at Matt. "Thank you again. I'd never have gotten out of there if it hadn't been for you and Sam."

"Where is Sam?" Blair asked.

"He's gone back to check on Duke," Matt said, opening the fridge and grabbing a leftover sandwich. He eyed the French press longingly. "Is the coffee ready?"

"I need to add the water and let it sit for a couple of minutes." Blair motioned to the back of the trailer and raised her brows to indicate she needed to talk to Matt.

Picking up on the urgency in her expression, he gave a barely imperceptible nod and made his way to the bedroom. A moment later, she followed him and closed the door behind her.

"What's up?" Matt frowned. "Why all the secrecy?"

"Remember that time you gave me Harvey's spare key to give back to him?" Blair whispered.

"You ... kept it?" Matt asked incredulously.

Blair put a finger to her lips to warn him to keep his voice down. "Yes, I did. It bugged me that we never got a chance to search Harvey's RV, with Sandy dying and all. And I know he was lying about those tennis shoes. So I decided to take a quick look around while he was gone. To be honest, I didn't even know what I was looking for at first. But then I remembered Hazel's note and how she'd written something about a mug and a face."

Matt scratched his head looking thoroughly confused. "She did?"

Blair blew out an exasperated breath. "I kept the note. It's in my purse if you don't believe me. The point is, I found—"

"Blair?" Whitney's voice drifted back to the bedroom. "I need to use the outhouse."

Gritting her teeth, Blair called back, "Coming!"

She leaned closer to Matt and whispered, "I found a mug with a wedding picture of Sandy and Harvey on it from 1979."

"And?" Matt demanded. "Where's this going?"

"The man in the photo is shorter than Harvey."

"I really need to go!" Whitney called out more urgently.

Blair studied Matt's reaction as she reached for the door handle. She could see by the look on his face that the gears were turning.

BY THE TIME Blair and Whitney returned from the outhouse, Sam and Reed had arrived. Blair tensed when Reed looked pointedly at her and tilted his head by way of greeting. She wondered if he'd told anyone about finding her in Harvey's RV. Or if he'd asked about Sandy. He struck her as the kind of guy who liked to dot his i's and cross his t's. Knowing him, he'd probably double checked her story.

"Harvey's back at the RV," Sam said.

Blair raised her brows questioningly. "Why didn't he come straight here?"

"He's covered in mud—he's cleaning up," Reed responded.

"We figured we'd go over there and save him a trip back out in the rain," Matt said, holding Blair's gaze as if willing her to see where he was going with this.

Her breath caught in her throat. Of course! It was a chance to take another look at the mug. Maybe even confront Harvey about it. "Good idea," she replied.

"What about Logan?" Whitney asked, throwing a nervous glance Reed's way.

"What about him?" Matt shot back. "He's where he needs to be until we turn him over to the authorities. He's going to prison, Whitney. What part of that don't you get?"

"I just don't think we should leave him out, that's all," she retorted, sounding miffed.

"It's good for him to have some time alone—to think. And he's gonna have a whole lot more time to do that behind bars," Matt said.

Blair reached for the French press. "All right, let's go. We can have coffee over at Harvey's."

HARVEY LOOKED MOMENTARILY TAKEN aback to see them all converging on his RV. "I was just about to head your way."

"No worries," Matt responded. "We thought we'd save you a trip."

"What's the word with SAR?" Sam asked, sinking down on the couch. "I take it they didn't attempt a landing?"

Harvey shook his head. "No, it was impossible in these conditions."

"And the drop?" Sam pressed.

Harvey frowned. "They made the drop, but the wind was so bad it didn't land anywhere near the SOS. They took off right after that. Visibility was next to nothing. I tried to look for the survival kit, but the mud was so slick I didn't get very far."

Disappointment radiated around the room in the silence that followed. They'd hoped to have radio contact by now, if nothing else.

"It's all right. They'll be back tomorrow," Blair said, trying to lift the mood. "Who wants coffee?" She got to her feet and made a show of opening and closing several different cabinets before fortuitously *discovering* the coffee mugs.

As she pushed down the plunger on the French press moments later, she wrinkled her nose at the distinctive burnt smell in the air. It couldn't be the coffee, could it? Glancing in the sink, she noticed that Harvey had been burning some paper. "What have you got going here, Harvey? Are you trying to start a fire or something?" she joked.

He flapped a hand dismissively. "Anything to save a trip to the dumpster in this weather."

Blair shot him a bewildered look. Who burned their trash in their RV?

"I can't believe you didn't set off the fire alarm doing that," Sam said, scratching his head.

Harvey gave a disgruntled shrug. "It was just a couple of scraps."

Blair carefully selected an assortment of mugs including the one with the photo of Sandy and Harvey on it and then poured the coffee and handed it around. She looked directly at Matt as she passed him the mug with the wedding photograph. He took a long draught of coffee and let out a satisfied sigh. "Ah, exactly what I needed. Hey, what have we got here? Sandy's and Harvey's wedding photo!"

Blair kept her eyes firmly fixed on Harvey, monitoring his reaction. A momentary flicker of surprise crossed his face before he quickly composed his features.

Matt held up the mug for the others to see and then

studied the photo more closely. His frown deepened. "No offense, Harvey, but you look kind of ... short." His voice faltered and Blair was impressed at how convincing he sounded at being surprised.

Harvey scrubbed a hand over his jaw and let out an embarrassed laugh. "Oh, that's Sandy's first husband. His name was Harvey too—a British guy." He hesitated. "He died in a car crash six months after they were married."

a strained silence followed Harvey's stunning announcement before Whitney exclaimed, "That's *such* a tragic story. Sandy had a hard life."

Harvey shot her a dark look. "We were very happy together."

"Oh, I didn't mean ... with you," Whitney stuttered, her cheeks flushing. "I meant with her first husband dying, and the cancer and all."

Blair stared down at the floor, her fingers so tightly wrapped around her coffee mug she feared she might crush it. The room appeared to be spinning around her—a thousand thoughts shooting through her head at once. Could it really be that simple—that Harvey shared the same name as Sandy's first husband? Harvey 2.0. It seemed he had an answer for everything. But it felt like one coincidence too many. She stole a furtive glance around the room full of strangers and their secrets. It was just like Reed had said—the important thing was to determine which of them was dangerous. They all had the potential to be. Even Matt. Whitney was right about that. He could kill a man given the right circumstances. He'd been trained to. But he had no reason to as far as she knew.

She considered each of the others in turn. Sam was tall and athletic, a wiry mass of muscle. He could take someone out if he had to. Harvey was older, but broad-shouldered and strong. And then there was Logan. His ego was big enough to drive him to murder. Doubtless, Reed, an experienced hunter, was well capable of killing. Whitney was the only one of the group that she could dismiss as a potential killer. The girl was too small, too lightweight, too fragile emotionally, and too much of an airhead to figure out how to cover up a crime she'd committed. But even she could parrot a cover story for someone else.

Sam threw Harvey a perturbed look. "How long were you and Sandy married?"

"Thirty-seven years." Harvey's voice quieted to a whisper. "I still can't believe she's gone." He pulled out a tissue and blew his nose.

Matt got to his feet and set the photo mug down on the counter. "It's been a long day. We should get some rest. I'm sure SAR will be back first thing in the morning,"

Sam nodded. "Even if the weather doesn't improve overnight, they can at least attempt to drop us another survival kit. And, hopefully, this time they'll hit their target."

AFTER A MAKESHIFT MEAL of meatless tacos and beans, Blair made up the sofa bed for Whitney and then retired to join Matt in the bedroom. She threw herself down on the bed and pinned a questioning gaze on her husband. "Do you believe Harvey when he said he couldn't locate the drop?"

Matt drew his brows together in concentration. "You don't?"

"Too many anomalies mounting up in Harvey's corner."

Blair leaned back against the headboard and drew her knees to her chest.

Matt nodded. "Yeah, what are the odds of Sandy marrying a man with the same name as her first husband?"

"Incredibly slim," Blair agreed. "If we had any Wi-Fi, I'd Google it, but I'm willing to bet it rarely happens. "I think you and I should go out tomorrow morning and look for the drop. Harvey might have stashed it somewhere."

Matt frowned. "Why would he do that?"

Blair pressed her lips together. "There might have been something in it he didn't want us to find."

"A sat-phone, maybe," Matt mused. "That would make sense if he didn't want us communicating with the sheriffs for some reason."

Blair wrinkled her brow. "Possibly. But I think there was something else in the drop he didn't want us to see. My guess is that's what he was burning in the sink before we arrived. I mean, who burns their trash in their RV? Only a desperate man trying to hide something."

Matt blew out a heavy breath. "I have to admit that was weird."

"It could have been rescue instructions from SAR telling us where to convene, and what time—directions to a pickup point or something," Blair went on. "Maybe he's planning on being the only one to show up. He never did like you being in charge. Perhaps this is his way of taking control."

"Or worse … he could be planning on killing us."

The knot in Blair's stomach tightened. "Either way, we can't trust him."

Matt scratched his forehead, looking worried. "If he's lying, he's good at it. I'll give him that. The lies just kind of flow effortlessly out of him. He doesn't lay it on too thick, doesn't try too hard to convince you. That's the part that throws me off and makes me think he's telling the truth."

"Which is exactly why he's been able to get away with it all this time."

Matt sighed. "All right, you and I will head out early tomorrow morning and wait for SAR to return. I'll have Sam tell the others to stay put until we come back."

Blair reached for his hand and squeezed it. "It's the right thing to do. We can't rely on anyone else to make contact with SAR."

Matt scrubbed a hand over his jaw. "Like I said all along, we can only trust each other."

Blair fell silent as she considered the latest developments. Even though help was now on the horizon, she had a nagging feeling they might not make it out of here alive if they didn't act with extreme caution going forward. Danger was all around them in the form of their fellow campers.

"I doubt I'll sleep much tonight and I know you won't either," she said. "I keep wondering about those tennis shoes. I think we should check what size Sandy's feet are."

Matt threw her a horrified look. "You're kidding, right? Do you have any idea what her body's going to smell like after two days?"

Blair repressed a shudder. "I'm sure you've dealt with worse. Besides, it's freezing cold out, that should lessen the odor." She reached into the drawer on her side of the bed and lifted out a packet of foam ear plugs. "We can plug our nostrils with these."

"Like that's gonna help." Matt covered his face with his hands and groaned. "I can't believe I'm even considering this."

"You know we have to," Blair urged. "It's the only way to find out if Harvey's lying to us about the shoes or not."

"I don't like it." Matt punched his pillow softly. "I think we should stay put until it's light out. Wait for SAR to put a plan into action."

"The way things are going, we could be dead by then."

Blair slid her feet to the ground. "We owe it to the others to warn them. Everyone's dismissed Harvey as a grieving widower. If he's lying about the shoes being Sandy's, then he's lying about everything. I'll go by myself if you don't want to come with me."

Matt tossed the pillow aside and got to his feet. "You know I can't let you do that."

They slipped out of the bedroom and padded softly past the sofa bed where Whitney was sleeping. After pulling on their coats, Matt unlocked the door, grimacing at the loud click it made. Whitney lifted her head and peered groggily over at them. "Where are you guys going?"

"Just to the outhouse," Blair said with an apologetic smile. "Go back to sleep."

Yawning, Whitney wriggled further down in her sleeping bag before turning over on her side.

Once outside, Blair made her way over to their truck and opened the back door to retrieve the tennis shoes.

"Do you have to bring those?" Matt asked.

"One, at least. How else am I supposed to know what size her feet are?"

Matt shrugged. "I doubt you'll be able to get them on—you know, rigor mortis and all."

"I don't need to put them on her. I can just measure them against her feet," Blair said, quietly closing the truck door.

"Don't turn on your flashlight until we get around the bend in the road," Matt cautioned, one hand on the gun concealed beneath his jacket.

They walked along the damp, dirt road in silence, finding their way in the pitch darkness by the sparse light of Blair's iPhone, which she tried to protect as best she could from the soft rain that was falling. As soon as they rounded the corner, they turned on their flashlights and made a beeline for Logan's and Whitney's campsite. Blair sucked in a breath at the catastrophic sight of the pine tree lying across the trailer with its twisted branches reaching out like claws—a sight that was twice as ominous at night.

"Whitney's lucky to be alive," Blair remarked. "It's a miracle the tree didn't crush her."

"She's dodged a bullet twice in the last few days if you ask me," Matt replied. "Logan's got all the hallmarks of a killer."

Blair fished out the packet of foam ear plugs and stuffed one in each nostril before handing the pack to Matt.

He followed suit and then nodded. "Ready?"

"Ready as I'll ever be."

Matt took a steadying breath and stepped toward Logan's truck parked a few feet from the mangled trailer. "Keep an eye out over your shoulder to make sure no one's on the road. I don't want to give anyone the opportunity to sneak up on us."

Blair glanced tentatively around in the shadowy darkness while Matt unlocked the tailgate. He shone his flashlight inside the bed and gasped, before stumbling backward, almost knocking Blair to the ground.

"Does it smell that bad?" she asked incredulously as she picked up the flashlight she'd dropped.

Matt rubbed a shaking hand over his jaw. "You'd better take a look and see for yourself."

Something in his voice disturbed her. She hesitated, tempted to abandon her plan to measure Sandy's feet, before mustering her courage. After making sure the foam plugs were firmly packed up each nostril, she gingerly approached the back of the truck and focused the beam of her flashlight inside the bed. The breath left her lungs as she tried to come to terms with what she was looking at.

Next to Sandy's tarp-draped body, lay a second corpse.

*B*lair staggered backward, covering her mouth with one hand to trap the scream threatening to erupt from her lungs. *No! It couldn't be.* The killer had struck again! Her knees felt like they were about to buckle beneath her, dooming her to the dark fear that held her in its grip. Matt grabbed her from behind and escorted her away from the back of the truck. Trembling uncontrollably, Blair sank down on a log next to the fire pit. "Who ... who is it?"

"I don't know," Matt said, rain dripping off the end of his nose as he scanned the campsite warily. "I need to pull the blanket off and take a closer look. It's a man—I can tell that much from his boots."

Blair let out a soft moan. "What if it's Rob?" She looked up at her husband despairingly. "Who else could it be?"

Matt's expression darkened. "Wait here. I'll find out. And stay alert."

Blair interlaced her fingers and pressed them to her lips watching with a mounting sense of dread as Matt approached the truck bed once more. He reached inside and yanked off the blanket that covered the man's upper torso and head. After a long moment, he rolled it up and tossed it back inside. His expression was strained when he returned to the fire pit and stood over Blair. "It's Rob," he said quietly, squeezing her shoulder. "Poor dude. I know I called him an idiot for heading out to look for his brother and all, but he didn't deserve this."

Blair's teeth chattered as she weighed Matt's words, trying to make sense of what could have happened. Nothing was ever as it seemed at first glance. Rob hadn't struck her as the reckless sort—more of a good old boy. Had he really gone off looking for his brother at all? Or had the killer outsmarted them once again? She got to her feet and darted another fearful look around. "Maybe Rob didn't write that note we found in the camper van. We don't know what his handwriting looks like. It's possible the killer left it to throw us off. Or forced Rob to write it. We can't be sure of anything."

Matt blew out a heavy breath. "So why leave the body in the truck now?"

"He's toying with us—letting us know he's in control. This is all a sick game to him." Blair smothered a sob, only too aware that any sound she made could alert a killer in the vicinity. "We're never going to get out of Bird Creek alive."

"We're not going down without a fight, I can tell you that much," Matt growled.

A glint of steel in her husband's hand caught Blair's eye. "Even a gun won't save us if he's ambushing people," she whispered.

"Harvey doesn't have a gun," Matt said.

Blair gave a despairing shake of her head. "Harvey couldn't have done this. Rob's been gone since yesterday. It must have been Reed. He only showed up here this morning. He's probably been stalking us for the past few days. And he basically accused us of invading his campground."

"So now you think Harvey's telling the truth?"

"No, of course not," Blair replied. "He's lying to us—about other things. I don't know what his reasons are. But Reed said something strange to me earlier. He said everyone's hiding secrets, but they were only dangerous if they impacted others." She chewed on her lip. "Now that I think about it, he could have been trying to warn me about himself. Maybe that's why he's a loner—he can't stop himself from killing."

Matt rubbed the back of his neck, surveying the campsite perimeter. "So bringing Rob's body back here was a trophy of sorts, to rub our noses in it."

"He wanted us to know Rob was dead, that's for sure," Blair said, throwing a nervous glance down to the road. She got to her feet and pulled out the tennis shoe she'd stuffed beneath her jacket. "I'm going to do what I came here to do. And then we need to get out of here."

She padded over to the truck and peered inside the bed, holding her breath. After pushing back the edge of the tarp, she pressed the shoe up against Sandy's frozen foot. Her heart knocked against her ribs. It was just as she'd feared. At least two sizes too big.

Swallowing hard, she threw a quick glance at Rob's body. A wave of pity crashed over her. With his broken arm, he hadn't stood a chance against the killer. Had he simply been selected as the weakest prey among them, or was there a more specific reason the killer had wanted him dead? Rob had suspected that Reed was stalking the camp. After all, he'd mentioned meeting the duck hunter and commented on how aloof and unfriendly he'd been. They might have crossed paths again when Rob left to search for his brother.

Matt walked up next to her and stared solemnly at Rob's body. "I wonder how he died."

Blair let out a defeated sigh. "What difference does it make? It's not going to help us identify the killer."

Wordlessly, Matt shone the flashlight over Rob's face and upper torso.

"Wait! What's that around his neck?" Blair asked. "I think … isn't that—"

Matt sucked in a sharp breath. "It's his sling. He was strangled." Silently, he closed the tailgate. "Let's get out of here while we still can."

THE THREE-MINUTE WALK BACK to the trailer felt like an eternity punctuated only by the eerie shrieks of owls and the occasional scuttling of rodents going about their nocturnal business. Blair breathed out a sigh of relief when they finally made it safely back inside and locked the door behind them. Whitney was snoring gently on the couch, her chest rising and falling, oblivious to the horrors that lay beyond the trailer walls.

After grabbing some water, they made their way back to the bedroom. They sat down, side-by-side on the bed, a sober silence descending between them as they took a moment to decompress.

"We need to figure out who the killer is," Blair said. "We can't go on like this."

"Or killers," Matt responded.

Blair threw him a disconcerted look. "What do you mean?"

"There could be more than one. We don't know for sure that any of the killings or Hazel's disappearance are connected."

Blair picked distractedly at a ragged fingernail. "So Reed might have taken out the elderly man on the hiking trail and then killed Rob so he couldn't identify him as a suspect.

Meanwhile, Harvey bumps Sandy off in some kind of mercy killing, and Logan murders Hazel in revenge for surveilling him."

Matt closed his eyes and rubbed his temples. "I know, I know. It's too far-fetched. The odds of multiple murderers camping at the same spot are worse than both your husbands being called Harvey. It's just that I can't make any connection between the killings."

For a few minutes, neither of them spoke and then Blair asked, "What's the significance of an Ace of Spades tattoo?"

Matt frowned at her. "Why do you ask?"

"Harvey has one on his wrist. I noticed it the first time we got together after we found the body."

Matt shrugged. "Could mean a bunch of different things —gamblers use it for good luck, gangsters too—even soldiers."

"I wonder if he has any other tattoos," Blair mused. "Tattoos tell stories. You know what they say, *a picture's worth a thousand words.*"

"Yeah, sometimes it is." Matt furrowed his brow, a faraway look in his eyes. "Do you have your phone on you?"

"Yeah." Blair said hesitantly as she slipped it out of her back pocket. "What do you need it for?"

"Pull up the pictures of the body we found by the hiking trail."

Blair threw him a befuddled look. "Why? He didn't have any tattoos, did he?"

Matt shook his head impatiently. "That's not what I'm getting at. From what I remember he wasn't a big guy. Stands to reason he had small feet."

Blair's jaw dropped. "You're thinking the tennis shoes might have belonged to him?"

Matt drew his brows together. "I don't know, yet. Just trying to connect some dots. It all began with him."

Pulse racing, Blair quickly scrolled through to the pictures of the body. She could feel the thud of Matt's heart as he huddled up next to her for a better view.

"It's impossible to tell the size of his feet from a photo, but he's definitely on the short side," Blair said.

"Yes, he is," Matt agreed in a grim tone. He tugged a jittery hand through his hair. "In fact, I think I recognize him. It's the man in the wedding photo with Sandy."

29

*B*lair let out a gasp and dropped the phone in her lap. She stared at Matt for a long moment, jaw askew, as his words slowly sank in. "If you're right, then Sandy's first husband was here at the campground. That means ... that means Harvey must have killed him."

Matt let out a troubled sigh. "That's what it looks like."

Blair dug her fingers into Matt's arm as another thought struck. "If the shoes belonged to Sandy's husband, then Harvey was behind Hazel's disappearance as well."

Matt frowned. "I don't follow. How do you figure?"

"She was on to him," Blair insisted. "She saw the shoes and the mug in his RV. She knew something was amiss. Harvey had to get rid of her."

Matt's expression hardened. "If he got rid of Hazel, it's possible he knocked Sandy off too."

"He might have, or the cancer could actually have killed her," Blair said. "The missing part of the puzzle is whether or not Sandy was in on the murder with him. Maybe they were lovers and planned to bump her husband off in a remote spot."

"There's no way for us to untangle all this," Matt said, stifling a yawn as he sank back on his pillow. "The important thing is that SAR launches a rescue attempt as soon as possible before anyone else dies. We need to get a hold of a radio." He fastened an earnest look on Blair. "Until then, don't breathe a word of our suspicions to anyone else at the campground. If Harvey really is behind the killings, he's extremely dangerous and he won't stop now in an effort to cover his tracks."

"Maybe we should enlist Reed's help after all," Blair suggested. "He's the only other person here with a gun."

"Too risky. We don't know that Harvey had anything to do with Rob's body turning up. It still leaves the possibility that Reed killed Rob."

SHORTLY AFTER SIX, Blair woke with a start. It took her a moment or two to orient herself and remember everything that had transpired during the night. She slid a hand across to Matt's side of the bed, but his cold sleeping bag was crumpled up like a discarded snakeskin. Had he slept at all? Surely, he hadn't left for the SOS point without her. Stifling a yawn, she hurriedly unzipped her bag and rubbed her eyes in an attempt to wake herself more fully before tripping her way out to the living area.

To her relief, Matt was seated opposite Whitney at the dining table, clutching an oversized mug of coffee. They glanced at her warily, as if she were a fragile creature who'd emerged from some kind of induced coma, which was exactly how she felt.

She slid into the seat next to Matt and reached for his mug. After swallowing a mouthful of bitter black coffee, she handed it back to him. "You told her … about Rob, didn't you?"

"Yeah." Matt studied the surface of his coffee as though searching for inspiration. "I had to. It wasn't fair to make her think we still suspected Logan. He couldn't have put Rob's body in the truck—he's been tied up for the past two days."

"I told you it wasn't him," Whitney sputtered indignantly. "He's not capable of killing anyone. It has to be Reed. Why else did he suddenly show up here? It's obvious he's been stalking the campground the whole time."

Blair exchanged a look of alarm with Matt. If Reed really had killed Rob, the last thing they needed was Whitney accusing him to his face. "You can't go around saying that. We don't have any evidence. And if it is him, we can't let him know we're on to him. If he's that unhinged, he could kill us all."

"But we have to tell the others that we found Rob's body," Whitney protested.

"We will," Matt assured her. "But Blair's right—we're not going to accuse anyone of killing him. We're going to act like we think the killer's still out there stalking us—and he might be."

"You and I should head up to the hiking trail and wait for the SAR drop before we break the news to the others about Rob," Blair said. "It's only going to freak everyone out and stir up more suspicion. We need everyone to stay calm until we're rescued." She fixed a solemn gaze on Whitney. "That means you have to keep your lips sealed until we get back. We can't risk anything happening while we're gone. Remember, Reed has a gun and he knows how to use it. He might have a whole armory in that safe beneath his bed, for all we know."

"Okay, okay, I get it." Whitney drained the rest of her coffee and got to her feet. "I need to get changed."

"You can use our bedroom," Blair offered.

"Thanks," Whitney said, grabbing her bag and retreating to the back of the trailer.

A loud rap on the front door startled them. Matt reached for his gun. "I'll get it." He ducked down and cracked open the blinds to peer out. "It's Sam."

He pulled open the door and a maniacal-looking Sam tumbled inside with Duke still on the leash. He tossed a distressed glance at Blair and then returned his attention to Matt. "I've got bad news," he hissed.

Matt held his gaze. "Rob?"

Sam gave a sharp nod. "He's dead."

Matt gestured to the dining table. "Sit down. We already know."

Sam slid onto the bench opposite Blair, his face blanched of color. Duke lay down at his feet and rested his head on his paws. Blair's nostrils twitched at the unpleasant smell of damp dog hair that filled the air.

"We discovered Rob's body last night," Matt said. "We went over to Logan's truck to see if the tennis shoes could have been Sandy's. How did you find him?"

Sam rubbed his calloused hands together. "I was walking Duke around the backside of the campsites. He kept straining on the leash when we went past Logan's truck. I thought it was odd because we walked by there yesterday and he was fine. On a hunch, I opened the tailgate." Sam furrowed his brow as if trying to erase the memory. "I can't believe it. What do you think happened?"

"That's what we're trying to figure out," Blair answered. "It's possible Rob never went to look for his brother at all. The killer could have written that note. Or maybe he crossed paths with Rob while he was searching."

Sam frowned. "It must have been Reed."

"We can't jump to any conclusions," Blair objected. "He's not the only suspect."

"Do you know how Rob died?" Sam asked.

Matt pressed his lips together. "Strangled, just like the other guy. The killer used Rob's sling."

Sam winced. "So it was a crime of opportunity. A random killing."

Matt and Blair exchanged a knowing look.

"Maybe not," Matt said, lowering his voice.

"What are you getting at?" Sam's gaze zigzagged from Matt to Blair.

"Keep your voice down," Blair urged. "Whitney's in the bedroom."

"Don't say anything to the others, yet," Matt muttered. "But I think the elderly man we found strangled is the man in the wedding photo with Sandy."

Sam's eyes bulged. "What?" he mouthed, casting a harried look in the direction of the bedroom. "Do you think Harvey killed him?"

Matt pinched the bridge of his nose. "It's looking that way."

"That means Harvey—if that's even his name—has been lying to us about everything," Sam said. After a beat of silence, he added, "If he killed Sandy's husband, maybe he killed Rob too."

"It's possible." Blair wrinkled her brow. "I remember Rob remarking once that he thought he knew Harvey from some-where. He might have mentioned it to Harvey and spooked him."

Matt rubbed a hand over his jaw. "Blair and I are going to head up to the SOS and wait for SAR to return. Harvey could have been lying about not being able to find the drop. We need to make sure we intercept the next one and get a hold of a radio."

Sam frowned. "Should I tell the others about Rob?"

"Not yet," Matt cautioned. "Wait until we get back."

He got to his feet just as Whitney resurfaced.

"Are you guys leaving now?" she asked.

Blair nodded. "Make sure you lock the trailer door after us. Sam will keep an eye on you while we're gone."

After donning their rain gear, Matt and Blair followed Sam and Duke outside and down the trailer steps. They froze at the sound of a booming voice. "That's far enough!"

Standing on the other side of their truck was Reed, aiming his rifle directly at them.

"Easy, man!" Matt said, positioning himself in front of Blair, one hand ready to draw his gun. "What's going on?"

"You're a pack of liars, that's what!" Reed thundered back. "You said you had nothing more to hide. All this time you were hiding another body."

Blair's heart pounded in her chest. "Please, put down the gun, Reed. Let's talk about this."

"Not until you start talking. Who is he and which one of you killed him?"

"If you mean the body in Logan's truck, he was one of the hunters camping up by the lake when the mudslide struck," Matt explained. "He was the only survivor, as far as we know. He recognized you—said you came by their camp."

"We put him up in your camper van," Sam added. "He left a note to say he was going to look for his brother two days ago. That was the last we heard of him—until his body showed up last night. We've no idea how he got there."

Reed scowled. "I put him there. I found him in a shallow grave beneath the brush at the back of my campsite." He panned his rifle slowly over them. "The bodies are piling up around here. One of you is a killer."

"You don't know that," Sam countered. "Someone could be stalking the campground—picking us off."

"Why should I believe that?" Reed sneered.

Blair stepped toward him. "Do we look like serial killers

to you?" She gestured to the others. "We're just a bunch of stranded campers. We came here to hike, relax, and enjoy the occasional fire pit conversation. And then the nightmare began. So you can either work with us to find this madman and stop him before someone else dies, or you can hold us hostage and take your chances against him on your own."

There was silence for a long moment before Reed lowered his weapon. "So what's your plan, or do you even have one?"

"Matt and I are heading up to the SOS point to wait for SAR," Blair said. "Sam knows a bit about how they operate. He's confident they'll attempt another drop with a radio."

"In the meantime," Matt added, looking directly at Reed, "You can help us out here by guarding the perimeter and keeping everyone safe." He hesitated before adding, "And making sure everyone stays put in their rigs until we get back."

A flicker of curiosity in Reed's eyes told Blair that he'd picked up on some underlying connotation in Matt's words. His eyes darted momentarily to Sam. Blair curled her hands into fists. He was homing in on the wrong target. Matt had warned her not to relay their suspicions about Harvey to anyone, but if they were valid, she needed to point Reed in the right direction before they left.

Matt raised his hand in a parting wave as he turned to go. "We'll be back as soon as we have an update."

"I'll check on Whitney after I feed Duke," Sam said, leading his dog back across the road.

Pulse racing, Blair held Reed's gaze as she walked by him and whispered, "It's not a stranger stalking the camp I'm worried about. Keep an eye on your other neighbor."

Reed's eyes darkened, and for a split second, Blair wondered if she'd done the right thing, if she'd trusted the right man, if her instincts had led her in the right direction, or into the path of the real killer. It was too late to retract anything now. He knew the stalker theory they'd fed him was bogus—that they suspected the killer was in the camp.

"I CAN'T HELP FEELING SOMEWHAT guilty about leaving Whitney alone in our trailer," Blair said as she caught up with Matt.

"She's as safe there as with us," he replied. "The killer struck on this trail before. He could do it again."

They fell silent as they concentrated on navigating the muddy path leading to their only real hope of rescue. Blair pulled her hood tighter over her head to keep the rain from running down her face. There was a risk of ambush heading up to the SOS point, but staying put in the trailer was no guarantee they'd be safe either. One way or another, they had to make contact with SAR if they were ever going to get out of there.

The boulders they had painstakingly hauled and arranged into an SOS were only half visible by the time they reached them. The unending rain had shifted more mud and debris, and only a broken message remained, an ominous reminder of how fragile their link to the outside world had become.

"Could be an hour or two before SAR shows up," Matt said.

"I say we look around and try and find the first drop," Blair suggested. "Survival kits are brightly colored—it's bound to stand out in this sea of brown. If nothing else, we'll stay warmer if we keep moving."

"We can try," Matt said sounding skeptical. "But the odds of us stumbling on it are slim to none."

"You're assuming it's lost—that it fell into a ravine or something. I still have my suspicions that Harvey might have found it. If I'm right, it could be hidden under some debris."

Matt zipped his coat up to his chin with an air of resignation. "All right. Let's do this."

For the next hour or so, they picked their way through the mud near the SOS, moving aside brush and branches in a desperate bid to find the survival kit Harvey had claimed he couldn't locate. Every few minutes, Blair cast a wistful glance up at the sky hoping to spot a rescue helicopter headed their way. Logic told her she'd hear the chopper blades before she saw anything, but she still found herself searching the sky almost as much as the mud below.

"This is hopeless," Matt moaned, kicking at an uprooted bush. "Let's get out of the dirt and find somewhere to sit."

Blair continued to sweep her eyes left and right as they made their way back out of the mudslide area. She lifted up random piles of brush in passing and peered beneath them, hoping against hope to glimpse something neon, but to no avail.

Matt gestured to a downed tree up ahead. "That's as good a spot as any."

As they approached, Blair noticed an unnatural-looking clump of mud beneath one of its branches.

Heart thudding in anticipation, she quickened her pace. "Look at this, Matt!"

Hunkering down next to the strange mound, she quickly brushed off some of the dirt and confirmed what she'd suspected—beneath the mud was a well-camouflaged neon orange bag.

30

*B*lair exchanged a knowing look with Matt as he dropped to his knees next to her, an expression of utter disbelief on his face. "You were right," he said, in a shocked whisper.

"This confirms everything we suspected," Blair replied. "Whoever that man in the RV is, he's not the real Harvey Ross."

Sobered by their discovery, they got to work at once brushing the caked mud from the canvas survival bag. The heavy-duty zipper was thickly coated with dirt and it took several attempts before Matt managed to yank it halfway open. Blair took over and rummaged haphazardly through the assorted medical supplies, rations, blankets, and water, searching for any communications equipment.

"No sign of a radio," she said tersely, her search growing increasingly frantic as her fingers scraped the bottom of the bag. "Surely they wouldn't have made a drop without leaving us an emergency radio."

"It has to be in here somewhere." Matt tugged the zipper open the rest of the way and started pulling out the contents of the kit, examining each item in turn and tossing it to one side. "Look at this," he said, holding up a laminated card. "It lists the contents: band-aids, fishing gear, aspirin, water receptacle, compass, hand saw—" Sucking in a sharp breath, he came to an abrupt halt.

"What?" Blair demanded, glancing across at the card in his hand.

"According to this, there's supposed to be a survival radio and a locator beacon in here." He locked eyes with her. "Harvey must have taken them."

Blair's pulse thudded wildly in her temples. She turned her attention back to the canvas bag and rooted around inside it one last time, just to be sure. But there was nothing in it that could be used to contact SAR—not even a single flare. She sat back on her heels and blew out a frustrated breath. "What do you think he's playing at?"

"I don't know for sure, but he's very much in control of the situation now," Matt said, sounding grim. "We need to get back to the campground. The others could be in danger. For all we know, he might be armed."

"What if SAR returns?" Blair asked. "One of us needs to wait here. It's more important than ever that we get help as soon as possible."

"We can't split up," Matt said. "Either we both stay here or we both go back."

Blair stared at the survival kit, torn between their options. They had a responsibility to warn the others that Harvey was dangerous—that he'd deliberately sabotaged the attempt to rescue them. At the very least, they had to make sure no one was left alone with him. Thankfully, they'd shared their suspicions with Sam. He would make sure Whitney was safe until they got back. And now that they had evidence of Harvey's deception, they might be able to enlist Reed's help to take him down by force.

On the other hand, Blair was tempted to stay where she was, knowing that SAR might show up at any minute. "Maybe we should wait here for a little longer," she suggested. "We desperately need to contact the sheriffs. We know they've seen our SOS and they're coming back. It's only a matter of when. They've probably been trying to contact us on the radio all night."

Matt scrubbed a hand over his jaw, a worried gleam in his eyes. "That's what I'm afraid of. What if Harvey's already been in communication with them? They might have given him rescue instructions—directed him to another area where they can make a landing. If that's the case, it's imperative we get back to the campground and make sure he doesn't go anywhere without us. Right now, he's our only link to the outside world."

Blair pressed her lips together, contemplating Matt's words. "You're right. He might have told them he's the only survivor, for all we know. SAR could land and pick him up and be gone again within minutes. We'd better get back and keep him under surveillance."

"We can't let him know that we found the survival kit," Matt warned her. "We need to pretend to be disappointed that SAR didn't show up again this morning."

"Let's get this survival bag zipped back up and out of sight," Blair said. "Just in case Harvey comes back to check on it for some reason."

They hurriedly threw everything back inside the waterproof bag and shoved it underneath the tree branch, then slathered it with mud to camouflage it again as best they could. The rain was coming down heavier than before, and visibility was severely hampered as they fumbled their way back toward the hiking trail, single file through the mud, Matt taking up the rear as usual. Blair kept up a steady pace, desperate to return to the campground and let the others know what they'd discovered.

All of a sudden, Matt's feet slipped out from under him and he let out a surprised yelp. Blair swung around to try and grab him, only to find herself face-to-face with an unsmiling Harvey holding her startled gaze in a deadly stare.

*B*lair took a shaky step backward eying the crowbar in Harvey's hand as her brain registered what had happened. Matt hadn't slipped on the muddy, root-ridden trail—Harvey had attacked him and knocked him out cold with a vicious blow. She opened her mouth to scream, but nothing came out. Either that, or the heavy rain was drowning out her desperate cry for help. Her brain sounded an inner warning that finally made its way down to her legs. She turned to run, but in a flash, Harvey overpowered her and shoved her to her knees in a muddy puddle. He stuffed some kind of a rag into her mouth and zip-tied her hands behind her back.

"Make a move and you're dead," he hissed, his heavy breath vibrating in her ear.

Her shoulders shook as she watched him roughly pat down Matt's motionless body. With a satisfied grunt, he removed the gun from the concealed carry waistband. "Fig-ured as much, him being military and all."

After rolling Matt over a couple of times into the brush, he dragged a clump of dead branches from the undergrowth and tossed them on top before striding back over to Blair and hauling her to her feet. She tried to cry out again, but only succeeded in choking on the rag in her mouth.

"I'm sure you've got plenty of questions," he drawled, swinging the crowbar maliciously in front of him, as if to remind her not to step out of line. "We'll have all the time we need to chat. Just remember, I don't need you alive. You're optional insurance. So if you turn out to be more trouble than you're worth, I won't think twice about disposing of you without as much as wasting a bullet. Understood?"

Blair nodded her head vigorously, blinking to clear her vision as rain lashed mercilessly against her face. She peered into the undergrowth hoping against hope that Matt was still alive but fearing the worst. Harvey gave her a shove forward and began marching her back up the mountain the way she'd come. With every step, Blair's dread increased. Where was he taking her? And what did he mean by optional insurance? She ran her tongue nervously over her lips as a terrible thought struck her. Had he killed anyone else at the camp-ground—all of them, perhaps? Maybe Reed hadn't fully grasped her veiled warning about Harvey, or maybe he hadn't believed her.

A short distance from the SOS, Harvey consulted a compass he drew from his pocket and then turned abruptly and began heading due east. A thousand thoughts collided in Blair's mind at once. No doubt he'd pulled the compass from the survival kit. He must have been in contact over the radio with SAR and arranged a rendezvous point. Was he planning to dispose of her as soon as he heard the chopper? Maybe she was only insurance in case someone happened upon them beforehand. Or did he plan on taking her on board with him?

Tears fell from her eyes, blending with the rain streaming down her face. Was her husband still alive, struggling to breathe beneath the brush? She hadn't seen the blow Harvey had landed with the crowbar, but Matt had dropped like a stone. Evidently, Harvey was convinced he'd killed him because he hadn't bothered to swing a second time.

After hiking for what Blair estimated to be the best part of an hour, they came to a large clearing. Harvey dragged her over to a small clump of trees on the perimeter and shoved her back down to the ground. He yanked the rag out of her mouth and held a blade to her throat. "Not that anyone's going to hear you, but if you as much as yelp, I'll make sure it's the last time you make a sound. Are we clear?"

She nodded, whimpering, "Why are you doing this, Harvey?"

He let out an amused snort, a cold sheen settling in his eyes that sent a shiver through her. "My name's not Harvey. But I think you already know that, don't you?"

"I … wasn't sure. I suspected as much." Blair swallowed down her fear, trying to steady her voice as she posed the question burning on her lips. "Did you kill him—Sandy's husband?"

He exhaled a long-suffering sigh as he sat down on a stump opposite her. "I made a promise. And I always keep my promises."

Blair frowned at him. "Do you mean a promise to Sandy?"

"To myself," he corrected her sharply.

"I don't follow." Blair gave a befuddled shake of her head. "Who are you, anyway?"

After studying her from beneath his brows for a long moment, he reached a hand inside his jacket. She tensed, terrified he was about to bring out the knife again, but instead he produced a folded sheet of paper. He opened it and held it in front of her. "Better read it quick before the ink starts to bleed."

Blair's eyes darted across the page, her heart seizing in

her chest when she recognized the black-and-white, clean-shaven face staring back at her.

FBI 10 Most Wanted Fugitive
Deroy Stephenson
Wanted for escape and unlawful flight to avoid prosecution - murder
A reward of up to $50,000 is being offered for the apprehension of Deroy Kenneth Stephenson, pictured above. Deroy was serving multiple life sentences for the murders of his parents and sister when he allegedly killed a prison guard and escaped from the Metropolitan Correctional Center in Chicago in the early morning hours of January 19, 2020.
SHOULD BE CONSIDERED ARMED AND DANGEROUS WITH VIOLENT TENDENCIES, AND AN ESCAPE RISK
If you have any information concerning this person, please contact your local FBI office or the nearest American Embassy or Consulate.

"Seen enough?" He laughed raucously as he scrunched up the soggy flyer and threw it in the dirt between them.

Blair stared at him, the horror of what she had read slowly taking root. "The flyer—that's what you were burning in the sink, wasn't it?"

He shrugged. "There were a bunch of them in the survival kit. Maybe the sheriffs thought the campground was full and we'd go around posting flyers on all the trailers like good citizens do." He laughed again and shook his head.

Blair scrunched her eyes shut, willing herself to remain calm. This was worse than anything she'd imagined. The man was a violent fugitive—one of the FBI's 10 most wanted, no less. She had no doubt that Harvey—or Deroy, as he was really called—was going to kill her at some point. He couldn't let her live now that she'd seen his face. She'd watched enough crime shows to know that. She had only her own wits to rely on if she was going to get out of this situation alive. "Why are you doing this?" she asked quietly. "Why did you have to kill an innocent couple on a camping trip?"

A gleam of hatred lit up Deroy's eyes. "There was nothing innocent about Sandy and Harvey. You've got that all wrong. They knew me since I was a kid, but they hung me out to dry. They lived next door to my folks. They're the ones who tipped off the police—told them they saw my car there the night of the murders. They even went to court and testified against me. Said my folks were always complaining about me hitting them up for money." Deroy paused, his lips curling into a cunning smile. "I swore I'd get my revenge on them. Like I said, a promise is a promise."

Blair's stomach churned at the thought of Deroy making a murderous escape from prison in a bid to hunt down an elderly couple who'd helped secure his conviction. All they'd done was try to get justice for their slain neighbors. And look where it had got them. She took a quick, steadying breath, determined to keep Deroy talking and distracted as long as she could. Maybe she'd get a chance to bolt for freedom if she played her cards right. "How did you access their RV?"

He gave a scathing laugh. "They made that part easy. I followed them to a gas station. Sandy went into the store to buy something. I slipped inside the RV undetected when Harvey was gassing up. It's amazing how little attention people pay to things around them."

Blair fell silent, contemplating the horror of Deroy's twisted plan for revenge. "Was Harvey alive when you arrived at the campground?"

Deroy let out a snort and nodded slyly. "Just think, you could have saved him if you'd known. Threatening to kill him was the only way I could persuade Sandy to pretend to be my wife when we pulled in here. She actually believed I was going to let them live."

Blair's throat clenched when she pictured the terror of Sandy's ordeal. "Did she really have cancer?"

Deroy gave a sinister nod. "Didn't take much to finish her off. I flushed her medications down the toilet and doped her up with Vicodin."

Blair shuddered at the callous tone his voice had taken on. "What about Hazel and Rob? Did you kill them as well?"

Deroy scowled. "Hazel stuck her nose in where she shouldn't have. She started putting two and two together—figured out I wasn't Sandy's husband. As for Rob, he was too observant for his own good. He recognized me. He couldn't place me at first, but I knew it was only a matter of time. I had to get rid of him before he shared his suspicions with the rest of you. I left the note in the camper van so you wouldn't go looking for him."

"What did you do with Hazel's body?" Blair asked, a tremor in her voice. "Did you bury her in a shallow grave somewhere too? Her family deserves to know."

Deroy gave a mirthless laugh. "What makes you think you'll be around to tell them?"

Blair swallowed down the bile rising up her throat. The threat was all too clear. She was expendable. Better to change the subject before he decided it was time to add to the body count. "I take it you've been in contact with SAR and this is where they're going to pick you up?"

Deroy laughed. "Not me, per se. As far as they know, they're picking up Harvey Ross, the sole survivor of the mudslide."

Blair gritted her teeth. "So once you hear the chopper coming, you'll kill me and dump me in the brush like you do everyone else."

Deroy seemed to consider this for a moment. "I'd love to dispose of you beforehand—it would make things a whole lot easier." He stood and squished the scrunched-up FBI flyer beneath his boot. "But I'm going to have the chopper fly me to an airstrip where a friend's waiting to take me south of the border. And I'll need a hostage to make that happen."

*D*eroy bent over, reached out a gloved hand and scooped up a handful of dirt. "If I'm taking you with me, we'd better get you ready for the show."

Before Blair had fully grasped what was happening, Deroy was smearing dirt all over her clothing, face, and even through her hair.

"Stop! What are you doing?" She tried to wriggle away, but Deroy only tightened his grip on her. With her hands restrained behind her back, there was little she could do to resist.

"Don't make this more difficult," he growled, "Or I might decide to leave you behind after all. And by now, you know what that looks like."

Blair took a shallow breath, lifting her face so her gaze was locked on his. There was nothing in his expression that made her doubt he would make good on his threat. Resigning herself to going along with whatever insidious plan he had to board the rescue chopper, she closed her eyes until he was done daubing her with mud.

"Much better," he announced with satisfaction, sitting back down on the stump. "Now that you look the part, we can work on your story. I had a lot of time in the slammer to get good at this, so I'm going to tell you what to say and you're going to repeat it back to me. Got it?"

Blair gave a reluctant nod of agreement, the foul stench of the ash-infused mud in her nostrils reminding her that Matt was still lying in the dirt along the trail—possibly in his grave—even as she was fighting for her life. What would he do if he were here now? His words swirled around inside her head.

If it's a game of last man standing, I intend to win.

He would want her to fight—to do battle to the very end and never give up. She had to rise above her fear, keep a clear head, and be ready for any opportunity that came her way to escape.

"Okay, listen carefully," Deroy began, self-consciously smoothing a hand over his beard, which Blair now realized was part of his fugitive disguise. "I came across you wandering around here in the early hours of the morning. You and your husband were sleeping in your tent when the mudslide came through and swept you both away. You survived and you've been searching for him ever since." He curled his lip at her. "Inspiring! A second survivor. The media will eat this up. They might even want to make a movie about you."

Seething inwardly, Blair glowered at him. "You're never going to get away with this. Someone will recognize you. They know you're in the area if they're distributing flyers. You were probably spotted on CCTV at the gas station."

"I'm not going back to prison—I can tell you that much," Deroy said with a venomous edge. "I've got nothing to lose if this goes south, but a young woman like you has everything to lose. If you want to live, you'd better play your part and play it well. If you try to signal anything about me to the chopper crew, I'll take you out, and then they all get to die too—courtesy of you. Now, let's go over your cover story again."

After making Blair repeat it back to him multiple times until he was satisfied she'd nailed it enough to sound convincing, Deroy got to his feet and began pacing impatiently, glancing at his watch from time to time.

Another half hour or so went by before Blair heard the distinctive sound of the chopper's blades once again—only this time, instead of hope, it drove a stake of fear into her heart.

Deroy squared his jaw and pulled out his knife.

Blair tensed, wondering for a moment if he'd changed his mind about taking her on board as a hostage and decided to dispose of her on the spot instead. But then he suddenly grabbed her by the elbow and yanked her to her feet. He cut the zip tie around her wrists before pressing the blade to her neck. "Remember, no funny business, or bullets will fly and we both die."

Blair gave a jittery nod, watching with trepidation as he pocketed the knife and drew out Matt's gun. She gritted her teeth at the sight of it—a symbol of betrayal of trust. She hadn't wanted Matt to bring it in the first place, and the irony was that it was now at Deroy's disposal—they had unwittingly gifted the killer an ace.

The chopper came into view over the tops of the trees and hovered over the clearing, red taillight flashing through the lashing rain. It was a small four-seater, a volunteer rescue chopper, by all appearances. Blair sucked in a breath as it began its descent, pitching to and fro in the wind. Miraculously, it set down without incident and, a moment later, a youngish-looking EMT stuck his head out the door and motioned them over.

"Looks like the pilot's not going to turn off the engine," Deroy said. "Can't say I blame him for not wanting to hang around in these conditions. Let's go."

Blair winced as he grabbed her and pulled her body tight to his, marching her in front of him like a human shield with the gun pressed to her side.

Her legs felt like spaghetti, but she forced herself to put one foot in front of the other, terrified he would put a bullet in her if she stopped walking for even one minute. Her life briefly flashed before her, but she refused to dwell on the memories, the significant milestones, the faces she held most dear. Time was running out. She needed to stay in the moment. She had to try and make some kind of move between here and the helicopter. She had no doubt that Deroy was deadly serious about not going back to prison. If there was any kind of shoot-out, or trouble in the air, they were all destined to die unless she did something to stop this nightmare unfolding.

Every nerve in her body felt as though it were on fire as she concentrated fully on her abductor. He would have to act more casual as they neared the helicopter or it would look suspicious. The minute she felt his grip slackening she would dive to the ground and tackle him. If she could throw him off balance, she had a fighting chance of getting away from him and running to the helicopter, zigzagging like Matt had taught her to make it more difficult for Deroy to get a straight shot at her. Surely the pilot would have a gun on board for protection, if she could only make it to the chopper.

Time seemed to stand still as she mustered her courage, adrenaline building up inside as Deroy pushed her toward the rotating blades. The EMT peeked through the door again to check on their progress and, for half a heartbeat, Deroy's death grip slackened.

Seizing her opportunity, Blair hurled herself to the ground smashing into his legs with all the ferocity she could muster. As Deroy toppled backward, she scrambled to her feet bracing herself for a counter-attack. Seconds later, a crack like thunder rang out over the clearing.

---

33

*B*lair stood glued to the spot, waiting for the searing pain of the bullet to hit—a pain that never materialized. Her gaze fell on Deroy, lying motionless in the mud, limbs splayed at an odd angle. A gasp escaped her lips when she realized she wasn't the one who'd been shot, and Deroy wasn't the shooter.

She spun around and peered at a figure approaching through the rain, hoping and praying it was Matt, that somehow he'd survived the attack and come for her, that he hadn't taken his last breath beneath the brush after all as another hapless victim of Deroy's twisted campaign of revenge. Her hopes were dashed a moment later when Reed strode into view clutching his rifle.

"Are you all right?" he asked tersely, scanning her for injuries before turning his attention to Deroy crumpled in the mud at their feet. Reed took a knee and felt for a pulse. "He's gone," he confirmed, rising with a stiff grimace on his face. "That was a gutsy move you made. You gave me a clean shot."

"You listened to my warning. I wasn't sure you would,"

Blair said, her voice faltering. "Thank you for believing me. You saved my life."

Reed threw her a sideways look, his expression softening. "I had to trust someone was telling me the truth. My gut told me you were a straight shooter."

Blair tweaked a wan smile that morphed into a sob.

"Are you sure you're all right?" Reed pressed, taking a hesitant step toward her. "You're covered in mud. Are you injured?"

"I'm fine." She wrapped her arms around herself in a bid to stop shaking. "I think he killed Matt."

"Matt's alive," Reed assured her. "I saw him myself. Sam's with him now. We heard him crying out for help and followed the drag marks off the trail. He said Harvey got ahold of his gun and took you hostage. Sam and I would have been here sooner but we didn't realize Harvey had left his RV. We were keeping an eye on the door but he snuck out the back window."

"His real name's Deroy Stephenson," Blair said. "He's an escaped fugitive. He was serving multiple life sentences for murder."

Reed gritted his teeth and motioned toward the chopper. "Here they come. Put your hands in the air. They'll need to identify us."

Tentatively, Blair raised her hands and watched as the pilot approached them, gun drawn, the EMT following a few steps behind with his bag. A welcome sight as far as she was concerned. It was over. They were safe now. They were finally going to get out of here. *Alive.*

34

att was evacuated out on the first flight and taken to the nearest hospital where doctors confirmed he'd suffered a severe concussion but fortunately no skull fracture as they'd feared. Blair broke down at the news, sobbing with relief that Matt had dodged death, not only in a desert halfway around the world, but also back on home soil where she'd mistakenly believed he would be safe.

"I was so terrified I'd lost you. It was just like when you were deployed all over again—that crippling fear that you were dead, and I'd never get to hold you in my arms again."

Matt smoothed a hand over her hair and pressed her to his chest. "It's over now, honey. You don't have to be afraid anymore. Bird Creek is a closed chapter in our lives. At least it will be once we get through Hazel's funeral. I'm not excited about reuniting with the other campers, but I'm gearing up for it."

Blair straightened up and blew her nose. "At least we won't have to see Logan again. He's been arrested and charged with second-degree rape, pending a court date. Whitney's pressing charges after all."

"Good riddance to him," Matt muttered. "I hope they lock him up for a long time. I'm proud of Whitney for developing a backbone."

"I think her parents were instrumental in getting her to see sense," Blair replied. "They stopped by earlier. They wanted to thank us personally for intervening—you were having your MRI scan. They were equal parts devastated by Logan's betrayal, and relieved that their daughter was alive after fearing the worst. They want justice."

TWO WEEKS LATER, Matt and Blair met up with Sam and Whitney, and their respective families, at Hazel's funeral. It was a bittersweet reunion, one Matt had initially been reluctant to participate in, but that Blair had insisted was the least they could do for Hazel's family. After all, Hazel had spent her last days on earth with them. At least her family had a body to bury, which was some small comfort. Search and rescue had gone in with cadaver dogs as soon as the weather cleared and located her body in a shallow grave not far from the campground. They'd also retrieved Sandy's and Rob's bodies from Logan's truck. A crew had been dispatched to begin the daunting task of locating the hunters' bodies, but it could be weeks before they finished combing through the path the mudslide had taken, with no guarantee they would ever find their remains.

"I'm so sorry for your loss," Blair said, shaking hands with Hazel's three adult sons and their wives at the reception after the funeral service. "I only knew your mother for a short time, but I really liked her. She was a strong woman, tiny but with a big personality. I think she tried to warn us about Deroy with the note she left. She must have been musing over it when he struck, and she had the foresight to stuff it down between the nightstand and the mattress, hoping someone would find it."

Hazel's eldest son, Michael, gave a knowing nod. "It sounds like something she would do. She lived fearlessly. When she retired from nursing, she wanted to take on a new challenge. She loved being a private investigator. We all worried about her doing it alone, but she assured us she only took on jobs she felt were safe. Surveilling cheating spouses isn't inherently dangerous. She couldn't have known she would stumble upon a fugitive in the process." He smiled sadly. "I guess her investigative instincts kicked in. She sensed something was wrong and she wanted to help that poor woman in the RV. She paid the ultimate price."

Blair shot a concerned look Matt's way, hoping the words wouldn't trigger him. Funerals were particularly hard. They'd agreed to pay their respects and make as early an exit as possible without appearing rude—using his concussion as their excuse. Matt's doctor had advised him to rest as much as he could and avoid too much stimulation in the coming weeks. The irony of it wasn't lost on them. It was the same advice that had set them out on the road and landed them at Bird Creek with a murderous fugitive to begin with.

"Thank you again for looking out for my daughter," Whitney's mom said, walking up to Blair and squeezing her hand. "She said you were very kind—like a mother to her."

Blair smiled back at her, the words warming her heart with a special kind of meaning. The drugstore test she'd taken yesterday confirmed what she'd suspected. She was going to be a mother. She'd wanted to wait until the circumstances were right, but she realized now that kind of thinking was futile. Life was unpredictable, and fragile, and if you didn't embrace the moment, you risked missing out on your dreams entirely. The past couldn't be undone, and Matt might always struggle with the repercussions of war, but the future she'd been trying so hard to control couldn't be predicted either—all they had was now.

After saying their good-byes, Matt and Blair made an unobtrusive exit and climbed into their car for the return trip home. With Hazel's funeral behind them, it was time to make some decisions on moving forward. The transportation authorities had told them it would be several months before the road into Bird Creek was rebuilt and they could retrieve their vehicles, which left them in a bit of a quandary. They'd toyed with the idea of foregoing the rest of their vacation and pulling the launch date for their landscaping business forward. But in the end, on the advice of family, friends, and doctors, they'd opted to take a little more time to rest and recuperate instead.

"So where do you want to go to get away this time?" Blair asked, as they pulled out of the parking lot next to the church where the funeral reception had taken place. "Preferably somewhere that doesn't involve fire pits and outhouses. If you still want to go to Alaska, I say we rent a cabin this time."

"How about Hawaii?" Matt suggested. "We could do Airbnb. Kick back for a couple of weeks and catch our breath."

"Hawaii?" Blair laughed. "I can't picture you with a lei around your neck. I thought you preferred the mountains and the adventure of staying in a new place every night."

Matt threw her a rueful grin. "Too many messed up people with the same idea. All things considered, I'd rather wrestle with sharks in paradise than fugitives in forests next time around."

"Messed up people hang out on beaches too, just for the record," Blair said.

Matt reached across and laid a hand on her belly. "Yeah,

but at least they're willing to let the sun heal their scars. You keep reminding me I'm not at war anymore. It's time to stop running from the best that life has to offer—beginning with the three of us."

THE CABIN BELOW

Ready for another suspense-filled read with shocking plot twists and turns along the way? Check out my psychological thriller *The Cabin Below* on Amazon!

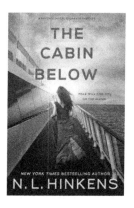

What happens on the water, stays on the water.
Or so they thought. Allison and her handsome, charismatic husband, Doug, are on a Caribbean cruise to celebrate their tenth wedding anniversary. But the steady stream of idyllic photos and happy hashtags they post online is hiding a

dangerous rift in their relationship. Allison has long suspected that Doug is having an affair. Despite his impassioned denials and smooth-talking alibis, she's unconvinced of his innocence and determined to dig for the truth, no matter the cost.

And she's not the only one delving into their secrets. The couple they've befriended on the cruise has been watching them. And they've come to a disturbing conclusion of their own. When Allison disappears the night before the ship docks back in Florida, they bring their terrifying suspicions to the police.

But the truth about Allison's whereabouts proves even more shocking than anyone imagined.

- An addictive thriller brimming with twists and a stunning conclusion! -

---

Do you enjoy reading across genres? I also write young adult science fiction and fantasy thrillers. You can find out more about those titles at **www.normahinkens.com**.

A QUICK FAVOR

Dear Reader,

I hope you enjoyed reading *You Will Never Leave* as much as I enjoyed writing it. Thank you for taking the time to check out my books and I would appreciate it from the bottom of my heart if you would leave a review, long or short, on Amazon as it makes a HUGE difference in helping new readers find the series. Thank you!

To be the first to hear about my upcoming book releases, sales, and fun giveaways, sign up for my newsletter at **www.normahinkens.com** and follow me on Twitter, Instagram and Facebook. Feel free to email me at norma@normahinkens.com with any feedback or comments. I LOVE hearing from readers. YOU are the reason I keep going through the tough times.

All my best,

Norma

BIOGRAPHY

NYT and USA Today bestselling author Norma Hinkens writes twisty psychological suspense thrillers, as well as fast-paced science fiction and fantasy about spunky heroines and epic adventures in dangerous worlds. She's also a travel junkie, legend lover, and idea wrangler, in no particular order. She grew up in Ireland, land of make-believe and the original little green man.

Find out more about her books on her website.
www.normahinkens.com

Follow her on Facebook for funnies, giveaways, cool stuff & more!

BOOKS BY NORMA HINKENS

I also write young adult science fiction and fantasy thrillers under Norma Hinkens.

www.normahinkens.com/books

THE UNDERGROUNDERS SERIES - POST-APOCALYPTIC
Immurement
Embattlement
Judgement

THE EXPULSION PROJECT - SCIENCE FICTION
Girl of Fire
Girl of Stone
Girl of Blood

THE KEEPERS CHRONICLES - EPIC FANTASY
Opal of Light
Onyx of Darkness
Opus of Doom

Follow Norma:

Sign up for her newsletter:
https://books.normahinkens.com/VIPReaderClub
Website:
https://normahinkens.com/
Facebook:
https://www.facebook.com/NormaHinkensAuthor/
Twitter
https://twitter.com/NormaHinkens
Instagram
https://www.instagram.com/normahinkensauthor/
Pinterest:
https://www.pinterest.com/normahinkens/

Made in the USA
Las Vegas, NV
16 September 2021